The Ink
Bridge

ALSO BY NEIL GRANT

Rhino Chasers

Indo Dreaming

From Kinglake to Kabul
(Neil Grant & David Williams, eds)

The Ink Bridge

NEIL GRANT

ALLEN&UNWIN

SYDNEY•MELBOURNE•AUCKLAND•LONDON

Australian Government

This project has been assisted by the Australian Government through the
Australia Council, its arts funding and advisory body.

This project is supported by the Victorian Government through Arts Victoria.

First published in 2012

Copyright © Neil Grant

Every effort has been made to trace the original source of copyright material
in this book. The publisher would be pleased to hear from copyright holders
of any errors or omissions.

All rights reserved. No part of this book may be reproduced or transmitted
in any form or by any means, electronic or mechanical, including photocopy-
ing, recording or by any information storage and retrieval system, without
prior permission in writing from the publisher. *The Australian Copyright Act
1968* (the Act) allows a maximum of one chapter or ten per cent of this book,
whichever is the greater, to be photocopied by any educational institution for
its educational purposes provided that the educational institution (or body
that administers it) has given a remuneration notice to Copyright Agency
Limited (CAL) under the Act.

Allen & Unwin
83 Alexander Street, Crows Nest NSW 2065, Australia
Phone: (612) 8425 0100, Fax: (612) 9906 2218
Email: info@allenandunwin.com, Web: www.allenandunwin.com

A Cataloguing-in-Publication entry is available from
the National Library of Australia: www.trove.nla.gov.au

ISBN 978 1 74237 669 1

Printed in Australia by McPherson's Printing Group
Cover illustration & design by Joe Leong
Text design by Bruno Herfst, set in 10/14 pt Wilke

The paper in this book is FSC® certified.
FSC® promotes environmentally responsible,
socially beneficial and economically viable
management of the world's forests.

*For Emma, Matisse and Calum – children
of immigrants. And for my ancestors
who lived and died on the Badbea cliffs.*

*And for Sardar Shinwari
who is still finding his way.*

Omed had the Buddha's eyes and a tongue that refused words. His was the silence of caves; the false peace that descends when a mortar shell rips apart a building. His was the stillness of bald mountains and long beards and the paths cleared by bullets; the quiet of a long-bladed knife.

Did this all begin with Omed? Or did it start with me at fifteen, shouting for answers; words running sour in my mouth, bleeding to whispers in my throat, evaporating in numbed ears. Those ears: my dad, my invisible friends, teachers that either didn't care or cared too much.

It is easy to look back and see all the pieces and the joins between them. The shards that could one day form this story. The tricky part is getting them all to fit together. It is like building an arch.

An arch begins with foundations, dug deep into the earth, filled with concrete. Then, the columns rise side by side, curving in space until they almost touch. They are cheating gravity and need to be propped. It is then that the most crucial part is laid. The keystone slots neatly into the curve and spreads the load to the two columns. It is what links them and holds them in place.

Our two stories, built word by word, in parallel, rise alone and unstable until the keystone is located and placed to make them strong.

I am searching for that keystone. Without it I cannot begin to build. It is buried in cold sand; it is bruised by wind and slivers of ice. I am searching for Omed. I know if I find him then I find the final stone. Then all this looking back can stop.

I have learned you cannot live in the past and the present at the same time. It takes too much energy to carry the dead. There is only one path out and that is forward. Omed knew this, but in the end he was forced back. Maybe that was the end of him. If this is true, I need to know; because his story and mine are waiting to be linked.

Today I am in a big tin bird, droning across the acetylene sky. Clouds are nothing, vapour that this plane discards as it shunts onwards. I press my palm to the perspex window and I can feel the ground below. My country, dusted crimson, auburn, citron, umber. It is a mandala viewed from above. Tiny roads and dusty tracks vomit into dry riverbeds, cloud shadows smear the land. The bleached bones of cattle and kangaroos settle into dirt. Somewhere on this landscape, his tracks are still there, after all this time.

I remove my hand but the imprint stays for a moment – a ghost of a time that has already passed. Like our stories – his and mine.

Hector Morrow
En route to Kabul

part one

Omed

OMED NOORI WAS FROM BAMIYAN and had always known the two statues. They were carved into the mountain and had once borne the faces of his people, the Hazara – eyes like *badam* kernels, the soft, high cheekbones. They had stood for over fifteen hundred years and had seen the coming and going of many invaders who hacked at the stone and plaster with swords as they passed. The Taliban were just another annoyance.

Omed shifted so he could get a better look. If he was seen, he would be shot and left as a warning to others. The Talibs were boring holes – in the ragged stone feet, in the rock behind the heels, up higher in the long folds of stone clothes. The men, local Hazara pressed into the dangerous work, swarmed like bees, slipping in little parcels of poison, hanging on ropes tied round their waists, spinning down, chins grazing the pebbled rock. There was Tahir, the father of Hamidullah and Zohra. And the baker, Sadiq, whose family were killed in their beds.

The Talibs lounged in the niches and doorways, and in

the gloom of the ancient caves with the paintings of flying gods. They picked at their teeth with their fingernails and aimed their rifles at the men on the ropes. Omed had seen them in the *chaikhanas*, the small teashops in the main bazaar, with their greasy turbans marking the walls, sucking at glasses of tea through small, hard sweets. They would get boys to dance for them and they would smoke hashish and opium. They were not as pious as they pretended to be.

The statues stood as they always had, silently taking in the broad sweep of hills and the broken bricks of town, waiting like mutes about to taste a stick. Years before, tourists would come from America and Germany to stare at the Stone People. Omed and his friends would offer themselves as guides, pulling them by their sleeves up the narrow staircase that led behind behind the statues. At the top the foreigners would point and click at Bamiyan – the fields of vetch and wheat, the tall poplars that lined the streams, the blue minaret of the mosque that was a bright eye among the dusty buildings. Above everything rose the snow-covered mountains of the Koh-e Baba range; heroic saints with their long white beards.

He would take the money he earned home to his mother and the words – *bitte, danke schon*, please, thank you – he would present to his father.

But as the troubles grew worse, the tourists had stopped coming, and the river of their ideas and language, the pebbles of money, had ceased. The Talib had closed Omed's school, leaving only the madrassas with their endless teachings of the Qur'an.

Now there was nothing to do but eat the dust and wind, so Omed and Zakir had come here to the feet of the Stone

People to find out what the whole town was talking about.

Each Talib, with a beard longer than a fist, was bent over fuses. Their fingers moved quickly, twisting and pushing tapers, occasionally wrapping the loose ends of their black turbans back into place. They were absorbed in the work of God. They had cleared the poor people who lived in the surrounding caves, shouting that they would remove the abominations from the mountain side.

Omed could see one of the cave people, Anwar, rolling wire between the charges. Anwar lived alone between the great statues. He had a goat, and a roll of old carpet on which to sleep. Although he was not very old, his beard was greying and he had a habit of chewing on the loose end of his turban so it was always soggy.

In the mornings, after he had fed the animals and swept the yard, Omed would squat beside Anwar as he washed from an old pink watering can, rubbing the freezing water over his face and neck, blowing his nose into his hand. Anwar would brush his teeth with his forefinger and then his thumb before taking a long look out at the valley.

Omed would come for the soft flat bread Anwar cooked in an oven dug into the ground in front of his cave. Anwar would slap an oval of dough against its wall and pick out the sparks that clung to his eyebrows and beard. The bread was the best Omed had ever tasted. The stories he listened to out of politeness.

'The two statues are called Salsal and Shahmama, the father and mother.' Anwar passed Omed a slab of bread, hot from the oven. Omed tossed it from one hand to the other to cool and then took a bite. It tasted of smoke and wheat, the breath of harvest.

Anwar continued, 'The father's face was once made of wood and covered with gold so it shone like the sun. Such was its brilliance that it was covered with a cloth. The father's eyes were made of rubies, the caves behind them, lit with fires. In the evenings men would chant behind the mask and the cloth would be removed. Salsal's eyes would pierce the whole valley with their light.'

The bread was good and Omed wanted more, but he could see that Anwar had only made two and was about to eat the second. Anwar rose off his haunches. 'Come, we will go inside where it is warmer.' He swung the blue curtain aside and they went into his cave. On the back wall were the remains of an old painting. Omed touched the curve of lips in the lamp glow, feeling the soft plastered surface next to the rough rock. The soul had been removed from this one with a quick blow from a hammer. Anwar poured tea from his battered kettle into two glasses.

'They will kill them you know,' said Anwar.

'Who?'

'The Taliban will kill Salsal and Shahmama.'

'But why?'

'Because they are like us.'

One of the men looked up from his work and over to where Omed and Zakir hid. 'Go, you Hazara dogs!' he shouted, and threw a handful of rubble in their direction. They ducked behind the stone wall, hoping that he wouldn't follow with a stick or a foot. Or a bullet.

The Taliban twisted the wires and connected them to the plunger. Omed pointed to one stern-looking man and whispered in his friend's ear, 'That Talib has a face like your mother.' The man had a long scar that had conquered his nose and lip, tearing them sideways. His single eyebrow was so thick it collapsed on his eyes.

Zakir punched his arm. 'He looks more like your sister.' Zakir lied – Leyli was beautiful and Omed knew how she and Zakir looked at each other.

Omed wrestled him to the ground, but Zakir was stronger, always stronger, and soon had him pinned.

'Surrender,' Zakir said as he looked down on him, his long fringe dangling above Omed.

'Never!' shouted Omed and with a grunt tried to push his friend away. Then the ground shook once, twice, and Zakir slumped onto him. Omed felt slices open on the back of his hands and pieces chip from his scalp. Stones drove into the ground around them and when they finished falling, dust coursed over them like bitter fog. He coughed, fighting for air, pushing his face into Zakir's shoulder to filter out the fine powder.

Eventually, Omed pushed Zakir off and rose to his knees. He felt the back of his head and looked at his moist fingers where blood and dust had mingled to a brown sludge.

It reminded him of the day the Talib shot his father. The bullet had passed through his back and disappeared. Like magic. He had fallen on his face, his nose breaking on a grindstone. Omed had been fourteen. The ground in their yard quickly sipped most of the blood, leaving only a dark stain that the chickens kept pecking no matter how often he beat them with a stick.

Omed smeared his own blood between finger and thumb. 'Zakir,' he croaked. The world was dim, muffled. He coughed and spat up a dirty lump. 'Zakir.' He crawled over and shook him.

'Zakir. It's over. The Stone People are gone. Zakir?' The words were strange echoes inside him.

He rolled Zakir over.

The rock was the size of a hand held flat and was shaped like the head of a spear. One edge reminded him of a sea-shell he had once seen in the bazaar, sharp and serrated. It had broken through his skull, neatly, allowing in flies.

Omed shook his friend, but he was as limp as a newly slaughtered goat. His tongue slipped from between his lips, followed by a rivulet of black fluid, too dark to be blood, too dark. *No. No!* Omed gripped his own head. Everything burned. He grabbed his friend against his chest. He shook him. *Wake up . . . wake up . . . wake up.*

He got to his feet. It was a dream, he knew it. It was a dream and in it he was invincible and terrible and fearless. He climbed over the wall, the piles of fallen stone, shouting at the Talib, calling them pigs, and worse. There was blood in his eyes, behind his brow, in his ears. His temples felt thin.

They looked up from their business – slapping each other on the back, congratulating, pointing with their feet to the fallen gods. Then they turned with curiosity to the scream-ing boy.

Omed ran at them, the stone in his hand; the same stone that had removed his friend. He brought it above his head as he came, shouting. And for a moment he saw the fear in their eyes and felt the power of it. Their mouths stretched like wire. Muscles on their necks shivering.

He struck the first on the bridge of the nose and felt the bone collapse. With the second, he pulled the stone up in an arc, tearing soft cheek muscle. He bit the face of a third. Then it was only a hazy mess of screaming, stabbing, kicking, spitting, hair and flesh and earthy blood in his throat and the clouds whirling. But when the power left him, five Talib remained.

He spat at them again as they held him into the dirt. He spat and yelled in Pashto, bad words that his father had never allowed. He could hear them muttering about punishment until the tall one with the scar took over.

Hold him.

To Omed it was only a whisper, like wind stripping out winter trees.

The blade was curved and as long as the thighbone of a sheep. It was chipped but sharp, he noticed that as it came closer. That and the metal glint, the patches of rust blooming, the brass hilt turning to green.

His tongue, hold his tongue.

He felt the fingers enter. He tasted steel and gunpowder, and the smell from when the man had toileted and not washed. Omed withdrew his tongue deep inside, but they punched him hard so he lost his breath. And the man drew his tongue out like a worm. As he did, the one with the scar went to work with his knife, carving under with the tip. He felt his tongue break free of its harness, loll on the floor of his mouth. Blood drained into his throat. He drank it, tasting iron and anger. Then he fell heavily into dreams.

He had gone to Darya Ajdahar – the Valley of the Dragon – with Anwar. It was the year his father had been killed and he had needed to escape his house and its mud-walled compound. That awful stain.

They had climbed onto the roof of a battered bus, swatting flies and hunkering down among the rough bags and bunches of chickens. The Grandfather of Mountains – the Koh-e Baba – was dusted in snow so it looked like the soft lining of a cow's stomach. But the sun was a gold platter on the tablecloth of sky. Omed breathed the cool air, forgot, remembered, ate a chunk of Anwar's good bread.

When they reached Darya Ajdahar, they climbed down from the bus and walked slowly up the dusty slope. Anwar made sure he and Omed stayed between the coloured stones that showed the safe path between the landmines. The back of the Dragon was long, blocking the valley, its snout facing towards Bamiyan.

Omed's father had told him the story, as it had been told to him, and to his father further back into the past, under the bowing roof of their old house.

The Dragon had been the scourge of Bamiyan with its violent, bloodthirsty rages. It had held the valleys to ransom until the King had agreed to offer up food and camels, and a young girl, as a sacrifice each day.

Hazrat Ali, the son-in-law of the Prophet Mohammed, had stood before it as it breathed acres of fire. And with a circle of his sword, Zulfiqar, the rolls of flame became tulips that dropped to the ground at Ali's feet. The Dragon was much maddened by this impudence and reared its terrible head, screaming in anger until the bedrock of the valley shook and the sky boiled with clouds. But Ali stood his ground, and when the Dragon slumped in exhaustion, he thrust with Zulfiqar and sheared the animal down its back. With that act, Islam had triumphed among the people of the valley.

As Omed and Anwar climbed higher the rock turned white.

'We are at the Dragon's head,' said Anwar. 'See, these are its tears. And look here, its blood.'

Omed placed his hand on the cool rock, touched the tears, touched the blood. He brought it to his lips where it tingled, slightly salty.

'Come, we must go higher.'

They climbed again until they were on the Dragon's broad back, where the sword of Ali had cut the mighty beast in two. Mist puckered the edges of the sky. The mountains dragged it around them like a cloak.

Anwar grabbed Omed's head, pushing it to the gap in the rock, the Dragon's mortal wound. 'Here, listen,' he whispered.

And Omed heard it then. A soft moaning from deep within the beast. A long mournful dirge, something more awful, more heartfelt than a wail. It was the sound of sorrow, of emptiness, of loss.

Anwar had been embarrassed by the boy's tears. He had pressed a cheek of bread into Omed's palm and retreated to the nearby shrine to pay respect to Hazrat Ali. Omed looked at the bread, then at the darkening sky and his friend circling the stone and mud shrine. He slowly touched the bread to his lips and slipped it into the Dragon's wound.

Omed came to his senses in the room he shared with his brothers. His mother was sitting beside his bed ripping a sheet and sponging blood from his chin and clothes.

'Oh, Omed, what have you done? First your father and now you. Is there no end to this? How heavy is my misfortune, Omed?'

Omed tried to answer, to comfort her, but there was too much pain.

'What must we do now? When you are gone there will be no one to protect us from the Taliban. Is this our family curse?' Her fingers worked the cloth, tearing it into long strips, dabbing at the blood.

His sister Leyli came into the room, a jug of water in one hand, their two-year old brother Liaquat on her hip. She had wet stains on her cheeks. He reached for her hand, pleading with his eyes. *It will be all right, Leyli. I will take care of all of you.* Liaquat looked down at him and smiled.

'Om-om,' he said, reaching down with his small, sticky fingers to Omed's. But Leyli pulled him away and left the room. The rags that served as curtains swept inside on the light breeze and he could hear the shouts of their neighbours. How long had he been asleep? How had he got here? Had the Talib finished their sport with him?

It was then that Wasim ran in. This brother was two years younger and his mother's favourite. Sometimes it caused them to fight, this unfairness within the family. Wasim always said that Omed had been his father's jewel. *How lucky I am, to be the favourite of a dead man,* Omed thought.

Wasim's face was red and streaked with sweat and dust. His chest heaved as he spoke. 'They are coming, Omed. They found where we live and are seeking revenge.'

Omed swung his legs off the low bed but, as the blood leapt into his head, he almost fell to the floor. He grasped the low table and willed himself up.

Wasim pulled at his shirt. 'Quick, Omed, we must go.'

He made for the door, the world swinging madly, light dancing off the walls. He felt his mother's fine-boned hand on his shoulder. How his father had loved those hands, sung their praises as they swept and sewed and cooked and caressed them all. In the end what did it matter, all those loves, when they could be taken so quickly?

'Omed, my son,' she whispered in his ear. 'I knew it would come to this. I was cursed for my happiness. When those around me saw such hardship, I felt only joy. And now it is my burden to know only sorrow. But you, my strong young son. You are young enough. You can escape. Take this money.'

She pushed the notes into his hand. He knew this money and where it was kept. It was to guard against hard times. In years gone by, his father would pull out the loose brick in the wall and pack the notes behind it.

Omed shook his head and pushed the money away. This would end his family.

'Omed, you must take this. Without it you will die here. As a mother I cannot allow it. You must live for all of us. Is it your duty now, Omed. You are the eldest, it is your responsibility.'

But this was not a responsibility that Omed wanted. The blood of his whole family on his hands, on this dirty pile of money and the torn reminder of his tongue.

'They are coming!' shouted Wasim. He could hear the jeeps and howling dogs and the rattle of Kalashnikovs.

'Take it!' screamed his mother and her face was so twisted by despair that he grabbed the money and turned towards the door. He stopped to give her a final kiss, but Wasim pulled him by the arm.

'They will kill you,' he hissed.

In front of the small window of their house, Leyli held Liaquat. Her dark eyes pierced Omed's for a moment. Liaquat began to cry and she hugged him close. She pursed her lips and with a jerk of her head bade Omed to go.

They ran.

They hid until dark in the bombed-out *chaikhana* where Bollywood movies were once played on an old television. Now there was only the smell of rat piss and piles of rubble. All afternoon they waited, hot and scared, shrinking inside a cave formed by a broken poster board and a fractured slab of concrete. Omed could hear shots from the area of the mosque, near where his family lived. The muezzin was silent.

The gossip around town was that their Tajik neighbour was a Talib spy who would sell anyone for a handful of wheat. Omed hoped it was a lie. His mother surely would have burned the bloodied bedsheets in their stove. The proof would be turned to smoke by now.

When the moon began its climb over the stone niches where the Buddhas once stood, Omed and Wasim crept out of their bunker, throwing long shadows against the cracked walls. There were only rats and dogs on the streets; no one felt safe when the Taliban were out for revenge. If they didn't find the right man, any would do.

The houses lay like row on row of bared teeth, lamps glowing behind them. They heard the sound of a child crying, a chicken woken from sleep. Every noise was a soldier with a gun and a beard and a new lesson.

Omed knew it was too dangerous for his brother to go any further with him. He pulled him by the sleeve and shook his head.

Wasim's eyes filled with tears. 'It is not fair, Omed. I am small without you. What can I do against the Talib? I cannot protect our family.'

Omed spun him round and pushed him in the small of his back. Wasim shouted after Omed as he ran. 'I hate you, Omed. It is all your fault! Do you hear that, I HATE you!'

But as Wasim's voice faded he heard a last desperate sob, 'I love you, my brother. Don't leave us.'

Abu the Turk lived in a tiny mud-walled house in Qala-e Dokhtar – the Palace of the Daughter. The palace had lost its glory to centuries of war. The walls were shattered, a rusted truck formed a dark beast in the square, its head lolled forward on a broken neck. In the arches of the old caravanserai, a donkey shifted restlessly. Omed put his hand on its flank to calm it. A person moving under the cover of night was to be mistrusted. There were old guns propped behind every door.

Abu the Turk had moved to Bamiyan fifteen years before, but had never learned more Dari than was necessary. As the wars bit deeper into Afghanistan, he grew richer. His body stored fat while those around him dwindled. And if you needed anything, Abu would get it – for a price.

Omed raised his knuckles to the door made from flattened oil tins, nailed to saplings. As he knocked he heard the sound of bottles and a voice tossing a curse into the room. Abu the Turk's face appeared, his yellowed eyes roaming beyond Omed and into the moonlit street.

'What you wish at this hour? You wish us shot?'

Omed saw the man's eyes stop at his bloodied chin.

'You are this boy. This boy the Taliban wish kill.'

Omed nodded, for the first time seeing a new problem. Without speech, how could he hope to make this man understand?

'I am wanting not troubles. This too big troubles.' Abu the Turk began to close the door, but Omed pushed his arm between it and the wormy jamb.

'Go away!' Abu growled.

Omed showed him the wad of notes. At this Abu's eyes widened and he sucked his top lip noisily. 'Welcome to my home,' he said, grabbing Omed by the shoulder and pulling him inside. He quickly scanned both sides of the street before shutting the door. The house smelled strongly of onion and lamb fat. Abu dragged a chair from the side of the room and placed it beside the table. He turned up the lamp.

'Let us talk business,' he said rudely, not offering food or drink or the usual polite exchange of words. He leant on the table and roughed his beard with the back of his hand.

Omed cracked open his mouth to show the bloodied remains of his tongue. The cold air stung him.

'Ha,' said Abu, 'I will do talking for two. You need to get away, far. I have man to help. But it will take money. Much money.'

Omed held out the pile of afghani his mother had given him. They still held the mustiness of the wall. Abu grabbed the money and fingered the notes, his lips moving numbers around.

Finally he glared at Omed. 'It is not enough. It is never enough.'

Closing his eyes, Omed pictured his death. It would not be quick like his father's. They would tie him to a car and drag him towards Kabul. Or they would hand him a stick and make him prod landmines from the tracks. The fear of that alone would make you shit in your pants.

'But I am good man. You have heard this, no?'

Omed nodded. *Of course*. Anything.

'And because of this I will do a very big favour. I know one man. He is smuggler but he will be leave tonight from Kabul road. You must meet him and give to him this.' Abu the Turk went to a tin on a shelf and pulled a slip of paper from it. On the paper was printed a small inked picture of an animal he had never seen before, like a long-tailed goat walking on its hind legs. Omed pushed it deep into his pocket and got up to leave. Abu the Turk caught him by the sleeve of his jacket.

'Many have left, boy, but who has returned? Think on this. Maybe death is better.'

Omed shook off the man's hand and opened the door.

'By the old Russian tank, Kabul road,' Abu called after him.

'They call me the Snake,' he said, shining his torch up to his misshapen head. 'Because of this.' He slipped his tongue from between his lips. It was blue and forked at the tip. There was a strong smell on his clothes that Omed recognised as opium smoke. His father had warned him of these men who slept in a cracked shell of a house, smoking poppy paste in turns from a sheet of foil. Of course it had made him want to see it for himself.

Once he had gone there with Zakir, and together they had squinted through the boarded windows into the dim room. There were three men inside. One was lying on a cot and groaning, the frame of his body bent at wrong angles, his tongue pushing at his lips. Another smiled like an idiot at the ceiling. But the third man, he looked directly at them.

'Come inside, little brothers,' he wheezed, beckoning with a fistful of sticks. They had run. But Omed remembered the smell.

One of the Snake's pupils was tiny, no bigger than a poppy seed, the other as large and dark as a pomegranate's. He showed Omed the short-bladed knife tucked into his belt and the blunt-snouted handgun in his coat pocket.

'To stop bad men,' he said, patting it. As he laughed, his forked tongue sprayed spittle.

He led Omed to a truck parked behind the abandoned tank. The moon was like a *naan* ripped in half and in its light Omed could see the tray, framed with crooked wood and covered with a dirty sheet, patched and torn in places. Through the open mouth under this frame, the red glow of a cigarette burned.

'Don't be afraid,' the Snake said, pushing him towards the truck. 'This way to freedom.'

He laughed again. A hand reached down and grabbed Omed's. It pulled him off the ground and into the truck. Then, without notice, the engine growled into life and the truck jerked forwards. The far off lights of Bamiyan shrank to pinpricks and were swallowed by the night. It was as if the stars themselves had been snuffed.

Omed's nose stung with cold. He wanted to sleep, but the road was rough and the wooden bench grew harder and harder. The faces of the people next to him were swathed in shadow but he could hear them talking, whispering as if they were being listened to.

After an hour, the truck groaned to a halt and the Snake got out. Omed pushed the cloth aside. He could see the outline of Shahr-e Zohak — the City of the Serpent-head King. Suddenly, a bearded face loomed up from the shadows. The tip of a Kalashnikov pressed against the bridge of Omed's nose. He closed his eyes and pictured his table at home, the chipped cups and yellow glow of the lamp. He pictured the Buddhas, the faltering sway of the poplars, he could taste Anwar's bread in his mouth and hear the sighing breath of Wasim asleep in their room; then his shouting, *I HATE you!*, Zakir's torn body, his father's blood, the slain Dragon. He pictured his mother crying over his memory. She would never view the body. It would be dumped in the river like a donkey's carcass.

He opened his eyes and looked into those of his executioner. The man stared back and spat at the ground. Then the Snake came to the back of the truck and tucked a fat roll of money under the gunman's rifle strap. The man turned away.

They drove on. No one spoke. Not even a whisper.

They reached Kabul as morning came. The air was filled with dust and smoke and the sound of the muezzin, calling the faithful. They kept on driving, forgotten by God.

Kabul was full of broken buildings and rubbish. Dazed goats stumbled around the streets, chewing on plastic bags. Sewage flowed from houses and onto the streets. Flies hummed into the truck, drunk on human waste, and crawled in noses and mouths. People moved as though they were in a dream, carrying dirty water, suitcases, plastic limbs, guns. Omed saw a dog with three legs being axed to death by a boy, and piles of books on fire. Open jeeps roared past with Talib, beards, rifles, cuts for eyes. The Dragon's groan could be heard under toppled slabs of concrete, in the call of rifle fire, his pain could be seen on the twisted face of a mother cradling her broken child. The Dragon was dying and only in its death throes could it atone for its violence and stupidity.

The truck bumped through the streets of Kabul, stopping only once more for the payment of bribes. It was night again when it reached the border of Pakistan.

The Snake ordered everyone from the truck. Omed could see the checkpoint ahead – a faint glow with the shadows of trucks and buses moving past like ghost ships.

'You must go through alone,' hissed the Snake. 'I will meet you on the other side.'

There were over twenty men, women and children standing in the dark and no one said a word. Everyone watched like sheep as he jumped into his truck.

But Omed was not going to be left alone on the road. He ran back and, pulling the door open, grabbed the Snake's arm. The Snake went for his knife with his other hand. In the dull glow of the cabin's light Omed could see the Snake snarl, his front teeth rotten and black.

'Freedom is that way,' he said and pointed to the border with his blade. He leant forward and pushed Omed out of the cab and into the dirt.

Omed had nothing. He crossed into Pakistan with only the clothes on his back.

THE CANVAS OF OMED'S TENT flapped. The winds were getting cooler, a sign that winter approached. When he had first arrived, it was summer and Omed had never known such heat. In Bamiyan the summers kissed the back of your hand. In Pakistan the sun roared and bit.

Out of the door, he could see the dust-riddled camp coming to life. He didn't know if he had the energy to get out of bed. Today would be the same as yesterday – a series of watery meals and then the waiting. For what, he did not know.

He was between worlds – without family, without money to move towards freedom, without the promise of safety to return to. His life had been cut in two and he was caught in the chasm the sword had made down the Dragon's back.

He rolled over and saw the old man in the next bed staring at him. He was called the Poet of Kandahar.

The old man's skin was yellow and thin, like the best parchment. His hair was white and he had a fine, curved nose. A pair of hands were gathered at the top of his blanket like two birds – the veins and blotches written in some old, lost language.

There were calluses on his thumb and forefinger and often he would quote poetry, snatching from the sky phrases in fine Persian. The Poet's words could fold like smoke in the air between them. Omed would close his eyes and try to block them out, but they were so beautiful that they fell like drifts of leaves inside him.

Others had learnt to keep their distance from Omed. They thought he was mad, with a ripped scar of a tongue and his wild eyes. Omed was glad of the silence. Words were at the heart of his misfortune. They had killed his father.

Omed's father had been a scribe. He had typed English words for villagers, filling in forms and writing letters for those with far-off family. The work had grown less and less and then finally, like an old well, it had dried completely.

His old black typewriter was missing the letter 'e' and the words were chopped in strange places so that for years Omed would think of English as a language with many gaps. At times he could still picture his father crouched over that machine with its clicks like the noise of scissors slicing the air, or a cricket's song as he pulled the paper free. Those papers swarmed with letters, lines of ants, nose to tail, left to right. The gapped words he would come to later, hand-writing 'e' after 'e' until the code was complete.

Copies, he would make with carbon paper, coated on one side with ink. Omed would often come across his blue fingerprints on teacups or on the corners of a book. In these smudges, he had lived in their home long after he died.

His father had believed in words, in their power to heal. He was working on a translation of local legends, and of poems and songs. Their lives had been busy with the strange mutterings of English stories, Persian and Greek legends. Odysseus did battle with the Cyclops between the evening meal and the creaking silence of bedtime. Winnie the Pooh lived in the Hundred Acre Wood, but also in the dusty mountains and landmined fields, and beneath the cupped wood of the kitchen table. As he sipped tea from a flowered cup, his elbows resting in the hollows that had formed there, he would tell of Majnun and his love for the fair Leyli that ended in madness and despair.

That low table had been a place of magic and Omed would lie beneath it and imagine himself in those storybook lands. With his eyes shut, the characters would leap about. When he was six, he had smuggled their kitchen knife under the table and carved his name up on the sky of his story-book world: *Omed*, in fine Dari script and then in English.

When the Taliban arrived they had told his father that the Qur'an was the only book that was needed. Sharia was the only law and it was swift and merciless. Amputations, stonings, beatings, executions.

His father had been a writer, a thinker of dangerous thoughts. But who would imagine that a thought, that stories or words, could be so dangerous they would get you killed. Omed understood it was his words, raging and rebellious, that had angered the Taliban more than his punches and kicks.

ℯ

The aid workers in the camp tried to help. But Omed refused. Silence was a wall, a fort. It held his misery from others and it protected him from himself. The foreigners said they could try to contact his family. But it would be of little use. If they were alive why would they come here, without money, to this half-place? It was better if they dreamed of him breathing the air of a new country; of their son, their brother, safe and happy like the Snake had promised. How could Omed live with the shame of his family on his head?

The Poet was still staring at him. His eyes were unearthly blue, the blue of the tiled mosque at Mazar. He was a Pashtun and Omed could not forgive what the Pashtuns had done to his people. But he could not muster hate for this man. He was far different to the hard Talibs that had come to his town.

As a younger man, the Poet had wandered Afghanistan, living as he could in the shrines of saints and gathering the stories of the land. For a while he stayed in the village of Deh-i-Ahangaran, near Bamiyan. Here he had learned to speak Dari nearly as well as his native Pashto.

'Why do you never talk, grandson?' he had asked soon after Omed had arrived.

Omed had opened his mouth and showed him his mutilated tongue. Since then they had shared a tent for many months. And each day the Poet asked the same question as though it were a riddle for Omed to solve, but his meaning was hidden in cloud.

This day the old man wet his lips slowly. 'There are other ways to speak,' he said. 'You must remember that words are our chance at forever.'

Outside the door, whirlwinds of dust whipped between

the tents, and the sky squeezed out the palest blue. This was not the sky of home.

'We are so much the same, grandson, you and me. I feel this,' the Poet continued. 'Our sin is imagining a better world.'

Omed never understood his tears when they came. But, again, they were hot on his cheeks. The Poet's face cracked open like a boulder touched by lightning. His eyes glittered and his lips parted in a smile. 'There is a better place than this. And better than the place we know as home.' He rolled his body upright and planted his feet on the ground.

'What is home anyway?' he said, looking at his toes splayed on the mud floor.

When he spoke again, it was in a whisper. 'The Russians killed my wife and children. That is where it began. I became a mujaheddin when I believed there was a war worth fighting. When that war was over there was another to take its place. The joyless feast of killing, on and on. So I sold my rifle and bought myself a book of fine paper and a pen. I turned to words. Now there is nothing left for me in Afghanistan. Nothing but death. We need life around us to live, grandson. We need people who love us and we need words.'

He paused and laid his hands on Omed's knees.

'We have all lost someone. It becomes a matter of what we do next. Once the grieving is over you need to calm the fire in your mind.'

The poet began to cough. His shoulders jerked and, finally, he spat into a cloth. Then he pressed the tears from his eyes and continued.

'I wanted to go to Australia, I have a nephew there. He writes to me of the ocean, how warm it is and how salty, and when it touches the shore the waves reach for the sky.

In the winters no one dies, there is always food and no one tries to shoot him.

'I have the money. It is enough, and I have found a way. But I fear I am too old to make the crossing. Look at me. I would never last. If I reached the shore of Australia, the waves would finish me.' He sputtered a laugh that ended in another fit of coughing.

When the coughing ceased, he reached out and placed his hand on Omed's, covering it with the cool sea of his skin, the whirlpools of his knuckles. 'So I will die here,' he said and swept his arms around him as if the tent walls were invisible and he was showing Omed the makeshift shops and the new mosque they were building from rough-sawn planks and dented ghee tins.

At night it was difficult to sleep. Radios droned; men hunched over them, ears cocked to music that soiled the air with noise. People walked round the camp, smoking and talking to themselves. Omed was scared of the night, because without the colour of day, his world tightened around him. First the dead would come to drink his breath and fill him with poison. Then, he would see his father, a bullet lodged between his shoulder blades, the flesh angry purple around the hole. Zakir's head sliced in two. His mother beaten, eyes hooded with bruises. Leyli, Wasim and Liaquat without food or laughter, fingers raking the soil for roots to boil in soup. The poplar trees were burning, withered corn trampled under boots. And again and again the Buddhas rained stones into the yellow streets.

At night, cold wind entered the tent and clawed at his

blankets. Omed would ball up on his stretcher and shiver until the first wheat-stalks of dawn pushed themselves into camp. The days and nights were the same – stretching on like a thousand-acre desert.

And one day it all changed. Omed and the Poet were sitting, as they did often, in the sunshine, on a rock that sat flat on the ground like a gravestone. The Poet had chosen this rock for its view up and over the camp to the mountains far off in the distance. Beyond these mountains, beyond the Khyber Pass, lay Afghanistan.

Omed had taken to joining him in this silent watching, even though it achieved nothing but a stillness of mind that allowed thoughts to creep in like bandits. Occasionally, the Poet would speak, just one word and there it would sit like the very rock beneath them.

Ali was a simpleton. Some said he had always been this way; that he had been brought up among the dogs in his village. Others said that he had been created by the Taliban who had held him for a year when he was a boy, dressed him in silk and made him dance. Either way, it made him a vessel that was easily filled with other people's nonsense. Sometimes it was the mullahs' craziness about jihad and sometimes it was just wild gossip that Ali carted from tent to tent. No one took him seriously.

'They have blown up America!' he shouted as he strode towards them.

The Poet turned his profile to watch Ali as he approached. His walk was an excited shuffle, a stumbling jog that made the torn hem of his kameez flap.

'They have blown up America. God is great.'

The Poet spoke. 'Who has blown up America? And what has it to do with God?'

'The Arabs have done it. They have killed the enemy.'

'Wait!' The Poet seemed angry. 'What has been blown up? The Americans are not our enemy.'

'The buildings are down. They have destroyed America by crashing planes. This is jihad. God is great!'

'Silence, you foolish boy. God's work is not war.' He got up and stretched out his legs. 'Come, Omed, we should go to the bazaar. They have a television there, we can see what is happening.'

They made their way to the main bazaar. The streets were alive with stories. Two planes had crashed into New York. America had fallen. And Ali's words burnt into them. *Allahu Akbar! God is great!*

The television set was in a filthy *chaikhana*. The Poet ordered a tin pot of *chay* and a dish of boiled sweets. They stood at the counter, crowded with the other men. There were two glass towers, black against the sky. Thick smoke belched from one. As they watched, a plane flew into view, banked, and was lost inside the building. Flame tore across the screen. The images of the plane crashing and the buildings burning, then falling were replayed again and again. Omed looked at the Poet. What did this mean? What was happening? He was used to war, the real war that had savaged his life for as long as he could remember. He knew what burning steel and lumps of stone could do to a living person, how much blood there would be, the terror and confusion of noise. He had grown up with the reality of war. But this was new for the Americans. It gave Omed a great sadness. People should not have to know these things.

The Poet was crying. The other men shook their heads at him, smirking behind their fists. *The old man is crazy*, they said. *He is soft. These people are far away. We do not know them. Why should we cry for them? What have they done for us?*

'We should cry,' the Poet said. 'Because if we don't we are not human.' He pointed to the screen where people were leaping from the burning buildings to their deaths.

The Punjabi *chaikhana* owner spoke up. 'This is not a movie we are watching, brothers. This is war. The Americans will come looking for who did this. And if they cannot find him, they will take something else.'

'What do you know of war?' shouted a small man on crutches.

'What do I know?' the Punjabi shouted back. 'I fought for Kashmir. You think Afghans are the only ones who know war. It is all around. And it is no good.' He spat on his own carpet.

'No good,' repeated the Poet, pulling his cap over his eyes.

And the war did come looking for them. Again. They heard reports that the Americans had flown planes to the caves at Tora Bora and bombed the hills to powder; that they had marched on Kabul; that the the refugees had fled south to Pakistan, crossing the mountains as refugees had done since the Russian times. The camp grew until tent seams burst. Food became scarce and, as it got colder, people died.

As the winter took hold, the Americans claimed victory over the Taliban, and the agencies tried to talk the people into going home. A hundred dollars was offered to each returning refugee. Buses were provided to cross the mountains. But it was common knowledge that the Taliban were still in Afghanistan. Omed knew one hundred dollars would not keep him safe from their reach.

Omed noticed the snow on the mountains as he returned from breakfast one morning. The cold had crept in like a beast, low to the ground, snapping the air. In the long winters of Bamiyan they had fire and song to keep them going. Here it was different.

The warmest place was beneath a blanket, so Omed got back in his cot and counted the holes and tears in the tent roof. It was quiet, just the far-off noise of a slow song droning from a nearby radio.

The Poet was in bed too. Omed noticed the strange colour of his cheeks – like *naan* dropped in water. He scrambled from under his covers and watched the Poet's shoulders, waiting for the rise and fall that would show he was breathing. But there was nothing. He put his ear to the man's lips but heard nothing.

Fear fell upon him like a hawk, tearing at him. The knowledge that once again he would be alone crushed his ribs and forced the breath from him. Bamiyan had been his world, he knew everyone and was known by everyone; he belonged there. Here, he only had this old man.

Omed shook the Poet and, as the old man rolled over, he groaned. But the groan was only his soul departing. He was cold as stone. Omed pulled at his clothes and moaned. He bit the back of his own hand and blinked away the tears. He would not allow this. He sat the old man up, his body already stiffening. He poured warm water from the stove over the Poet's hands and rubbed them. He buried his face in his shoulder and begged him to return.

Eventually, he went outside and sat on the cold ground to weep. The tears turned to ice on his cheeks, scouring them like glaciers. They turned to acid in the corners of his eyes. He was poisoned by sorrow.

He borrowed a shovel with a splintered handle and a worn crescent across the cutting edge. He piled the Poet's carefully washed body on a cart and wheeled it to a patch of ground beyond the camp. The cart had a squeaky wheel and as he travelled it spoke to him:

How does a corpse differ from a body? When does a man cease to become 'he' and become 'it'? Is this all there is after a life so full?

Cheap plywood coffins stood upright guarding the entrance to the burial ground. Refugees returning to Afghanistan would carry the dead back to the places of their birth so they would be buried in their own soil. This was impossible for Omed. The Poet had long given up on his country anyway. He owed no loyalty to his tribe, his village. Now his spirit was free of this earth. There was no fence around the burial ground, just a ring of stones to keep the dead from wandering.

Omed attacked the ground with the shovel. The soil was hard with frost and each strike shook his shoulders. His grief was made real by this. He dug until his hands blistered and burst, until the shovel handle was red with blood. He sweated and cried and couldn't tell the difference between the two. And when the hole was deep enough, he carefully lowered the Poet in.

He should have fetched the mullah to say the prayers, but the man had a reputation for greed. Instead, Omed spoke the proper words in his mind. It was all he could do. And with that done he pulled the blanket over the Poet's face and shovelled in the soil.

When the crying was over, Omed returned to the tent. Thieves had already been, pulling apart the Poet's meagre possessions, stealing what little he had. They had ripped the small book he used to write in and scattered it around.

Omed gathered the pages. There were pieces of poetry he had written throughout his travels. He found one from the Poet's time in the Bamiyan valley.

> *How high these walls,*
> *   but they cannot hold the sky*
> *How sharp the sword of the conqueror,*
> *   but it does not cut me now*
> *How cold the snow,*
> *   but it does not trick the spring*
> *How beautiful the Buddha's smile,*
> *   but it did not last forever*
> *How glorious is peace,*
> *   but war is trapped inside me.*

He had painted beautiful miniatures around the poem in the style of an ancient Persian text. There was the grandson of Genghis Khan, felled by an arrow in the Shahr-e Zohak. There was the Buddha's smile, waiting to be erased by the invaders from Persia. There was the Poet with the blue of his eyes and the power of his youth.

Omed crumpled the page to his chest. He would never get

used to death, no matter how many times it was paraded in front of him.

There was another page on the floor. It had been stepped on and partly torn, but Omed could still make out the words.

Dear Grandson,

It is without regret that I leave this world that has been both fair and hard to me. I had hoped to one day watch the waves reach the sky, but now this dusty camp will be my last memory. This dusty camp where I met you. If you have the courage and the inspiration for the journey to the waves, it is one you should make. Everyone deserves a chance at freedom, a chance at forever.

The journey will be difficult and dangerous, but there is one part I can help you with. The rest will be up to you, but I have confidence in you. You are strong and you have a fire inside you. Do not be afraid of your words. They are everything.

There is money. Below my seat is your chance at forever.

With great affection,

Your Grandfather

Omed sat with the page in his hand, letting his tears blur the words. He knew what he must do. He packed his bag and walked quietly out of the tent.

The Poet's rock, the one he sat on watching the mountains, mirrored the morning sun. Omed stood above it, remembering how the Poet looked and sounded. Omed's father would have liked him. He had courage and faith, in himself and in others.

The rock was warm, like a living thing. Rolling it over, Omed quickly scraped at the dirt with his hands. There was nothing. He grew furious, like a dog burrowing in the soil. The earth stung his blistered hands, it was cold and filled with sharp slivers of stone. Wounds opened and his fingers bled. He kept digging.

Eventually, his fingers struck something harder than dirt. He scraped around it until he could see the outline of a tin box. He wrenched it out, hugged it to his body and ran. Behind him, a ribbon of shouting children and curious adults who had gathered while he dug wound through the camp. He ducked into a tent and hid, his heart leaping in his chest.

As the gang of people ran past, Omed swallowed his breath. He was afraid that any movement or sound would give him away. Blood shouted in his ears. His head whirled. Then, as the last of the stragglers darted after the trail of dust, he breathed again.

'What have you there?' asked a man's voice from an unlit corner.

Omed jumped and brought the box closer to his chest.

'I am a friend,' said the voice. 'Why does everyone follow you?' it asked. 'What do you have in your box?'

The voice was thicker than smoke. It bristled with the sharp points of daggers.

Omed pushed the box inside his shirt.

'Friend, it is me,' said the voice and the Snake stepped out of the shadow. 'There should be no hard feelings.'

Omed showed his teeth, hard against each other.

The Snake grabbed his arm. 'Wait, I have news of your family.'

The box slumped down inside Omed's shirt, fell to his stomach. He fought to stay on his feet.

The Snake smiled and nodded. Omed could see his forked tongue, sneaking up behind rotten teeth. 'Yes, yes, news of your family.' He slithered beside Omed, wrapped an arm around his shoulder.

'They send their greetings,' he said.

Omed narrowed his eyes.

'And of course their love,' he added hastily. 'That as well, of course.'

The Snake stepped uneasily from one foot to another. 'They are well. They are very well; excellent, I would say. But as for me, I am not so good. Things have gone badly for me and it was impossible for me to stay in Afghanistan.' He looked up at the roof of the tent. 'Running a business such as mine requires a great amount of money. I have to pay *everyone*,' he hissed, through gritted teeth, 'to make sure things run smoothly.'

Omed shook his head, but the Snake ignored him and carried on. 'I have big debts. Debts to people that it is not good to be in debt to.

'So is it not funny how fate throws us together? Both without a country. Both hoping for a new life. We should help each other. Maybe what you have in your box could aid us in our escape?'

Omed shrugged off his arm and tried to leave, but the Snake grasped at an elbow and spun him around. 'Do you think I am a fool? Do you think I have not been on this earth long enough to read people's faces. This is my business! I *know* what is in your box.' His face softened again and his large eye shone like the moon reflected in a stagnant pond.

'I am sure we can both profit from this situation,' he said, his voice suddenly soft as milk. 'You have no idea how to escape this place, but you have the money to do it. I have no money, but all the contacts and plans. If you help me, then I will help you. It is a simple deal.'

His face was lumpy with smallpox scars. Omed didn't trust him, but what option did he have?

'It is up to you and how much money we have as to where we go. Where do you wish – Sweden, America?' There was a pause before he asked, 'Australia?' Omed pursed his lips, and the Snake's eyes slitted for a second as he saw he had won a small war.

'Australia is a beautiful country, full of fair-minded people. We will have a good life there. You will see.'

He moved forward and put his hand on the box, but Omed turned to block him, pulling his jacket over to cover it further.

'As you wish,' he said.

OMED AND THE SNAKE CROSSED the camp, walking until they seeped like two drops of ink into the starless night. No one would cry at night or think of them. No one would even know they had gone.

Sometime before dawn, Omed fell asleep and dreamed he was home. His father was sitting reading under the gentle light of a lamp, his mother softly singing Liaquat to sleep. He could feel the warm curves of his brothers at his back and belly, like punctuation, bracketing him. But when he woke it was to the pox-scarred Snake, smiling.

'Soon Lahore,' he said. 'Gateway to Australia – The Lucky Country.'

Beyond the Snake's lumpy profile, the dust of Pakistan rose in clouds. Men beat overladen donkeys down the road. The smell of sewerage swung out of villages.

In Lahore, the Snake found a room with one bed and mint-green walls flecked with blood. Huge scabs of paint hung from the ceiling and trembled as a sour breeze blew over them. Omed lay on the bed and watched television – Channel V from India. Girls with long blonde hair danced to furious beats while, outside, a thousand kites climbed above the city. It was Pakistan that had bred the Taliban, but Pakistan did not have the stomach for their ways.

The Snake swung open the door. 'I need one hundred dollars,' he said.

Omed shook his head.

'For passports. We need identities if we are to travel to Australia. We must have our photos taken. And then I need to go alone for the passports. Do you think these people will want a boy meddling in their affairs? I am known to them. You, they do not know.'

A grin slithered onto his face and his big eye shone like a coin. 'I see you are questioning if you can trust me,' he said, 'But the question you need to ask is not *if* you can trust me, but how can you afford *not* to trust me?'

The photo shop was near the hotel. The air was filled with smoke and car fumes, music wailed from speakers. They were told not to smile. They were told the photos would be ready in three hours.

Back at the hotel, Omed lay on the bed and watched kites tumbling above the city. Even though the window was cracked and dirty, and the curtains ravaged with holes, the kites signalled the beginning of spring.

Omed thought of the time an American had bought him a kite. He was wealthy. Omed and Zakir had known it when they saw him – his jacket with button-down pockets, the thick boots, the metal bottle he sipped water from. It was before the Taliban, before they banned kite-flying, when the skies of Bamiyan were hung with diamonds of coloured paper.

e

'Watch this,' said Zakir as he smacked the dust from his hat and walked straight up to the foreigner. 'Yo lak kite?' he asked.

The American had squinted at him. Zakir only partly blocked the sun. He took a sip from his bottle. 'Some,' he said.

'We lak kite.' Zakir pointed his thumb at himself and then Omed.

'Good for you, boys,' said the American and got up from the low wall he was sitting on.

Zakir followed. 'I lak kite. We lak kite. Please to buy.'

The American turned. 'Look, you seem like nice kids, but if it's all the same to you I'd rather not buy you a kite.' The man pulled at his shirt collar. 'God, it's hotter than the devil's underpants out here. Thought it'd be cold. Expected snow and ice.'

Omed could see the man was uncomfortable; he tugged on Zakir's sleeve. 'We should go, Zakir. The American does not want to buy kites.'

'Omed, be brave. If you want something you must ask for it. This is the way of the world.'

It was true, Zakir was much braver than him. He led while Omed followed. He would be a great man one day; Omed knew this and kept close to Zakir in the hope that some of his friend's bravery may come to him.

'Meestar, come, one kite.' Zakir walked backwards in front of the man.

'Look, son, you think I'm made of money? Sure I've come to look at your statues from halfways around the world, but I'm just a poor sucker like you, just born in a different country is all.'

Zakir shook his head. Omed could almost hear the strange language rattling around in Zakir's brain. Omed was the one who knew English. He should talk to the American. 'One kite, meestar,' Zakir said. 'One kite.'

The man stopped walking, bit his bottom lip. 'I'm too soft for this place. Too soft. They said before I left, why not Europe, why India, Afghanistan, Pakistan, why there? They were right. Too soft.' He stared at Omed. 'Spose you'll be wanting one too, huh?'

Omed smiled at the man.

'I must have "sucker" tattooed here in big letters across my head, in Dari, Pashto, Urdu, Hindi and just about every other language under the sun. Sucker, that's me.'

Zakir led the way to the kite shop. They picked the biggest, the brightest. They got large spools with powdered glass thread. Omed's was fire-red and perfect, but when he got it home his mother made him sell it back to the shopkeeper so they could buy bread for the family and a sack of lentils and a flyblown neck of goat.

Even when his father had lived, there were often times when they were hungry. Words were worth little. Less even than half the value of a kite, which was all the shopkeeper would pay.

The American caught him two days later near the river. 'Where's the kite?' he demanded. Omed just shook his head and pretended he didn't understand, but the shame he felt, the overpowering disgrace of his poverty, made him want to weep.

The man shouted after him. 'That's gratitude for you, hey.'

'I need the one hundred dollars now,' said the Snake, getting up from a lopsided chair.

Omed opened the tin. The rolls of American dollars were faded black and green, torn and shabby. Pulling the rubber band from one roll, he peeled off five twenty-dollar bills. The Snake's small eye widened until the pupil was as big and black as a lychee seed. Omed stuffed the remaining money back in the tin and handed over the one hundred dollars.

'I will return with the passports,' said the Snake as he left the room.

After he had gone, Omed wondered if the Snake would return or if it was just another trick to milk a stupid village boy of more money. He cursed himself for being so unwise. But as the time passed he realised that to be free of the Snake was worth a hundred American dollars. He would just have to find the path to Australia by himself.

Dread struck at him with heavy paws, sharp claws sunk into soft flesh; his stomach spilled outwards. He was a village boy who had landed beyond the horizon of the known lands. He had seen the world only through his father's books. And how little those words had prepared him.

The kites outside clashed. The powdered glass strings cut against each other. One drifted off. Torn by a violent wind, it spiralled up to meet the dark clouds that had formed over

Lahore. Rain, in huge spots, stained the streets. Soon all the paper kites were drawn back to earth.

Reaching under his pillow, Omed pulled out the tin box. He ran his hands over it and felt the roughness of rust under the swirls of his fingerprints. He slipped a small finger into a hole that may have been made by a bullet. Omed opened the box and stared at the rolls of dollars pressed against each other, like bodies. He removed the bands and spread the notes over the bed, faces of high-browed men staring back at him. Solid, square faces hacked from stone. Some bearded, others balding or with hair rising like clouds from their mountainous scalps. For these faces, men would kill. These slips of paper could mean freedom or death.

Omed piled the notes into groups of faces. One dollar – white hair, solemn as a mullah. Five dollars – rock jaw, fringed with beard. Ten dollars – high forehead, strange shirt. Twenty dollars – wild poet's hair. Fifty dollars – stern, beard too short to please the Taliban. He counted all the piles and stored the number in his head. Seven thousand, five hundred and ninety-six American dollars. More money than he had ever seen in his lifetime. How had the Poet of Kandahar collected it all? He looked as poor as anyone. It was a lot of money. If Omed could return home, his family could live like kings.

But he could never return home. Even seven thousand, five hundred and ninety-six dollars could not stop a whistling bullet from a Kalashnikov.

The Snake had robbed him of one hundred dollars already and they had spent money on a bus journey, the hotel and on bribes. Out the window, Omed could see people bending, sitting, pacing, stretching, scratching. Any of them, all of them, could steal the money. It was not a rich place; some people would kill for half the amount. Omed pulled the shabby curtain across, tearing a corner in his haste. The burden of the money was too great and he fell onto the bed, his lips touching faces and numbers.

'Of course I would return,' said the Snake as he sat down in his crooked chair. He couldn't keep his eyes from the bed filled with dollars. 'Here!' He threw Omed a Pakistani passport.

The photo was his, but the name was Mohammed Afghani. Omed held the passport to his face and pointed to the name.

'Oh, I am so sorry,' said the Snake. 'I will take it straight back and tell these men that the Shah of Hazarajat is displeased.' He cleared his throat, drew the curtain and spat into the street. 'Would you be so stupid as to allow a name to stand between you and freedom?'

Omed shook his head as he stuffed the notes back into the tin, closing the lid tightly.

'Listen, my friend.' The Snake's voice softened and he put his arm around Omed's shoulder. 'If you would trust me and let me hold the money for safekeeping, our journey would be a smooth one. With you clutching the purse, I cannot protect you.'

Omed shrugged his arm off and pushed him away. The Snake growled and shoved Omed onto the bed, where he clipped his head on the wooden edge. The Snake's eyes were bloodshot, whites the colour of ghee. He brought his face close to Omed's. There was hashish smoke on his breath. A forked tongue slid along the broken edges of his teeth.

'You should be careful. A boy alone in a foreign city is

subject to many dangers. A boy with a lot of money could be at risk. A boy with no history, no family, could disappear like water into the earth.'

The Snake grabbed the box and walked to the door. Omed's world went red. Like the last day of the Stone People. His blood burned in his arms and thighs. Omed leapt at the Snake's back and as they fell to the ground, the Snake's face smashed heavily into the door. He rolled over and his fat tongue, with the split tip, lolled out of his mouth. Blood wept from a cut above his eye, onto the stained carpet.

Omed prised the dirty fingers from the box. Then, grabbing the Snake by his heels, he dragged him towards the centre of the room and opened the door. He jumped the stairs two, three at a time and ran into the street.

He ran, dodging trucks and motorbikes; cracked concrete and oozing gutters blurring beneath his feet. His feet slapped the ground, beating out a rhythm that kept him moving. His breath was sharp, his heart lunging in his chest. There was no time to think about where he was going. He just kept running.

And then he stopped. He waited while the image of the Snake drained to a spot in his memory – the vision of him lying, bleeding on the hotel floor. Omed knew he wasn't safe. Even with the Snake gone, there was no one in Lahore he knew or trusted. The streets were slick with pollution and the dark glances of strangers.

He slipped into a shop and ordered a cola. It was the first time he had tasted such a drink and the bubbles were a surprise. But he sat, sipping it through a straw, until it was finished. Then he crunched the rough lumps of ice and swallowed them as well.

The light from outside lurched under the wide canopy

at the front of the shop and crept as far as it could into the shaded interior. But at the back of the shop there was almost complete darkness. As Omed stared into this gloom, his eyes gradually made out the blurry half-shapes of men lying on bunks in a darkened room. In one corner a man, with a towel wrapped around his head, scrubbed at his teeth with the frayed end of a stick. The more Omed looked, the more he saw – a whole world looming out of the darkness. People sleeping, eating, playing cards, dreaming, drinking, washed by shadow. Omed turned and the light from outside stung his eyes. Did they ever stray into the sunlight?

Omed slid the box off the table and between his legs. Reaching in, he pulled out the roll of dollar bills and unwrapped one. He went to the counter and paid. The man looked at the dollar bill, held it up to the sun and nodded. He muttered something in Urdu. The word *money*, the word *boy*. Smoke from a cigarette curled from behind the jars of melted sweets. He pointed with his long nose towards Omed's box. Omed hugged it to his chest and turned from the man, not waiting to receive change. Omed could feel the eyes of the shadow-people on his back.

The sun was like a flash of gunpowder. Omed blinked against it, everything fuzzy. He felt a hard grip on his elbow and a rough hand clamped across his mouth.

'I should kill you and take your money. That would be the clever thing to do. No one knows you are here. You are no longer a person. I should kill you.' Omed flinched. The rough bristles on the Snake's chin grazed his neck.

'You cannot even speak,' he whispered. 'What use are you?' He felt for the money box inside Omed's coat. 'I could have all the money for myself.'

The Snake held the knife at Omed's back below his ribs where it would slide easily into his kidneys. It would be a painful death and a slow one. The knife was a silent weapon and Omed was sure the Snake knew how to use it.

A string of Urdu words came over his shoulder and the Snake spun Omed to face the man from the shop. In the same quick movement, the knife dissolved and the Snake placed his hand onto Omed's shoulder. He spoke to the shop owner in Urdu and Omed recognised the words: *uncle* and *nephew* among the complicated syllables. He slapped Omed's face affectionately and smiled.

The shop owner's eyes narrowed and he asked Omed something. He felt the Snake's grip tighten on his shoulder, so he nodded. The owner smiled warily and walked back to his shop.

'You did well,' hissed the Snake. 'Maybe you are of some use after all. A man travelling alone is suspicious but an uncle and his dear nephew, well that is another matter.' He let go of Omed's shoulder. 'You should give me the money,' he said. 'It will be safer.'

But even with the danger of the Snake and his thin-bladed knife, he would not give up the money. It was not his, it was the Poet's, and it was for one purpose only. Omed held his arms tightly around his chest.

The Snake shrugged. 'Well, I shall keep the passports,' he hissed. 'That way we each have something the other needs. That way we are locked together.'

The aeroplane was Malaysian, a red and blue kite on the tail. The seats faced forward like a bus, but the plane was wider and cleaner than anything Omed had ridden on before. Omed tightened his seatbelt until it hurt. He needed to go to the toilet, but he was afraid to enter the small room. Voices crackled out of the speakers above his head – in Malaysian and English, but he struggled to understand. They were flying to Kuala Lumpur, a small red dot many thousand kilometres away. They would skirt the mountains of India before crossing the sea. Then they would fall from the sky into a new land.

When Omed was young, he would watch the steel birds crossing the skies – fat-bellied Antonovs and the sleek darts of Russian MiGs. Once, he and his friends came across wreckage scattered over the rocky ground in the Kakrak Valley. The pieces were so heavy that, between five of them, they could not roll even the smallest chunk. How the machines clung to the sky was unimaginable.

Omed's flight crossed the plains of India at night; towns winking up through dust and smoke like fiery eyes. The clouds were tinged with moonlight as the brocaded edge of a fine kuchi skirt. The plane was among the stars, one of them, a comet across the blue-black night.

Inside the plane a movie was playing. Everyone's ears were wired to their armrests, their eyes stuck to the flickering images on the screen. But Omed could not bear to separate his eyes from what was passing below – cities full of people, sleeping, hiding, robbing, praying, escaping, dying. Town after town after town. As many people as stars.

Then came the sea – a liquid struck by the morning sun and spinning out forever. Omed had never seen water in such a great amount before.

As a boy he had visited the five lakes of Band-e Amir with his father. They had travelled from Bamiyan by bus, all day, walking the final two hours to avoid the mined road. The lakes had been a terrifying blue, caught like snatches of burqa in the folds of skun hills. The water, when they reached it, was cool and refreshing. They had camped overnight in a cave tunnelled into the cliff by Band-e Zulfiqar – the Sword of Ali. Him and his father, and a holy man, a *pir*, all wrapped in shawls against the cold. In the morning, they woke to the sight of the sun turning the water to sky.

It had been their final journey together, and Omed had never forgotten the blue lakes; the red painted stones where the landmines lay; his father's hands tearing bread for breakfast; and the kind words and soft face of the *pir*.

His father sat with the old man for a long time, writing his stories in the small green book he always carried with him. Omed had grown bored and walked down to the lake where giant fish circled in the deep water. When his shadow fell on the surface, they scattered.

Omed walked out on the shallow ledge and peered over the cliff that plummeted into the deepest blue. His shadow radiated spears of light and dark from the sun. It reminded Omed of the paintings of the Buddhas.

Suddenly, his foot slipped and he fell into the deep water. It was so cold that it stole his breath. The air was replaced by water. And he was sinking. And the surface seemed so far away. Too far. And he stopped fighting. He could see the beauty. He could hear voices, soft, fluid, like the water itself.

Above, there was an explosion of white. And from out of it a dark figure moved towards him. It was the *pir*, his long beard trawling behind, filled with bubbles. He dragged Omed up, towards the light.

On the shore, his father's worried face bent over him. Omed coughed the lake from his lungs, shivering. The water had been inside him, all around him, it had been everything.

This was his memory of water.

Below the metal bird, tiny boats rose and dropped on waves. Islands swelled like mountains from the cloudlike sea. Omed could not believe the world was so big. He had read of such things – towns, cities, oceans, countries, people – but a reader can only imagine with what he already carries inside. His father had said, *Omed, you cannot make a cup without clay*. You cannot make something from nothing. By seeing, he could gather clay.

The strange magic of the plane made him crazy. He believed for a moment he could see his future; him standing on the beach in Australia with waves that reached to the sky. His toes curled into wet sand and the sun warmed his neck. He could smell salt as the Poet had described. There were white flocks of birds tumbling though the air.

It was as though the plane was swimming through milk. Skimming towards a city – a dot on the smooth shiny map on the screen.

The plane slowed and lurched through the cloud, dipping its wings at the lights of Kuala Lumpur. When the runway grabbed for them, the plane swooped gracefully and, kissing it softly, delivered Omed back to earth. Passengers tumbled from the gullet of the tin bird, faces as rumpled as their clothes.

The man behind the desk yawned until his nose ran, looking at Omed's photo and then at him and back to the photo. 'Mohammed Afghani?' he asked. Omed nodded. The man held the photo up and then, as pearls of sweat ran into Omed's eyes, he brought his rubber stamp down hard on a fresh page.

Omed's worn shoulder bag travelled slowly beside fresh, plump cases on a long belt. Inside was everything he owned – a few old clothes bought with the bag at the bazaar, a lump of cheap soap. Omed had sewn the rest of his money into his coat while the Snake was sleeping. Stitch by stitch he would unpick it and unfold stone-faced men into the Snake's hand, buying his freedom a dollar at a time.

As they shuffled through the doors and into the thick heat, two men stepped in front of them. One had a bad limp, his friend wore reflective sunglasses. They spoke quickly in the Hazaragi dialect of Omed's homeland. The Snake turned them by their shoulders and walked away so they could talk without Omed overhearing. He stood and waited like a dutiful nephew. Like a lamb waiting for the Eid feast.

Suddenly the two strangers marched quickly towards him, grabbing his bag, and his arm, and shoving him towards a waiting taxi.

'You ride in front. I must talk with your uncle.'

Omed opened the door and saw a man with skin so dark he seemed to be made entirely of night.

'Jalan Tunku Abdul Rahman. Short way only, we are not touriss,' growled the man with the sunglasses as he followed the Snake and the limping man into the back of the taxi. His English was clumsy in his mouth. He smacked the driver on the neck. 'And we pay air so turn it over.'

The driver looked at Omed and smiled, flicking the switch so the air conditioning moaned into life. He reached for another switch and a small statue on the dashboard was suddenly haloed in red and green flashing lights. The men behind snorted and Omed heard the word *kafir*. The statue was a Hindu god, its head heavy with a gold crown and in its right hand a thick spear with a heart-shaped head.

Although he had been brought up in a land where there was but one God, Omed knew from books that in other countries people worshipped different deities. In India there were elephant-headed gods and those with many arms and heads. He had heard the mullahs talk of these idols, deride them, and denounce them as demons. The people who followed them were infidels and beyond salvation; for them it would not be a smooth ride into the afterlife.

Omed was raised a Muslim and taught tolerance. His father had said the many gods of the Hindus were all aspects of one God and that all people's belief in something similar united them. For these words the Talib had delivered him to his God.

The driver saw Omed staring at the tiny figure on his dash. 'Lord Murugan,' he said to him, continuing in English. 'He is my God. Number-wan. I love him wery much. He is helping me when no one else can.'

The driver reached for the radio. The tinny wail of a Hindi song struck the cold air inside the taxi. It was like two strange currents meeting in the fork of a river and the whirlpool they created made Omed's head turn circles. He had not slept on the plane, which added to his dizziness. He closed his eyes for a moment.

He bumped awake in a crowded street in front of a crumbling hotel. The Snake reached in through the window and pinched him on the cheek.

'Hurry,' he said.

The taxi driver held out his hand to Omed.

'It was nice to be meeting you,' he said.

'Come on!' yelled the Snake.

Inside the hotel, Sikhs in neat blue turbans were sipping large mugs of beer. Tourists were rubbing sweat from their cheeks onto the shoulders of their short-sleeved shirts while around them, paint sloughed from the walls in leprous sheets. The creaking fans did not even wake the heavy air.

They put their bags in a room then ate lunch at a wooden table in the dining room. The waiter drew white bibs around their necks and brought hot steel plates of meat, over which he poured gravy until the tablecloth was spattered with meat juices. Omed picked up his knife. It was a weapon that didn't belong at the table. He pushed at his meat. The weather was too hot for this food, full of blood and fat. The Snake tore at his meal, grease spilling down his chin, while the two Hazara drank beer and smoked. All around, men and women became noisy and drunk.

'Why do you wear a coat?' one of the Hazara asked him. 'You are sweating like an ox. Take it off you idiot!' But the coat was the only thing between them and Omed's money.

They demanded Omed pay for the meal.

'You are a rich boy. We know. Come on rich boy, pay for your brothers!'

Omed paid and excused himself, slipping out of the dining room and upstairs to the room. He dropped heavily onto the bed, falling asleep quickly and without dreams.

He awoke, sweating, gasping for air. Where was he? He had dreamed of home – the square of mud wall with its single loose brick, the sight of the table through the doorway. But he was far from Bamiyan and that feeling tore at him, forced a strange howl from his throat.

He opened the window onto the noisy street. The night air was as unbreathable as oil, insects clouded round the streetlights and hawkers had set up stalls on the footpaths. Omed noticed the taxi driver sitting alone at a small tea cart.

He shut the window and left the room, creeping past the dining room where the Snake and his companions were shouting over a table of bottles. Omed crossed the street, dodging scooters and buses, ignoring the calls of men to buy their food, cheap watches and plastic shoes. The taxi driver was sipping a glass of water and he did not see Omed approach. Omed reached out his hand for the man's shoulder but withdrew it. The man turned as if he had been touched.

'My friend, it is wonderful to see you,' he said, flashing his brilliant smile. 'Come, sit, I will get you some foods.'

Omed raised his hand to object.

'You must share something with me. A tea?'

Omed nodded and the driver called to a stall owner, '*Teh tarik satu!*'

The stall owner poured the tea from one jug to another, drawing the jugs apart to froth the milk.

'Pull tea,' the driver laughed. '*Teh tarik.*'

The stall owner drained the tea into a plastic bag and slipped in a straw.

'Come, we will walk and talk,' said the driver. 'I have some time to finish.'

He saw Omed hesitate over the bag. 'It is okay,' he said,

his head rocking loosely on his shoulders. 'You drink. This good *pull tea*. I am only not drinking because of fasting. Only water today, I must regretfully announce, and for the last forty days. And we must walk because walking is good for talking. It is helping words to spill.'

They walked down the busy road, blending onto the street when the footpath became too crowded.

'You must call me Puravi for that is me. It is meaning *horse*.' He laughed loudly as he leapt into the path of an oncoming bus. Narrowly avoiding death, he turned his body at the last moment so it was only his thick black hair that was swept up by the smoky breeze. The driver leant on his horn, but that only made Puravi laugh louder.

'See. See how sure-footed I am. Like a horse. I am sorry if I am scaring you, but I am only having fun. Tonight is a special night, my friend, and I am very full of happiness. Is it not wonderful?' He paused, waiting for a response from Omed. 'You do not speak, no matter, I will speak for both of us.' He laughed again as they crossed the road by a mosque.

'People say if you want a lawyer who can talk you must hire an Indian. For this you do not pay by the word. But I am only a taxi driver. Still I have come far. Is not the city beautiful at night? Do the lights not shine like jewels? Look, some of them have fallen into the river.' He pointed at a dark serpent of water that had sprung up beside them. 'Even she is beautiful at night. Now we cannot see the plastic bag and dead dog and mud.

'Hindus have great respect for the rivers. Mother Ganga in India sprouted from Siva's hair. Siva is very important god and Ganga is important river. See this bridge.'

The bridge was a dark hump with the river easing under it.

'That is way across without trouble. No need to get wet foot. From one sides to next sides, no problem. You want to see the highest up bridge? I can show you this no charge, but we must go by my taxi as it is far.'

While they drove, Puravi allowed a plastic pocket of photos to gush onto the seat between them. They stopped at traffic lights and were immediately surrounded by motorcyclists, pushing to the head of the traffic. Puravi switched on the light and pointed at the first photo.

'This!' he said pointing at the photo. 'My wife Ambuvali. Is she not beautiful?'

Omed nodded. Her gold jewellery shone against her dark skin.

'Ambuvali meaning *piercing eyes*. See the shape of her eyes.'

Omed bent closer, studying the photo, her kohl-rimmed eyes.

'Eyes like arrow tips. Like *vel*, the spear, of Lord Murugan.' He touched the photo with his fingers and then moved to the next one. It was of a small child, a girl with the thick black hair of Puravi and the arrow-tip eyes of Ambuvali. As Omed looked from the photo to Puravi, he noticed the man's lips disappear under his beard. Puravi shoved the car into first gear and rushed away from the lights. The motorcycles were like a swarm of angry bees around them. When the bikes had gone, he whispered, 'This is my daughter.' He closed the wallet and held it against his chest for a moment, steering with his free hand. 'This is a special story. This one is miracle.'

Puravi eased the taxi into a space in front of an open-fronted restaurant. Glazed ducks hung from hooks and food was being tossed in huge curved pans over roaring gas burners. The cooks in dirty white singlets mopped their brows with rags thrown over their shoulders. Puravi took Omed by the hand along the dark street. Above them and beyond, a dark giant of a building peered over its brother's shoulder into the valley between the shops and houses. The buildings pierced the sky like swords.

'My daughter,' said Puravi, coming back to the story. He leant against the doorway of an old shop and his face was split by shadow. 'Her name is Inimbili because we knew when she was born even her cry was sweet. That is her name – *sweet voice*. Inimbili is hard to be born and Ambuvali she almost dying with the strain of it. I thought I would lose everythings, but Inimbili, she is born and everyone is happy and I am dancing and sometime I am drinking whiskies and people they are looking at me differently now and I am proudly because I am a daddy and the world looks different. You understand?'

Omed shook his head slowly and Puravi shrugged. 'I have this very big feeling inside me and sometimes it is too proudly and I am angering God. I do not know. Maybe it is because I am having too much happy and this is not my karma.'

He stopped and twisted his lower lip with his fingers. 'My Inimbili, she is getting sickly. She is burning feverish and I am too stupid, too stupid, to get doctor quickly. I do go, but later. I run, I get doctor, but then it is too late.'

He rubbed his face in the crook of his elbow, his eyes were shiny. 'It is too late. I am stupid.'

Omed wanted to put his hand on the man's shoulder. After a moment they resumed their slow walk. Rain drifted down from the two towers, castles against the purple-black of the sky, a new bruise.

'Ambuvali she is crying for two years. Every night, you cannot believe this noise, this kind of sorrow. I am drinking whiskies again, but this time not for dancing, not for happy. For sad. Ambuvali she is wanting for another baby, but I am afraid. What if I lose her? Then I lose everythings. But she says, "You must be brave Puravi, because if you live with fear you lose what is goodly in life." She is very clever, my wife. She could have been doctor, or lawyer. Maybe in a next life.

'So we try for baby, but no baby. And the doctor, they say there is problems inside and it is not possible any more for baby. And I say to Ambuvali, "It is not possible, Ambuvali, we must accept this and be happy." But she says, "No, Puravi. No! I will not settle for this. Go and pray to Lord Murugan." And I go and pray, but secret I am afraid because if Lord Murugan grant us this wish then I must do Thaipusam, this is one Hindu festival, with *kavadi*. You know this *kavadi*?'

Omed shook his head.

'If wishing is granted you must carry *kavadi*. It is like a tower – a mountain – joined with hooks to body. Inside there is rice and milk for offering to Lord Murugan. There is much pain if you are not fully in trance. For this you must fast carefully, eat only vegetables and curds, no meat. You must take meditation for forty days and desist from bad thoughts and pleasures. You must not even shaving.' He rubbed at the coarse bristles on his neck.

'Down by the river they bathe you and join you to *kavadi* and then you must walk to Batu Cave. It is two hundreds and seventy two steps and it smells of bat smells, but on Thaipusam when we pray to Lord Murugan with our bodies, the air is full of camphor and sweet incenses and the people chant "*Vel...vel...vel...*" and everybodies is dancing and it is most magical. And I take these many steps to the temple of Lord Murugan and I feel no pain, not even from the spear in my cheeks because it reminds me of the love of my God because he has given Ambuvali and me another chance, another baby.'

They crossed the road under the huge buildings and walked around the sleek glass until they met them head on.

'See the bridge,' said Puravi, and Omed followed the tip of his finger to a point not quite halfway up the two towers. 'Two brothers with one arm out to the other, that is the sky-bridge.' Puravi put his hand on Omed's shoulder to show him what he meant. 'Is this not what a bridge is for? For reaching and touching? Once this bridge is built then it is forever and you can cross it any-such time.

'I have been up there and it is incredible I tell you. I have been standing on that bridge looking down right here.'

Omed looked up at the bridge, the arm flung out between the Brothers, and wondered what the world looked like from up there. Above the bridge, the buildings towered upwards until they narrowed, like the sharp peaks of mountains. Omed thought back to when he had watched the American towers collapse while he was in the camp in Pakistan; the terrible frailty of standing alone. The Brothers were stacked in each other's shadow, but there was something comforting about the bridge and the way it reached out and touched, this connection making each one stronger, more stable.

When his brother, Wasim, was young, he was a follower. No matter how Omed and Zakir twisted through the poplars, Wasim would find them. They would hear his sobs behind them in the wheat alleys, from behind boulders and bombed tanks. And when they returned home, Wasim clutching at the tails of Omed's kameez, Omed would be scolded. *Look at your brother. Why is he wet? His pants are torn.*

Wasim couldn't leap the streams on the handle of a shovel. He couldn't make it to Anwar's cave or over the two-plank bridge that led to the bazaar. He was too little.

The lights of Kuala Lumpur were bright. Too bright. If Omed climbed to the top of these buildings would he see the Koh-e Baba? He knew the distance he had travelled, but the mountains of Afghanistan were high.

Omed felt Puravi's hand on his shoulder. 'I must go now my new friend. I will take you to your hotel, but I must warn you, the men who you come with from airport, they are not good men. I have seen them before. Be very caring of yourself.'

At the front of the Coliseum Hotel, Puravi allowed the taxi to creak to a halt. Omed shuffled some money from his pocket.

'No, my friend.' Puravi pushed his hand back. 'This is my pleasure surely enough. Remember the bridge, how it is for crossing and reaching. Remember me when you are far away. Remember my luck and remember yours.' He reached over Omed and flipped open the door.

'My friends have gone to arrange transport.' The Snake took a long drag on his cigarette, it crackled and spat clove sparks into the room. He'd had no opium since leaving Lahore. He was sweating, yawning, shivering. Omed thought he may die and it filled him with hope and dread at the same time.

'We are going to Indonesia, but it is too risky to fly. Our passports are cheap. If you had given me more money, I could have bought better ones.'

The Snake batted at some unseen thing with his palm.

'So we will take a boat. We can easily get into a port where the people checking have lazier eyes and emptier stomachs. They can always use a little money.

'To travel, it is necessary to grease the wheels. Today we go to Melaka. We will meet my friends there. They are arranging a boat.'

While the Snake was organising a car for Melaka, Omed sat in the tiled bathroom and unpicked his coat. Slipping several hundred dollars from their hiding place, he carefully restitched the lining.

The Snake returned sweating, clawing at his clothes. With him was a small Chinese man who had a statue of the Buddha in jade around his neck. Omed remembered the stone Buddhas and how quickly the Talib turned them to rubble. He saw the slice in Zakir's head, the dark blood and flies. And felt the terrible weight of Zakir on his chest as the dust had spilled over them.

'We should go,' said the Snake, snapping Omed back into the moment.

At the rear of the hotel was the Buddhist's car. Three long-haired boys in black T-shirts were leaning on the bonnet and the man pulled out a few small notes and handed them over.

'*Jaga Kereta*,' the Buddhist said, watching them lope back down the street. 'Car guard. They say the money is for them to guard our cars, but it is more so they do not scratch.' He shrugged as if to say, *What can I do? It is the only way.*

The Buddhist spoke English, but his accent was hard to understand. It was fortunate that the Snake spoke little other than Dari and some Urdu. He would need Omed to translate. They were like two leeches, living off each other and hoping to be the last one alive.

Omed's father had insisted that he learn to read, write and speak English. He pestered the few tourists that came to Bamiyan, to practise with his son. They sat with their long hair and torn clothing, listening as Omed had talked. 'Allo meesta. Waatees yar naam? Ma naam ees Omed. Woodju laak tea? I am gooboy.'

'It is the language of the world,' his father told him. But Omed had argued that he never wanted to leave his country, his family and friends. The world outside was of no interest. What use was English in a country filled with so many languages of its own? His father had pointed to a butterfly outside their window. 'Do you think a caterpillar knows that one day it will need to fly?' he asked. So many wise sayings. So many words.

The streets of Kuala Lumpur were busy with trucks and buses and bikes and people. Everyone was going somewhere and where the noise of traffic thinned, the shrill rattle of insects rose. Indian men scuttled down roads on motorbikes laden with plastic bags of bread. Families of Muslims with clean felt hats and white headscarves rode scooters to morning prayer. Chinese taxi drivers shouted at each other from cars swarming like flies over the carcass of the road.

The sun roared over everything, beating down on children playing in the deep gutters, bouncing off white buildings, tearing at the scabbed backs of dogs. When they reached the highway and the rain came, it was not in light drops, but in fat balls that burst on the windscreen like jackfruit. The rain drummed so heavily that they had to slow so the driver could see the way. He clicked his tongue and swore at the skies in Chinese as the car planed like a boat down the highway that had become a river.

In Melaka, they drove past the old red buildings and to the dock where bundles of wood and slabs of heavy rubber lay waiting to be loaded. The port was full of plastic bottles and sticks and smelled like a toilet.

The Snake seemed unsure of his directions. By now he was twitching violently and retching. They stopped and asked a group of small boys, who pointed to the end of a wharf where an old boat was tied. Omed pulled out some notes and paid the driver. Only after the man kissed his Buddha for his good fortune and drove off, did Omed realise he had paid in American dollars what he should have paid in Malaysian ringgit.

This was the first boat Omed had seen up close. When he was a child they would make little boats from paper, floating them out onto broad puddles, or down the streams between the wheatfields, until they became too heavy with water and sank.

Omed knew trucks and buses, where the dangers lay: from landmines, bad driving and poorly made roads. But the ocean was a cold and unfamiliar highway they could slip beneath and be lost forever. Omed had never learnt to swim. Like learning English, it had seemed a foolish pastime. Afghanistan was a country without knowledge of the sea.

The man with the sunglasses and his friend with the limp hurried across the deck. They grunted their greetings before helping Omed and the Snake over the narrow plank and onto the boat. Everything stank of diesel. Wet ropes were coiled like huge snakes against the cabin. They were introduced to an Indonesian man named Malik who was bent over an oily motor. He pointed to an empty spot on the deck and went back to his business.

Without notice, the Snake's friends jumped off and the engine coughed awake. They nosed out of the harbour as night tugged at the corners of the sky.

The lights from shore winked, smaller and smaller, before being clenched in the tight fist of the night. They passed small fishing boats with petrol lamps and saw the huge ghost-shapes of cargo ships bellowing into the swirls of fog. The sea was as dark as a bullet wound. The boat's bow dipped in and out, scooping handfuls of water onto the deck. Omed sat and shivered under the starless night, fearing the cabin, where the Snake was sitting shivering, crying, smoking. Where he would be trapped when the boat edged under the ocean.

About two hours after leaving, one of the boat crew brought Omed a package of rice and a plastic cup of water. The man opened a hatch on the deck and shone a torch below. Then he threw packages of rice into the hole.

Omed crept over and stood beside the man, peering into his torch beam. The whites of a hundred eyes flashed. Sheep, he thought at first; then, cows. But slowly Omed recognised a hand, an arm cradling a human baby, the highlighted curve of a human cheekbone. This ship was a cargo ship and it was exporting live humans.

The hold was a tangle of bodies – human on human – and the heat rose from them like a breath of hell. The sourness of their unwashed skin escaped into the night air as packets of rice rained down on their heads.

The man with the rice nodded at Omed and then down to them. Omed shook his head, imagining their nails clawing at the underside of the deck as the boat filled with water. He backed away, covered himself with his coat and blocked out the world.

The darkness of the coat was like his memory of the movie theatre in Bamiyan – little more than a TV in a darkened *chaikhana*. The screen flickered and came to life. Omed's mother was spooning softened rice into Liaquat's mouth. Liaquat with eyes soft from tears, wearing the embroidered Mazari cap Omed had bought from the gypsy traders. Leyli was singing in the courtyard. He could hear the soft touch of her broom on the dust and the fragile quiver in her voice. Wasim was looking from the window to the Buddha, Salsal, across the fields and bridges, past the ripening wheat and clover. His face was golden, the soft hair on his neck picked out by the afternoon sun.

Try as he might, Omed could not wish himself into the scene. Just as he could never wish his father back.

He tore the coat from his head and breathed desperately, as if he had almost drowned. The boat's nose leapt and plunged. Omed's life was as unstable as this boat. If he stepped to the left or the right, he would leave the world without a trace. But he must keep going. Australia was a light on an island across a black sea. He was moving slowly towards it.

IN JAKARTA, A STREET CALLED Jalan Jaksa wound like a serpent through cheap hotels and restaurants. It was a crossroads, a place of waiting. In Jalan Jaksa everyone was waiting for something. From the tourists who had not yet found the escape route to Sumatra or the temples of Yogyakarta, to the refugees like Omed, who hoped for news of a boat to take them to Australia. Everyone was dying a small death; each hour they stayed, the foul air and hopelessness tore their simple wishes from them. They sat and drank tea and beer in the heat and dust, and swallowed with them the fumes from cars and motorbikes. There were prostitutes – men and women – waiting too, and hoping, like the refugees, for better luck, for a clearer sky, for a chance.

The hotels in Jalan Jaksa all bent their shattered necks towards the street, their curtains hung like folds of skin from the windows. Dogs shat and died and raised puppies among the sheets of cardboard and plastic bottles. The drains ran with green water. Smoke clung to the hot, heavy air.

There was nothing to do but eat and drink and wait, and

repeat this day after day. They had been in Jakarta for two weeks and nothing had happened. The Snake had lost his foul temper and the shakes that racked his body at night. Each day he faded into the smog, returning before lunch, smiling and fluid, with his good pupil a tiny full stop in his rheumy eye. Omed could not smell opium smoke on him, but he knew that vacant, sleepy look.

The Snake said Omed's money was not enough. He said it would be at least five thousand dollars for a safe boat for one person. Omed counted the presidents and found there to be little more than that amount. This meant one of them would be left, marooned in this half-place, this waiting land. The Snake said he had contacts in Australia that would find him work and then he could send for Omed. It would be quicker for him, he knew the system. But Omed knew his tricks.

So, he tried to find a boat by himself. He did not know the right people, the right palms to grease. Every door was barred. And each day the refugees who had found agents disappeared and left him there, waiting.

Each day cost money. And every day Omed's coat got lighter. The faces of stern American presidents slipped from his hands to money-changers and then to the deep pockets of the hotel manager, shopkeepers and restaurant owners. Every day his chances got smaller and smaller, and he knew he could not make it on his own; he was tied to the Snake with a wire that caused him much pain. The contacts the Snake eternally promised, never appeared.

Some days they saw the unlucky ones. They, in turn, saw only their feet as they tramped the dirty road. Motorbikes swerved to miss them, honking horns, but they never flinched. They were ghosts, not people, who had boarded boats with the last of their money spent and never made it to Australia. Some returned only with stories that they told as they begged for change or food.

Omed was sitting alone having tea one afternoon when he saw Yusuf. It had been two years since they were children in Bamiyan. They had not been friends, not in the strictest sense. But Yusuf was someone from home.

He looked far older than his years. His clothes were frayed and his eyes were like puddles. But it was definitely Yusuf.

Omed jumped up from his table and, rushing to the street, caught Yusuf's arm. He cowered as if Omed was going to strike him. Omed pointed at himself and smiled; surely he remembered.

Yusuf looked at Omed for a long time as if peering through smoke.

'Omed?' he said eventually.

Omed nodded.

'What are you doing here?' he asked.

Omed shrugged.

He swallowed painfully, and said, 'If you buy me a drink and some food I will tell you my story. I cannot give it to you for free, my friend, even though it shames me. I have not eaten in four days.' Omed took his elbow and drew Yusuf back to the table. He ordered two teas and a plate of flat noodles.

Yusuf ate greedily, sucking the noodles from his fork and slurping his sweet tea. Between mouthfuls, Omed caught fragments of story. 'I almost made it, Omed.'

He looked up from the rim of his empty cup. 'May I have coffee?' he asked.

Omed ordered and it arrived with a sludge of condensed milk in the bottom of the glass. Yusuf scooped four spoons of sugar into the coffee, stirred, then added another.

'The Australians do not like us. We were forced back to Lombok. I would dearly love another plate of noodles, Omed, if it is not too much trouble. I will pay you when I have money, though I do not know when that may be.'

Yusuf started his second bowl of noodles, but he doubled over with cramps. Gradually, as the cramps rolled from him, he continued. 'Everyone says Australia is the Lucky Country. They say the people are fair.' Yusuf laughed, but his eyes did not laugh with him. He started coughing and held his chest. 'But it is not true. Maybe if we could reach the Lucky Country then things would be good. But we may as well be landing on the moon.' He took another fork of noodles and a slurp of his coffee.

'And now I have no more money, Omed. I am kept alive on foreign charity. I will be sent home and I will die at the hands of the Taliban.' He looked at his own hands as if they were foreign to him.

The two boys sat quietly for a while, the humid air still and heavy. Then Yusuf asked, 'Is that where you are going – Australia?'

Omed nodded.

'Do you have an agent?'

He shook his head.

'Then you may as well swim. Even if you know who is running the boats, it is impossible. Those agents are worse than dogs. They care only about your money.' Yusuf dabbed at the corners of his lips with a cloth.

'Maybe it is better a quick bullet from a Kalashnikov than

your body slowly filling with water. Have you seen these boats? They are not fit for animals!'

Omed thought of the Poet of Kandahar for the first time in weeks. He recalled the Poet's dream of standing by the ocean. Then he remembered the boat from Malaysia. Humans crammed like beasts inside the belly of the ship, the waves eating at the fragile wood.

'You will die. Or be returned here to a living death.'

Omed paid for the food and drinks. He took Yusuf's hand in one of his, clasped his shoulder with the other. Yusuf looked into his eyes and repeated softly, more a plea than a statement, 'You will die.'

As Omed walked back to his hotel Yusuf shouted after him, 'Why do you not talk? Omed? Omed!'

When Omed got back to the room, the Snake was lying on the bed. He snorted himself awake and blinked for a moment with his different-sized eyes turning like wheels under his hooded lids.

'I have some good news, Omed,' he slurred.

Even though Omed had known him since his very last night in Bamiyan, he still did not know *his* name. He would always be the Snake – to be respected, but only from fear, and never to be trusted. The Snake sat up on the bed and rubbed his stubbly face. 'I have found a boat.'

Omed waited.

He added, 'For both of us.'

Omed held his breath.

'For five thousand.'

He threw his arms around the Snake. The man smelled like stale milk, but Omed did not care.

'I must have the money now so I can pay the agent,' he said.

As Omed took his arms from him, he said, 'It is best that I go alone.'

Omed shook his head.

The Snake sucked air through his bad teeth and said, 'As you wish.'

The Snake led Omed down the hotel stairs and back to the noise and heat of Jalan Jaksa. He smacked the roof of an auto-rickshaw and showed the driver an address. They pushed inside and breathed the heavy fumes as the vehicle crept into the traffic.

Jakarta raced through the window at them. Omed's eyes wept, his nose burned and ran rivers which he mopped with his sleeve. The driver's knuckles were blue with tattoos. He had a plastic doll with pink hair hanging from his mirror, a sticker that read *Dagadu* under a big eye on the dashboard. A bead of sweat trickled down the man's neck to the dirty towel draped over his shoulders.

They stopped in front of some shops and the Snake said gruffly, 'Pay him!' He crossed the footpath and disappeared up a crooked flight of steps. Omed paid the fare and gave the driver no extra.

Then he walked up the stairs until they dissolved in gloomy darkness at the first landing. There was a light burning on the flight above. As Omed neared this light, he saw the Snake talking with a turbaned man on a thick pile of rugs. The walls were hung with carpets. Omed recognised tribal designs from Afghanistan and some similar to the ones he had seen in Lahore.

'This is Omed,' said the Snake.

The Carpet Trader nodded at him, but said nothing. Omed knelt on his rug. The fibres were coarse and they poked through his thin pants. He dared not move.

'You wish to go to Australia?' asked the Carpet Trader in Dari. It was good to hear the language, so unlike the throttled Indonesian syllables.

He nodded.

'You are from Bamiyan?'

Omed nodded.

'Bamiyan is a beautiful town,' said the Carpet Trader, stroking his thin beard. 'Why did you leave?'

'The Taliban were trying to kill him,' said the Snake.

'Can the boy not speak?' spat the Carpet Trader.

'His tongue is useless. The Taliban.' The Snake shrugged and said no more.

The Carpet Trader flared his nostrils and Omed felt a handful of whipworms working inside him. The man was bad.

The Carpet Trader muttered, 'Those Talib dogs, they have ruined everything.'

The man picked up a small glass of dark coffee. On one finger he wore a thick gold ring with an emerald as big as a cuckoo's egg. 'Why do you want to go to Australia?' he asked.

'He has heard it is a beautiful country,' said the Snake, leaning forward, holding Omed's shoulder, 'And that the people are fair-minded. There is no war there, no killing.'

The Carpet Trader turned to the Snake and said, 'The young believe there is a perfect world waiting for them.' He stared at Omed. 'But it is only money that can buy this perfect world.

Money can protect you from your enemies. Money can set you free. It can buy dreams.'

Omed ran his finger over the lining of his coat.

'He has money. Five thousand American dollars.'

'Pah! You will buy yourself a cheap dream for that.'

This man disgusted Omed. He pushed himself to his feet, but the Carpet Trader grabbed his wrist and pulled him back down. His uncut nails bit into Omed's skin. He brought his face so close that Omed could see the huge grimy pores on his nose, the hairs that flared out like brushwood from a cave.

He growled through gritted teeth, 'Humility is favoured by your elders. Remember that and you will do better in this life.' He threw Omed's hand back into his lap. Then he got up and left the room.

Omed hung his head. He had come so far, but then destroyed his chances with a foolish act.

The Snake slapped the back of Omed's head as he left. After a moment's silence, Omed could hear the Snake arguing with the Carpet Trader on the other side of the thin wall.

'We had a deal!' shouted the Snake.

'I do not make deals with insolent boys.'

'You do not understand, I must get to Australia. There are people waiting for me in Afghanistan. People who would kill me.'

'What makes you different from any other refugee? Do you think I can go home, that I can earn a living back there? Do you think I like it here with strange food and strange people surrounding me? Police who require bribes? My countrymen, who have turned to beggars, pleading with me every day? The dangers from rival agents? Do you think I have a choice?'

'But you will go home one day,' said the Snake. 'Once your pockets are full of dollars. Once you have pushed a thousand boats to the ocean, you will go home.'

'One day, maybe we can all go home.'

'Me, never. And the boy – his father was killed and he would have been next. He can never go home. I know the one that he shamed, the Talib dog, and that man has a long memory. It is not just a matter of money to us. It is that we wish to live.'

'We are the same, you and I. For us, money is like air. Do not pretend that it is otherwise.'

For a moment there was silence in the next room. Then the Snake cleared his throat. 'You are right – we are the same. And a man who is like me should recognise a good deal when he sees one. Think on this: when I am in Australia we can make some good business.'

'I always know a good deal. Its sweetness is like honey on the tip of my tongue.'

'Come closer, I will whisper to you.'

Omed could hear only the hum of traffic and the table fan whirring, ruffling papers as it turned its head around the room. The Carpet Trader snorted, laughed loudly. 'We are fruit from the same tree, you and I,' he said.

When they walked back into the room, the Carpet Trader bent down to Omed and said, 'You are lucky to have such a friend as this.' And then he chuckled.

The Snake smiled, his smaller eye disappearing beneath his brow, the large one a bitter moon cloaked in fog.

'The boat sails tomorrow. I need the money now,' said the Carpet Trader.

Omed slipped off his jacket. It was really too warm for

Jakarta, but he had sweated and kept his chance at freedom. He moved quickly to grab the Snake's knife.

Both men drew back, waiting for Omed to lunge at them. But instead, he carefully slipped the blade under the stitching in his coat and removed the remaining presidents. He placed them one by one, facedown on the floor.

The Carpet Trader licked his lips and began counting. He folded each hundred dollar set as he went, ending up with fifty piles and a small collection of loose notes. Pulling a steel chest from under a nearby table, he unlocked it and put the money inside.

'You can stay here tonight,' he said. 'I will charge you only what you have given me. From now you will have no need of money. When you reach Australia you can get a job that pays well and live like an Australian.'

The Carpet Trader's room was hot. He and the Snake puffed on cigarettes until the air was bloated with smoke. Omed rolled himself into a carpet. It was brown and gold, from a village near Shibar, he recognised the strong, square *gul* – the stylised flowers blooming in the pile. Breathing the dust of his homeland deep into his lungs, he wished for the morning.

It arrived like a surprise, bursting through the cracked windows and changing the carpet colours like autumn leaves. Omed lay watching them unfold in the new light and thought of small fingers working handmade looms in villages high in the mountains. Children nearly blind by the age of twelve, tying knots handed down to them by generations of weavers. Each design a carefully guarded secret, with codes to be learnt like songs. Designs as much a part of the landscape as rocks or trees. Had these carpets been smuggled like him, with salt water staining their dry fibres? Was this the end of their journey or just another stop on the long road?

'Wake up!' yelled the Carpet Trader as he kicked Omed roughly in the back. A trail of smoke followed him out of the room. Omed roused the Snake and dragged him down the steps. The Carpet Trader waved down a taxi and they sped off.

'Where are we going?' asked the Snake.

'To freedom!' shouted the Carpet Trader and threw his head back and laughed.

The Snake smiled grimly and Omed remembered when he had used these same words as he pushed him into the truck bound for Pakistan.

After half and hour of threading through traffic and narrow streets, they arrived at a place called Sunda Kelapa. The docks were busy with ships unloading rough-sawn timber. Whole forests sailed into the harbour, the boats sipping water over their low sides. Men reloaded them with mattresses and tins of paint, crates of Coca-Cola and beer.

Gangs of boys and girls ran up to the taxi and thrust model ships through the open windows. '*Pinisi*, mister! *Pinisi! Pinisi!* One hundred tousands rupiah, mister.'

The Carpet Trader threw open the door, knocking two of them to the ground. He pushed the others out of the way and strode onto the dock.

Omed and the Snake followed him to a steel boat. Even though it was heavily rusted, it looked strong and for the first time in weeks, Omed had hope in his heart that he would make it to Australia.

They squeezed in beside bags of cement. As they pulled

away from the wharf, the Carpet Trader's taxi threaded through the tangle of cars, buses and bodies, back to his carpets and the papery silence of Omed's smuggled presidents.

The boat was smaller than the one that had carried them to Indonesia. The Snake and Omed were the only passengers and there were three crew members and a captain who steered with his feet from a tall chair in the cabin. He dodged small boats and piles of floating rubbish as they sailed from the port.

The boat made it to the rolling sea and hugged the coastline of Java past smouldering mountains and the tiny canoes of fishermen. The sun pushed through starched clouds and blistered the wooden villages lining the beaches.

One of the crew brought bowls of hot noodles and beans. They sat with their backs against cement bags and ate. Omed finished and crawled to the front of the boat. He tried to imagine what Australia was like. In his mind, he saw wide beaches, smiling people, kites, waves reaching for the sky. It had been hard to imagine waves of this size when the Poet of Kandahar had first told him of Australia. Now, he understood them, the way they pushed and rolled under a boat. Their power and their grace. How hard it would be to fight against them.

The Snake slept, the larger of his eyes slightly opened to the sun. Omed wondered what he had spoken of with the Carpet Trader, how he had persuaded him to get them both on this boat.

Omed watched the sun drop and night skulk like a thief round the corners of the sky. It stuck foul fingers into the valleys of the waves, dug itself into the boat. Omed shivered and wished for the sun but finally, exhausted, he fell asleep.

He dreamed again of his kitchen table. As he ran his fingers over the smooth wood, the knots opened like eyes. The eyes bled sap tears and behind them faces, torn with agony, opened hollow mouths. Their screams were silent, but Omed could feel the despair twist into his heart like shrapnel. And then the wood turned to water and waves sprung from open grain, whorls twisted down to the ocean floor where the bones of people rattled. The faces on the table were covered by the waves, stone faces, cracked, masked, eyes lit by fires, mouths sucking like fish as Omed reached his hand into the water, but it burned as if it was fire. He turned to the faces of his mother and father, but they were smudged by darkness and he couldn't make them out and this was the forgetting, this was the heart-killing sadness of distance and time, and his brothers and sister drew behind as if they did not know him. He fell backwards into the table, into the water, and even though he reached his hand out for his mother she turned her back and walked to the door as the waves grabbed his shoulders and he tried to scream, but the water was in his lungs and it was soft like honey. It didn't hurt. It didn't hurt! It was over.

He was a spot of light on the sea floor. Fish worshipped him. He no longer had to live like a rootless person, shifting like the clouds across the sky, never resting. Omed had found his new home. He looked across the ocean bed – it was covered with points of light, people like him, small stars.

'Omed. Omed.' The Snake was bent over him. 'We have to change boats. This is Lombok Island. This is the plan.'

Omed stood. They were moored to a dock. There were chickens, goats, bright bundles of cloth, drums of diesel, baskets of fish. There were faces, bodies in bright cotton, bicycles, clusters of happy children fishing and diving into the oily water.

'You have to get off here,' said the Snake and shoved him towards the plank connecting them to shore.

He looked at the Snake, trying to know what was going on behind those mismatched eyes. Omed was still furry with sleep.

'Come on, you must go to the other one.' He pointed to a small fishing boat. 'I will follow.'

Omed blinked his eyes and tried to clear his mind. The Snake was a fat twist of deceit. How could Omed trust him? But there was no one else. He walked down the plank and crossed the jetty to the other boat.

The boat was small and made of splintered wood. There were twenty people crowded onto the tiny deck. Surely it could not sail to Australia?

The man in the wheelhouse smelled of alcohol and had a dirty rag tied to his head in the manner of a turban. He was eating a tin of fish with a bent fork. These sea-people were all the same. How casually they approached their dangerous work. Was it because they had little respect for water? Or was it simply that they knew the sea, and its many moods, so well? Omed had no choice but to trust them.

The man pointed with his fork to the open deck. Omed sat beside a mother and her two little girls. She smiled at him.

'Are you going to Australia?' she asked in English.

He nodded, thankful again for having learned these English words. Long ago, they had been an unwelcome gift from his father and the strange travellers to Bamiyan. Now, with his father dead, the gift would only ever be for Omed's ears. Even if he landed on the shores of Australia, these words would never be tested on his tongue.

'We have travelled from Iraq. My children have not seen their father in four years. They do not remember him. In two days we will meet him.'

Omed smiled at her. He liked the way she cradled her children to her, protecting them from everything. It was the thing that every child should know.

She turned her children's heads into her breast. 'I am scared. My husband writes that he is in prison in Australia. He warned us of this journey also. But we did not have money for a bigger boat. There were too many people to pay. Still we must go. What else can we do? The children must know their father.' She touched her girls' hair with the tips of her fingers. 'We have been lucky so far and *insha'Allah* we shall continue to be.'

Omed thought of all the money he had spent getting to that boat. Of all the strange palms he had greased.

'The luckiest ones travel on that boat,' said the mother. She pointed to the boat that was pulling out to sea. The boat Omed had just left. As it turned its nose seaward, Omed noticed the Snake huddled among a group of people. They locked eyes for a moment and Omed spat into the sea. If there had been bullets Omed would have sent them to him. If there had been a knife he would have thrown it. His spit was swallowed by the ocean, pathetic in its smallness. It was all he had.

The boat sailed away and the Snake became a stain, a smudge, a spot, a pinprick and then he was gone.

They had been a long time at sea when the waves became mountains. The boat was tossed like a stick in a snow-melt river. Two people were lost overboard – a child and an old man. No one dared to try and save them. Inside, all prayed for a quick death.

The boat rose on the waves, trying to spear the clouds with its sharp nose. It fell, gulping water over the decks, washing people from side to side. Fearing they would be swept overboard, Omed tied the mother and her two children to the anchor chain with some thick rope. The sea was furious. It was endless peaks and chasms. The captain was crazy, shouting into the wind. They were in his hands.

The mother grabbed Omed's shoulder. 'Please save my girls. If I die, please save them. Help them find their father.'

Omed promised with his eyes, but they were so full of fear and water that he was sure she didn't understand. How could he promise such a thing when his own death was so near?

People were screaming. Grown men sobbed and vomited through their hands. The wind stole prayers and whipped them into the ocean. This place knew no mercy. It howled into the faces of terrified children. It knew no shame, spitting in the mouths of grandmothers. Omed had fled the Taliban for this new hell. To die so far from his home and his family.

An old woman was dragged from the deck by a wave. Her arms stretched out above her head, her hands clawed at the air. Omed saw her hair float for a moment on the top of the water before swirling under. A young boy screamed after her, jumped from the arms of his sister into the sea. The world was insane. Omed could make no sense of it anymore. The rules had been changed. Chaos replaced order. The sky became the ocean. Language was screams. Omed rocked on his haunches, his hands over his ears. He sang into his mind, into this new broken world. A cradle song, a lullaby. His mother's hand reaching down for him. Her soft voice. His tears, the seawater, all the same.

The boat began to break. The captain ran from the wheelhouse and dived into the ocean. He shouted at the waves. Wood tore apart. Oil ran over the decks, whipped to brown froth on the sea.

The boat's back snapped like an old tree. Water raced into the hull. The motor choked. People scrambled to abandon the deck. The mother was tearing at the knots that tied her and her children to the anchor chain. Omed's knots. *His* knots.

He scrambled towards her. The boat ducked beneath the waves. Rose again. He crawled like a crab over bodies and broken wood. Towards the mother, the children, his carefully tied knots. The deck plunged and Omed slipped forward until he was jammed hard against the side of the boat. Suddenly he was thrown free and rolled through the sea. When he clawed to the surface, it was to angry sheets of white water. The boat was gone. The anchor was gone. The children and mother were gone. Omed was alone with a thousand peaks and valleys, grey and black and white; and the howling, stinging, tearing wind.

A piece of wood became his world. On one side, the words POTONG DI SINI, that he read over and over to quieten his mind. The strange words meant nothing to him but they meant everything. They were something human to focus on. On the other side were the intricate swirls left by worms. It was layered like a biscuit. Light then dark wood sandwiched to form a piece as thick as his thumb. If he lay flat, it almost floated, but it was more comfortable to lie with his cheek against it and his body dangling into the water. Every now and then he would drag himself up to warm a piece of his body in the sun.

There was nothing to eat or drink. It would be a slow death. Unless the big fish came. Omed had heard whispers of them on the boat. They were twice as big as a man, their teeth were daggers, their skin was steel. He prayed that the big fish would take him.

The ocean was sleeping off its rage; it was as flat as his sheet of wood. The sun shone onto the mirrored sea and stripped the skin from his neck. The only sound was a light knocking as if the ghosts of the storm wished to use his raft as a door to escape the ocean.

Omed's kitchen table was a boat filled with strangers and he was a small boy locked to one side with his legs hanging below; his knees knocked like broken tree limbs and the moon was shining through his window. But it was springtime and the sun was burrowing through cloud and it touched the tips of his fingers as he paddled them in the broad still water. He was awake and asleep. He was filled with the hollow feeling of not-knowing and a thirst that he could not quench despite all the water that surrounded him and then he dived beneath dreams and people he knew were there and there were plates of soft lamb and vegetables and jugs of cool mountain water and his father was alive. He was alive. And he sang his mother's song and watched kites drift in the turquoise sky, their tails snapped in the breeze and everything was hope. He was hope. The kites were black diamonds, the sun was a ball, the clouds were goats, herded from dawn to dusk grazing on the endless blue. Everything was blue or white and there was so much light, his eyes were burnt, his lashes were stuck to each other with salt and still he looked for hope, watched for the kites.

It was then they came. He saw their dark shapes first, twisting like coils of night within the sea. He plunged his hand into the water. As she rose, Omed could see her mouth, lips turned in a smile, skin turned grey. Her hair ran behind her in a wake. Her children tugged at her toes and clung to her breast as she rose to the surface. Her lips pushed above the water and Omed heard a gasp as she took the first taste of air.

Come down with us, she said reaching towards him with her thin fingers. *It is time to rest. Your journey is over, Omed.*

I am sorry, he called to her, but her ears, small, curled like two shrimps, were filled with brine. *I am sorry!* he shouted, touching his hand to his heart.

Her children rose so their eyes were pressed to the skin of the ocean. They had grown webs between their fingers and toes.

Come, said the mother again, straining up with her hand to rest it on his arm. But as Omed recoiled from her touch he could see sorrow flood like a shadow into her eyes.

She said, *It is a long and difficult path you have chosen. But remember us. Wherever there is water we will be there.*

With that, she spiralled down into the depths, towing her two children behind her.

Don't go, Omed cried. Rolling from the wood, he felt the water's cold shock. And he dropped to where it was black and there was no light and he felt the hunger and thirst falling away and the mother and her children smiled, sea lice gathering in the corners of their eyes. And he remembered long ago when he had fallen into the cold waters of Band-e Zulfiqar. And it seemed right that his journey would end this way.

And then he was rising, his body pulled above the ocean and he could see his world, his square of wood, lying flat and small on the endless blanket of ocean and he reached out his hand, but it was too far away.

And someone said in English, 'What's your name?'

They were surrounded by the sun. They smelled of soap and salt.

'What's your name?'

Behind them were stars and blue sky and red lines, white triangles. And faces he remembered from the boat – the captain, an old lady with weepy eyes, a small boy. But the Iraqi mother and her two children were not there. And he had tied the knots.

'What's your name?'

I am sorry, he whispered, but they could not hear him.

OMED DREAMED OF A LIFE that wasn't patterned by wire. A life that was not sealed behind two rows of steel fences. Every day he watched the wall and hoped. When he was out for exercise, he watched the sky. It was the home of eagles. Omed knew these birds, had seen them on the battlefields and killing grounds of home. They sent a shiver down his spine.

Out there was an endless desert, a sea of sand and rough rock where no man could live. Strange animals roamed the desert, snakes and giant lizards, the *kangaroo* that stood on two legs like a man and had the face of a sheep. They stared at Omed from outside the wire. This was no country for humans. Not here. They were trapped in a desert, an island within an island.

His father once said, *Words are a bridge that can save you.*

So Omed read. There were only a few books in the centre. But he found one on the stars and learned the tricky constellations that made up the roof of Australia.

At night there were many stars – a spray of them, thick like a shawl across the belly of the sky. But it was not like the sky of Bamiyan where as a child his father would point out animals and strange beings. Here the moon rocked on its back, stars flew across like tracer bullets.

He searched for the Southern Cross. This was the key to the way south. In the south lay cities and people, places where someone could hide; he had heard the guards talking.

As he read he practised his writing, scribing words onto lengths of toilet paper with a fine-tipped pen. He needed to write quickly or the ink would grow fat on the soft pàper. He needed to write in English because he needed to answer their questions. And how else would a mute speak?

At first they had thought he was deliberately silent and told him that things would go badly if he did not answer. When he had showed the mangled stump of his tongue, he saw disgust in the pucker of their lips.

There were always two and they spoke quickly. They had an interpreter, a Tajik who hated the Hazara and did not know his special language of silence.

The more Omed wrote his story, the less he remembered what he had written. Once the words had left his hand they were gone. They kept the paper and said it was their property. This was the way they stole his story.

It was important to remember everything exactly as it had happened. This was what they wanted. If something, even a small detail, was forgotten the two suited figures would give each other a solemn look, like sour mullahs, and the rat scratch of their pens would rise in his ears.

He knew enough to realise that these men held his life in their hands. At their wish, he could live beyond the wire. But again, it all came down to words and sometimes they were his friend and other times they betrayed him.

Words would haunt Omed at night. They would rain into his sleep like bullets. They would puncture his dreams with their tiny spikes, the punctuation marks worrying his wounds and infecting him with their madness. He would swallow words like *illegal* and *refugee* and *backdoor* and *process*. He would shout *poor* and *life* and *hope* as an antidote and the words he did not know in English he would whisper in Dari, in Hazaragi, in shame.

The detention centre was built for four hundred people, but fifteen hundred souls crouched under the tin roofs. There was no air conditioning even though the sun made the sides of the huts too hot to touch. Five toilets meant long queues in the mornings and evenings. The conditions turned people into animals, fighting and clawing their grief out on each other and themselves.

Omed watched as desperate people drank shampoo and carefully sewed their lips together to show the world how little their words meant. Such was their sadness, their sense of helplessness. He saw parents pull their children to their bodies in the hope they could protect them, but the poison was in the air, inside their minds.

The man who ran the camp wore a wide-brimmed hat to protect him from the sun. His shirt was pressed, the seams of his trousers sheared like blade edges to his polished shoes. His name was Jim Parasole and he was the whitest man Omed had ever seen. Even the albino, Omar, whom the village children would shout names at from behind the walls of Bamiyan was not as white as this strange man. When he had first seen him, Omed had wanted to touch his thin, pale eyebrows to see if they were real. But he would not be touched.

He was king here. In the old manner of kings. A ruler in a desert kingdom surrounded by his army of hard-booted men and the annoying presence of his subjects.

Omed had been brought before him only once, when he had scuffled over the book he was reading. The man who had wanted to take it, an Iranian, had not counted on the sharpness of Omed's nails. Omed had spent three days in the Management Unit for his crime.

One afternoon Mr Parasole stepped onto the red dirt and made his way to the front gate. Omed leant his face against the burning wall of the toilet block and watched. A truck drove to the gate and was let inside. Mr Parasole greeted the driver and walked with him as he opened the rear door. A figure stepped into the glare. A man. He was small and hunched, impossibly dark and dirty beside Mr Parasole. Mr Parasole talked to the smudge-person briefly and called a guard. As the guard walked the man inside, Omed recognised him.

The Snake looked back and smiled, his forked tongue reaching out and running over his bottom lip. Omed fought sickness. The Snake had condemned him to death on that wormy boat. Omed had tied the children to the anchor that had dragged them to the bottom of the sea.

Omed sat alone as he always did at mealtimes: the boy who couldn't talk, whose silence set him apart. He ate slowly, turning the pages of a book with his free hand. Around him, the clamour of language fell like a mortar barrage. He put his hands over his ears and continued to read.

Suddenly, a plate came down beside his book and Omed's gaze ran slowly to it. From there to a rough brown hand, nails bitten back hard, a tangle of hair on the forearm, scars, a cheap jumper with sleeves pushed to the elbows, the bristled neck, the jawline puffy and pocked, and then the eyes, one of them too big for the face, as if it had been plucked from the corpse of a giant.

'*Salam*. If I am not mistaken it is my young travel companion.' He leaned close to Omed, whose nose tightened on the smell of his sweat. 'Is it not wonderful that we meet again?'

Omed's heart thumped. It became so loud that the lights in the room dimmed. There was not enough air. He fought for breath. His book slid sideways and hit the floor. Then he was on top of the man. He had a fork. And suddenly there was little space between it and the Snake's good eye. The Snake pushed him back, but the fork drew four deep lines across his cheek before rattling across the room. There were faces all around. People shouted. Blood. The Snake's hands came around his throat. He could feel his windpipe crushing.

Omed gave up.

Time began a slow shuffle. Sounds echoed and faded. And so, he would cease to be. In this terrible nothing place so far from home. He felt relief that it would be over. Should a life be lived in this way? So much fear and running. So much death and waiting. He closed his eyes and the world vanished. Like the giant Buddhas, like his people, he would finally be scoured from history.

The guards dragged the larger man off. Despite himself, Omed pulled breath into his worthless body.

'You right there, buddy? You right?'

Omed went into Management. Where they put the suicides, the violent, the crazies. It was punishment and protection. A bright hell.

The lights were on all day and all night. There was no one to listen to, nothing to see, nothing to touch but the bare walls. With nothing to cling to, Omed's mind floated like an abandoned boat. At first he marked the passing of time with meals. He pressed his ears to the wall, eager for sound, any sound at all. Eventually, they became so finely tuned they could pick up the slightest noise through the steel. He could hear ants working the soil under his bed, clouds preparing rain, the sound of birds and singing and bells and the rush of wind through feathered wings and water trickling underground and his blood churning, churning inside. His mother came, telling him to be strong; saying his father had never given up, even when they finally came to kill him; he had not surrendered his beliefs. The guards came with questions and even Mr Parasole with his white, white skin, and his big hat. They said Omed had started the fight. There were witnesses. He should speak up. *He had no words!* They were well-fed and sweaty, beefy men, with thick necks. But he was alone on another ocean. Cool salt. Sun. Adrift with wraiths and water *djinns* and bird spirits and gods with trunks sewn with golden thread.

The Poet sang to Omed, his face long and wise.

A week can be a month and a month can be a year.
  It is that simple.
But time is never caught like a fly in amber.

It moves. It is a living thing.
And time dresses as it pleases.
  For one it is a quick dancer,
  its skirts spinning around.
For another it is an orphan
  dressed for a funeral,
  a slow march.
When there is too much time,
  then there is more.

Finally Omed was torn from the lighted cave. But he had cleverly turned himself into a curtain. They tried to open him, but he had gone; slipped into a world of his own making. He spoke with his parents as fluently as when he had a tongue. He knew everyone else to be ghosts: the guards with their pink fists, the swirl of inmates in dull prison clothes. Walls were everything to Omed. A thing only had value if you could hide behind it. Beyond the fences, he knew angry gods were marching, he could hear them stamping up a haze of dull desert dust, dragging the heavy souls of trapped men behind them. Omed slipped enough food between his lips to hold life. He spread oil through his hair and smelled of printing ink and the tin-tack odour of electricity.

The Water Mother came to him one day as he plunged his hand into the toilet to paste the walls. Her voice bubbled up.

Why have you not called for me, Omed? I have been wait-ing all this time. Look how my children have grown.

He was used to hearing voices, but there was a clarity in

this one that drew him closer. Eventually, he could see the outline of a woman, her hair bound to her head like a hank of seaweed. In the dark folds of her skirts, the faces of two children appeared. They were the colour of wet paper, a storm-cursed ocean.

I have a message from the Poet, Omed. He asks, 'Have you given up on freedom?'

He had not heard from the Poet in a while. *Tell me, what is freedom?* Omed asked.

She smiled and small fish glimmered between her gums. *Freedom is many things to many people. You have to find your own meaning. For your poet it was the waves that reached the sky.*

Omed slapped the water. *Waves mean death! I am free now. I am free from worry and fear. I am safe within this world.*

You call what you have freedom, but it enslaves you, she said. *You are not the master of this world that you have built. You are trapped. You have built a wall when you could have built a bridge.*

Then what is freedom? You must give me an answer.

It is a right. Freedom is an idea that you must make real. You must allow it into your life.

That is easy for you to say, snarled Omed.

The mother rolled onto her back, her children under her arms. Omed looked into their eyes – dark, shiny like mussel shells; impenetrable.

And then in the mother's eyes he saw a tiny image of his own mother, cooking and cleaning, and carrying wood for the fire. And at night, the house lit by candles, his mother stitching their torn clothes. He saw her clasping the photo of her husband to her chest as she watched her children sleep. He saw the faces of refugees trapped below decks on the boat bound for Sumatra. He saw Puravi, his willingness to suffer for the gift of new life. His bright steps, sure-footed as a horse, below the sky bridge in Kuala Lumpur. And finally, Omed saw his own father pecking words onto the page with his ancient typewriter. All those handwritten 'e's. All those people pushing forward even though the way was hard.

'Morning, Omed,' said the guard as he pulled out a chair and leaned on the back with his two big hands. 'They're offering packages for you blokes to go back home. Looks like things are improving in Afghanistan. The good guys are winning again.' The guard smiled and patted Omed on the arm. A month ago, Omed would have flinched at this contact, but he had gradually made his peace with the living and forced his mind back into some kind of order.

But he didn't know what to feel about this news. That the Taliban had fallen was a great thing, but how long would peace last in a country that has lived by war for years? The Talibs could outlast the Americans.

The Afghans in the Centre watched and listened to the story as it bloomed like a flower. The media reported that the new government was bringing peace to their country. The Taliban were finished. The country was going to enter a new time of peace and prosperity.

The Australian government offered money and a one-way ticket to Kabul. There would be planes instead of leaky boats. Everyone would go back to their villages like kings with presents and smiles. The country was safe, they were saved.

But the news that arrived by telephone – straight from the towns of Afghanistan – was different. The country was in chaos. Warlords ruled in remote areas. The Taliban were like wounded dogs, more dangerous than ever.

Omed would sometimes talk with the Water Mother and her children. They were different to his parents whom his mind, in its sickness, had called to bear witness to its collapse. These spirits were real.

As Omed cleared toothpaste from the sink she whispered, *Remember freedom, Omed. It is up to you. You owe it to your family to find a better life, to be strong and never give up. They have suffered to give you this chance, do not waste it.*

One day a tail of dust whipped across the desert. At the head of this storm were cars and vans.

The guards were assembled in blue overalls and black caps. Jim Parasole stood in the deep shade, watching, his faded blue eyes darting between his forces and the dangerous others. People, with cardboard signs and bright clothes, spilled from cars. They waved flags and shouted. After months of white walls and blue uniforms, spring had arrived.

They climbed the outside fences. The guards stared at each other and shouted into their radios. Mr Parasole pulled off his hat and held it in front of his chest like a shield.

Refugees climbed onto roofs, burning themselves on the hot metal as they scrambled up. Sweat pearled on the faces of the guards as they pulled on helmets.

A group of protesters tied ropes and chains to the fences and started their cars. Bars flew out leaving gaps big enough to squeeze through. The refugees tried to scale the inside fence, but guards tore at their legs and brought them screaming to the ground. But soon there were too many and one man made it across the razor wire and through the outside fence. Then another. Then six, then twenty. The crowd enveloped them.

The refugees were made bold by the promise of escape. Many were cut badly by razor wire, bruised and broken by the batons of the guards. But still they climbed and jumped.

Omed saw his chance and clambered onto a roof. From there he leapt to the high rail of the inside fence. The razor wire sliced at him as he slid his body through. He could see the gap in the outside fence, imagined himself there. A hand reached up for him and the tips of fingers brushed his leg.

He felt himself being drawn back. The tiny knives on the razor wire dragged through his flesh. His face scraped the metal bars as he fell. The guards were frenzied – scared and excited by the riot and the escapes. With one cheek in the dirt, Omed stared across the ground at helmeted men on horseback forcing the protesters away from the fence. He buried his face in the dust and wept.

Someone kicked him and he drew his legs to his stomach for protection. A baton wavered in the air and the guard gritted his teeth. Omed closed his eyes, but the pain didn't come. He opened them again and saw a second guard with his hand wrapped around the baton.

'Leave him,' he said. 'Can't you see he's already beat?'

It was the man who had given him the news that Afghanistan was once again safe.

As summer began, many people began starving themselves. It grew hotter, but they refused even water. Some were children.

And then there was another chance at escape. In the black before dawn – a time when the silence was the worst – Omed was shaken awake.

A voice whispered in his ear, 'They have come again. Go outside. I must tell the others.'

Omed blinked at the darkness as the shadow slipped out of his room.

He crept from his cabin into the night air. The desert sky was filled with stars. He could see the Southern Cross, low on the horizon. There were shouts outside the fence. Men's voices. They howled into the clear air and the noise echoed through the steel valleys of the Centre.

A man was pressed against an outer building. Omed joined him and strained his eyes into the dark. There was a silhouette of a car, smudges of people and the crunching of doors opening and closing.

'They are drunk,' a man said, chuckling. Omed recognised the Iraqi who had escaped during the spring protest. One of those that had been captured and returned, with his head bowed, to the Management Unit.

'You are wondering why they are here, no?' he said. 'Well, I think it is a good place to be drunk. No one to complain – just kangaroos, wild dogs and us dead souls.'

They both tilted their ears to catch the noises. A car barked into life, its headlights spearing into the desert. Behind it, in the red eyes of its tail-lights, a fog-bank of dust grew. Then came the tearing of metal.

'Quick!' said the man. 'They have broken the fences.'

They moved towards the steel and razor wire. Already there was a group of guards trying to protect the hole in the outside fence. One of them was trying to tug a blanket from the inside fence where refugees were pulling themselves over. On the outside, the car was already flying into the night.

'This way,' said Omed's new friend.

They moved to a patch of darkness where the searchlights couldn't reach. From there they eased along the fence until they were next to the battle. Every now and then a black figure would cut free from the blur of fists and feet and a torch would trace its path into the black desert.

'Now!' said Omed's friend and pulled him towards the fence. Batons came down like thunder, blood gushed, torch beams swept across metal and into the low bushes, footsteps thumped on the ground, his heart surged inside him. He tripped, stars whirling to the earth, sand pouring into the sky. The dark figure of a guard moved towards him and he knew it was over again.

The guard stood above him – a black tower. He smelled of aftershave, chewing gum and soap. His torch blinded Omed and he shielded his eyes.

Then the guard swung his light towards the inside fence, through the gap in the outside fence and into the desert.

'Go,' he said. 'Before I change my mind.'

The searchlight swept over them and Omed saw for a second that it was the guard who had saved him once before. He stood and held out his hand for the man to shake.

'Go!' he screamed.

Omed turned to run, but only got a few paces when a voice exploded from near the fence. 'Stop him!'

The lights hit him as he clambered up and over the blanket-covered razor wire. He got past the guards on the outside fence and ran into the bushes. The branches scratched at his arms, but he kept running. He fell over, got up, ran again. His breath burned like boiling water. A hand grabbed at his arm, swung him off his feet. It pulled him into a hollow – a collapsed burrow.

'You run like a bullock in a wheat field,' the voice whispered in Dari.

Omed knew at once who it was. That he could be so cursed to have escaped only to find himself with this man.

'It seems once again we are to travel together.' The Snake leant back on his elbows and sucked in the night. 'Can you taste the freedom in the air?'

Omed jumped to his feet, but the Snake caught him at the elbow and jarred him to the ground.

'Are you mad?' he hissed. 'They have lights. Soon there will be dogs. We need to keep low, travel quietly by night. I am a smuggler, it is my work. My family has done this business for centuries. Yet again, you will need me.

'I saw you reading the star book. You must know these skies. If you know the skies then you will know the land. And so I need you. It is much like old times.'

Omed struggled in the Snake's grip.

'Use your head, boy. We can travel together to the city. From there we can be rid of each other. It is a business arrangement. Nothing more. I am not asking you to like me.'

They ran most of the night, moving away from the lights of the nearby town. Finally, they lay in a dry riverbed, shivering with cold and exhaustion until the sun reached out with its broad arms and held the desert. As Omed waited for the sun to warm him, he watched an army of ants crawling over the sand, searching for water and food. How would they survive with nothing? The back of his throat already ached from lack of water. He swallowed what little spit he had, but his own body's moisture would evaporate soon enough.

They found patchy shade under a thin tree. The hours passed slowly. Omed tried not to move, to use any energy. There was a time, when the sun was at its highest, when even the ants stopped.

They began walking again as the sun dropped, following the point on the earth that the Southern Cross showed. The Snake talked, filling the open space with his voice as if he feared the silence.

'There is money to be made in Afghanistan again, I hear. The opium fields are blooming. Westerners are greedy for heroin. If only I could return home. And escape this hell.' He kicked at the dust that had turned from red to blue in the dim starlight.

They came across the corpse of a camel. Its legs spread out as if it had been flattened from above. The stench was overpowering, but Omed wondered if they could eat it. Wild dogs had torn at the carcass and Omed and the Snake heard their mournful howls.

'We must get away from here. The animals will be back and we shall be next on their table.'

The next morning it rained and they busied themselves finding small puddles in the rocks. The water tasted of the earth, but it was good. They made for a rocky outcrop before the heat of the day dried what little moisture they had gained.

Omed and the Snake crept into the shade of an overhanging rock and lay down. The ground was smooth and dusty. On the ceiling of the cave, paintings had been made from white and red earth. There were pictures of kangaroos and bird-headed animals, strange snake-necked tortoises, men with spears and the outlines of hands. It gave Omed some comfort to realise that they were not the only ones to know this place. There were also pictures of fish that swam before his eyes on cool currents.

He sat up suddenly. If there were fish then surely there was water.

'Where are you going, boy?' asked the Snake, his large eye appearing like a moon.

Omed waved him off and entered the glaring light. It made him dizzy and his head throbbed from thirst. The sun was high and it nipped the back of his neck as he skirted the outcrop, climbing over boulders and weaving through patches of shade.

When he saw the colour, he could not be sure if it was real. Suddenly there was green where there had only been red earth and blue sky. There were fringes of it peeking from behind rocks, creeping over the ground. Omed followed it and, as it became denser, he heard the sound of birds. Small birds, like the singing canaries in the bazaar. Not the fearful screech of the death hawks.

As he climbed onto a rock, he found himself overlooking a pond. The water was yellow-green, like the eyes of a cat. The branches of nearby trees pierced its surface. It was as close to paradise as Omed had known. He crept down and, sinking to his knees, began to sob; but his body refused to make the tears. The water was soft and cool on his lips. But it entered him like a knife. Too cold. Too much. He gagged. Rolled onto his back, clutching his stomach. When he recovered, he washed his face and his arms and sipped a little more, carefully letting it ease into his throat.

Once he had water his brain began to work again. He would leave the Snake on the other side of the rocks. He was old and lazy, he would sleep until death snuck up on him and rattled his bones. Then he would be rid of him. But what then? Omed knew the Snake would be his voice when they reached people. It was the same quandary that had plagued him since the camp in Pakistan. He hated the Snake, but they needed each other.

And so Omed woke him and led him to the water.

'For a village boy you are clever,' he said as he plunged his dirty body into the pool. 'What? Why do you look at me like that? Is this not a good place for a bath?' He sat up to his chin in the water, letting it drift in and out of his mouth. 'If there was food then this would be heaven.'

They lay on a slab of rock in the shade. Now his thirst had gone, Omed thought of *kabob*, *shorwa*, *pulao*, *naan*, *chay* and fat pomegranate. He could taste these things as if they were in his mouth. His teeth closed on the pomegranate seeds, they exploded on his tongue. His stomach twisted like a laundered shirt.

He tried to think of something else. Turning to the water, he noticed a small dark shape. It looked like the head of a snake. Slowly, it made its way to the bank and pulled its shelled body onto the sand. Omed got to his feet and jumped on the water-tortoise. He held it in his hands as it snapped at him with its beak.

'What will you do with it now?' asked the Snake, his tongue drugged with sleep. 'We should eat it.'

Omed looked at the poor animal flapping helplessly in his hands.

'Have you not the stomach to kill it? Here, give it to me.'

The Snake grabbed at the tortoise. But Omed pulled it free. He had never killed an animal to eat. He knew it had to be done quickly in the *halal* manner, with a sharp knife to the throat, and that the name of Allah must be pronounced over it. The animal must be completely bled. He had watched the butchers at work in the bazaar by the river in Bamiyan.

With a quick movement, the Snake had it in his hands and smashed it onto a rock. The shell split open and the Snake's greedy fingers were inside pulling at the live flesh. Omed was disgusted; the animal was *haraam* if it was beaten to death. But he was also hungry. He fought for his share.

There was no thought of cooking it. No time, no fire. Never had he eaten food in this way, but Omed knew it would keep him alive. How quickly the water-tortoise had turned from animal to food.

They were still hungry after the tortoise and they scoured the water for more. But apart from a few small, quick fish they found nothing.

Omed fell asleep on the rock and it was dark when he woke. He heard a familiar whisper from the water. He crept to the edge of the pond and saw the dark silhouette of the mother and her children.

You must keep going. This is no place for you. Keep following the stars.

Omed woke the Snake and although he grumbled, they drank their fill at the pond and started walking south again.

Omed looked at his feet. There were ripples. Dark red eddies. He looked at the air where the death hawks spiralled. He looked at the long straightness ahead. It sparkled like water – like a river – but the animals that came to drink at it had been buckled and shunted to death. Omed shook his head. It ached. Night was far behind them. They had given up its cover and its guiding stars. The guards no longer seemed their biggest danger.

He heard a noise. A low drumming. Behind him, the Snake sat in the dirt, his knees around his ears, his arms over his head. The drumming got louder and the Snake looked up. He licked his cracked lips.

The image shimmered like a dream. It had a big flat face, many eyes. It roared as it came. Omed took a step back. When it stopped there was a moment of quiet. A tick, tick, like fingernails on a *chay* glass. The buzz of many flies. They crawled inside his mouth and nose. Heat tunnelled up into his feet.

Then a door opened.

'You clowns tryin to get yersels killed?'

There was a blast of cold air and Omed wanted more than anything to be inside away from the sun.

'You fellas don't look so clever. Whaddya doin wandrin roun out here?'

The Snake opened his mouth, but his voice had dried to a frog-whisper.

'Climb up and I'll give yuz a lift to town.'

They got in. The seat was cloud-soft, the air was as chilled as a snow-wind.

'Get some sky juice into yer.' He handed Omed a canteen. 'Can't believe yuz are out here without water.'

They fell asleep almost immediately and when Omed woke the sky was on fire. The driver smiled at him with metal-strapped teeth.

'D'yer car break down, did it? Must've missed her on the road.' He looked at Omed, back at the road, back to Omed.

'You can't jus go swannin round out here. Stoo bloody hot. The sun'll boil yer scone off. Water's the key out here. See the body's up around ninety per cent water and you can't do without the stuff. Food you can live without, fer a while anyways, but water, now that's another matter entirely. Take this truck frinstance. Fill her guts up with diesel and then let her run dry. Fill her up again, bleed her, and she'll run as sweet as ever. But don't give her water and she's knackered. Motor'll seize tight as a drum. Same deal with your human body. Minus the bleedin, of course,'

He paused and looked expectantly at Omed.

'So where are you clowns headed? Gotta be Marree if yer headed north.'

North? They were headed south.

'Yer in luck if it's Marree cuz that's where I'm goin. Couple more hours of this road and I'll be puttin me head on me own pillow. Yuz are welcome to bunk in with me if yuz want.'

The driver rubbed his hand over his hair. 'Geez, you don't say a whole lot do you. Reckon it must be all that sun. It'll do that – rattle the old voicebox.'

He looked at Omed and shook his head until his helmet of hair quivered.

'Howzabout some tunes,' he said, stabbing a finger at the radio.

. . .twelve-thirty Tuesday morning. They are without food and water in the desert region surrounding the Centre. Authorities fear for their safety . . .

'Like you two, eh?' said the driver.

. . .anyone who has information about their whereabouts should contact police. People found harbouring the escapees can face up to ten years' prison—

'Enough talkin. Let's have some music. You like country? Course you do. Everyone likes country.'

The man pushed a tape into the player.

'This is Ted Egan. You'll love him. He writes about this land out here.' The driver swept his hand at the windscreen and the deep shadows outside. 'He knows it.'

The sound of drumming rolled into the space between them. And then a man singing.

'This song's bout an old camel driver – an Afghan. They built this country up from nothin and all they left behind was a few camels, some mud mosques and a bit of blood. Never got so much as a thank you.'

He pursed his lips and shook his head slowly.

'My grandad was a cameleer, y'know.' His eyes were on the road, but Omed could see he was looking beyond the halo of the lights, beyond the twisted bushes and dark shapes.

'He came here from Afghanistan some time in the early 1900s.'

The drums came through in the music.

'There was a lot of em here back then. Came to build the

railway north, put in stock routes, deliver supplies. Same as now, doin jobs no one else wanted. People hated em, even though they was the ones that brought the water and supplies through miles of burnin sand and rock, sleepin rough under the sky. One time my grandad and his two mates stopped to wash themselves at a waterhole; before prayer, y'know. So some old bugger cocky farmer up and shot his two mates and wounded Grandad. All over a bit of bloody water. He had that hole in his leg till he died. I could put my finger right in it when I was a boy.'

The truck's engine hummed; the Snake snorted in the dark air.

'He met Granny on a station up north. She was full-blood Aboriginal, tribal woman. She was young, maybe seventeen or eighteen and beautiful, thick hair, skin like midnight. I seen the pictures and she was a looker. Grandad was an old man by those days. He had grey in his beard, must've been forty, easy. But it was love awright. If not at first, then later. Grandad went properly and arsked the elders if they could marry, he was a traditional man, see. They okayed it, but the Protector of Aborigines, he said no. But they went ahead and did it anyways. Lived through some hard times because of that decision.'

His hands gripped the steering wheel tighter, his knuckles silhouettes of small hills.

'The problem is, people don't want other people to be happy. They see a bit of happiness and they gets jealous and want to stomp on it. A hundred years back cameleers built this bloody country. Now the cousins of those cameleers are in trouble and what do we do when they come here looking for a better life? We lock em up and toss away the key.'

The truck driver sucked in air through his teeth then spoke again. 'See this scar.' He held the back of his hand out for him to look. 'Know what a blue-tongue is?'

Omed shook his head.

'It's a kind of lizard. Pretty harmless sort of an animal really, but he can give you a hell of a nip if the urge takes him. Got this bite when I was knee high to a grasshopper. Summertime it was – week before Christmas. Thing with yer blue-tongue bite is that she comes back every year to remind you. Round Chrissie, this old wound starts weepin and givin me grief. That old blue-tongue got magic in his mouth all right. Seems to me we need a bit of pain to keep us rememberin.'

The driver went quiet after this and before long Omed was asleep.

When he awoke they were rumbling through the streets of a dusty town.

'Marree,' said the driver. 'Int she a beauty!'

Marree seemed little more than a meeting of brick and board and tin in a vast expanse of sand and rock. There was one fine building of two stories, with a shining new roof and a second-floor verandah thrust at the street like a hawker's basket.

But they didn't stop at that building or anywhere in town. They kept going until the houses got smaller and smaller and were built of less and less. Scraps of iron and stone, a rag of blue sky tied like a flag, sand running into doorways, tree stumps and plastic sheet windows.

The driver's home was built of sheets of tin. The flat roof held down by large rocks placed all over like landmines.

'This was Grandad's place. Built it with his own hands. Seen better days, the old joint.' The truck, as it stopped, pushed out a noise like a small animal being thrown to the ground. 'Used to live in Adelaide. When Grandad died, I moved back up here to take up what he left me. Found out a bit of me background. Dad never told me, guess he was shamed or somethin. Nothin to be shamed bout as I see it.

'Come on, I'll introduce you to the better alf.'

Omed shook the Snake awake and they climbed down from the truck, legs stiff in the morning cold. Small plants struggled from the rust-red soil and from tin cans hung with wire from the windows. The dirt path was swept clean and lined with small men in bright red caps.

'Gnomes,' explained the driver, shrugging his shoulders. He moved down the path. 'Let's see if we can rouse the missus.'

A door opened and a *missus* leapt out. She was very tall and wide and wearing a quilted pink coat. 'Haz, come here and give us a hug you old bugger. Missed you, I did. Missed you sore.'

They held each other for a while before Haz turned to them and said, 'And this is me new mates. Didn't get their names, but they was hitchin on the back road.'

The Snake stepped forward. 'Please to meet, Missus. My name Saladeen. This boy ankle.'

'Ankle?' said the woman.

'Uncle,' said Haz.

'Pleased to meet you, Saladeen. My name is Minnie.' She held out her broad hand to him.

'And this clown,' Haz pointed to Omed, 'doesn't say much. Reckon we'll just call him Rowdy.'

'Pleased to meet you, Rowdy.' Minnie's hand was rough and warm. She stood looking at them for a moment. 'Come inside. You look like you could use a cuppa.'

'They might need a place to stay too, Min.'

The Snake shook his head. 'No, we are to city.'

'Adelaide?' asked Minnie.

The Snake nodded. Omed had heard of this city too. It was one of the biggest places. 'Is far?' asked the Snake.

Haz and Minnie looked at each other and burst into laughter. Haz said, 'Yeah it's far okay. You guys really were lost, werncha. I'm stayin put for the next week or so, but there's trucks that'll be headin south. We'll get yuz a seat tomorrow.'

Omed and the Snake spent the night in the dark front room with the smell of kerosene and boiled potatoes. In the morning they ate a breakfast of eggs and thin rolls of meat that Minnie called sausages.

'Beef, not pig,' said Haz. 'You can eat em. They're safe.'

The day was already blinding, as they went outside to wait. It wasn't long before the truck arrived. A huge beast hauling trailers of cattle, packed tight. Omed and the Snake walked to the cabin. Haz grabbed hold of Omed's arm. He put his mouth close to his ear.

'You take care of yersel, okay. I dunno what mess you and yer uncle are in, but if ya need help then just sing out. Here's a number of a guy in Melbourne that can help you. Mebbe Adelaide's okay, but it's harder to find someone in Melbourne, if you get my drift.'

Omed understood less than half of what Haz said, but he took the paper and the fifty dollar note wrapped inside.

Minnie took hold of Omed and kissed him on the forehead. She pulled back and looked him in the eye. 'Betcher mum misses you, eh?'

Haz shook the Snake's hand. 'Take care of this young nephew of yours, you hear.'

Minnie folded her arms. 'Or you'll have me to answer to.'

Omed could see neither of them liked the Snake.

They got into the truck and as they drove away, Omed looked back at Minnie and Haz waving. It was a long road and they weren't there yet. Maybe in Melbourne they could finally rest.

part two

Hec

HEC WAS HERE AGAIN IN the waiting room. Waiting. Reading old copies of *National Geographic*. Traditional bridge-builders in PNG's wild country.

His dad had a hand in bridges. He knew about stress values, the importance of load and span. It was an old science built over centuries. When Hec was small Dad would show him pictures: the Bridge of Sighs in Venice where the prisoners would take their final walk; the Golden Gate hugged by mist; the Howrah in Calcutta with an eight-lane snarl of cars and double tram tracks.

They would drive down to the docks on winter's nights to look at the West Gate, its slow double curve, dark water gulping the small blots of light. It would snatch Hec's breath; so big in his small horizon that sometimes it crowded his night-thinking. That bridge knew sorrow, was built on bones, disaster after disaster, big and small, ending with theirs.

'Hector Morrow?'

He continued staring at the pages of the *National*

Geographic – men with penis gourds, women with sagging bags for breasts, kids with rivers of snot.

'Hector Morrow?' The receptionist checked her book. She coughed. 'Sorry, *sorry*. Hec. The doctor will see you now, *Hec.*'

He's no doctor. Not real. Just blood and bone and chicken innards. Mumbo jumbo.

'The doctor will see you…*now.*'

He went into the room. Creaky chair. He held his own wrist, counting the beats of his heart. The Mickey Mouse clock. Photos of the doctor's pasty kids at Dreamworld. A poster of that Disney castle somewhere in Europe.

'Hector?' It was him, Dr Feelweird in the same diamond-fronted cardigan, thin across the shoulders.

'Hec, Hec, Hec! I keep forgetting. Your dad told me, "Not Hector," he said, "He doesn't *like* Hector, Dr Freeboard." But I'm just an old jelly-brain sometimes.' He giggled – a big child with shiny scalp.

'So, Hec, what are we going to chat about today? Hey? How about it, Hec?'

The doctor looked at his notes. Actually flipped pages. Hec wondered what was written there. Hec had given him nothing. His dad maybe? It must have been him. Them. Conspiring behind his back. Trying to analyse. Trying to work out what went wrong. As if it wasn't obvious.

'Hec, if you don't want to talk then that's okay.'

One…catanddog…two…catanddog…three…

'We can just sit here like last time.'

And the time before that. Mumbo jumbo.

'But if you feel you want to let go, then here's a good place. I'm not going to judge you. Just let fly. Let those emotions out.'

The Doc had eaten tabouli for lunch. There was a fleck of parsley on his tooth, a grain of couscous in his mo. It disgusted Hec, made him want to punch those lips just to see what it was like. He had never punched anyone before, but he would make an exception for this moron with his lunch advertised on his face.

'Or... not. It's up to you.'

He walked back home under dusk's cover. Streetlights shocked into life behind him. The footpaths were slick with almost forgotten rain. It was March. Nearly a year.

When he got to the door, he pushed his key at the lock or where he thought it should be. In daylight he could see the scars where he had often missed. It was a log of these nights spent walking and coming home to silence and dark. Finally he found metal and the yield of the hole.

Inside there were coats on pegs and he slipped past them like a blind man, hands outstretched, feeling the darkness. He found the lounge room under the firefly glow of standby lights. It wasn't long before Shaboo found *him*, weaving through Hec's legs in a complicated pattern of cat knots. He picked her up and smelled warm fur.

The chalkboard hung on the wall by the fridge. It was the information superhighway for the house.

Home late. Dinner in freezer.
Dad

Hec could picture him, hunched over his drawings under the stark fluoros, his face streaked with worry lines, liver-blue pouches beneath his eyes. Hec's defence was to grow younger; Dad's punishment was to grow old.

He lay back on the couch with Shaboo purring, dribbling her happiness onto his chest. Healing him as cats were supposed to. Mumbo jumbo. Sleep.

He dreamed his dad was a landslide, eyes lost in spooling mud, his features jumbled, pouring past him. Rough hands that never touched him anymore grabbed at his shoulders. He had forgotten what that touch was, what his hands meant. When Hec was small they had been a fortress. Those hands so big. He had pressed his own palms against them and shuddered. They were like paws, fingers so thick, veins on the backs like cable.

Dad was whispering, shaking him. Whispering and shaking. Hec pushed the dream and the edges hardened, light streamed in, sound cartwheeled across.

He blinked, his eyes climbing the room, finally landing on Dad lying on the floor. Had he pushed him?

'What is wrong with you?' Dad asked as he pulled himself up, brushing cat hair from his pants.

'Have you had dinner?'

Hec shook his head, untangling the last fibres of dream, spinning them like fairy floss into the room.

'Lasagne?'

He shrugged and Dad went into the kitchen. 'Did you see the doctor today?'

He's not a doctor!

Hec heard the microwave humming a familiar tune. His dad came back in. 'He rang me, the doctor.'

Then why ask.

'I have to pay for his time whether you talk to him or not. I have to pay. A lot by the way. Quite a lot.'

His dad riffled through the grey remains of his hair. 'You have to snap out of this, Hec, it's doing you no good. I don't know what to do anymore.'

Hec got up slowly, dropping Shaboo to the floor. She landed on her side, disproving yet another myth. He went to his room, slammed the door and turned into a question mark on his ancient Wiggles doona. It wasn't long before the knock came.

'Hec, you can't hide from me. From this.'

I can, I can, I can...

'Hec, I called the school today. They said they'd take you back. They were pretty generous, considering what happened.'

Hec drew his pillow into his ears.

'Or... I have another plan,' his dad continued, lips pressed to the door so his words came out flat. 'I need to talk to you about it, but not like this. Come out, Hec.'

The door had no lock. It was a rule from before – no locks, no secrets. His dad could just come in. What stopped him? What invisible force held him on the other side? What stopped him crossing? After all, he was a bridge-builder.

'This won't go away, Hec.'

He heard his dad back away from the door. Hard heels on the bare boards. And something inside Hec wanted to call him back, but he didn't give in. He waited until the house grew silent, or as silent as an old house can, with its moaning walls, the arthritic creak of its joists, the caw of its doors. Their mangy possum shat bullets over the roof, a mopoke called. And finally after the churning of his mind stopped, Hec fell into an exhausted sleep.

Morning rattled like a tram down the street. There was a note on the chalkboard.

> **Fed cat. Home early.**
> **Will talk.   Dad.**

Hec poured a bowl of muesli and sat crunching it, spitting the raisins and chunks of pawpaw down to Shaboo who pushed them around with her claws.

There was a knock at the door. That was strange. No one came by these days. The knock came again, but Hec stayed seated, mouth open, mid crunch. He put his finger to his top lip to silence Shaboo.

The mail slot clattered open.

'Hector, you in there?'

Hec caught a whiff of clove oil. His dentist used clove oil in her rinse water, said it dulled the pain. *Rinse and spit.* Strings of blood and amalgam on the stainless steel. *Rinse and spit, it will help with the pain.*

His English teacher was a big fan of clove oil too. She must have bathed in the stuff because in period six English, you could hardly smell the whiteboard markers and the grey tang of old books. *Rinse and spit.*

'Hector, I know you're in there. I talked with your dad and he said you might be open to returning to class.'

Hec crept to the door and looked at the mail slot. A slash of violent red, teeth smeared with lipstick.

'Mr Jard didn't send me if that's what you're thinking, although he *did* tell me to let you know that you are required to attend school by law, he just said to remind you of that.'

Calypso's eyes appeared at the slot and Hec shrunk behind the jamb. 'I saw you Hector, open up and we can talk. I feel like an idiot.'

You are *an idiot.*

'I'm not leaving until you open the door, I want you back in my class, you belong there, you were so gooooood and that baobab essay you wrote in Year Nine it was extra-extraordinary and I mean it Hector, I do, I'm not just saying that because Mr Jard told me to; although, he did say to remind you of that and your Talent. He said Talent, Hec, Talent.'

Considering she was an English teacher, Calypso was a little shy of punctuation. She just kept trundling out the words until the class went comatose or the period ended. It was a fact you started life with so many breaths and when you reached that number, you died. Simple as that. Well maybe Calypso was jiggy with the theory and was planning a breathless charge.

'You need to start writing again, Hec, it's important. Words are our chance at forever.'

Forever?

'You have so much to say.' She sucked in a breath. 'Oh, there you are, that's better now we can talk face-to-face, sort of, it would be even better if you just let me in, Hec. Don't you dare shut this flap, Hector Morrow, I am warning you as a teacher, now please don't shut this flap, Hec...'

With the flap shut, Calypso was just a clove-oil ghost. A whisper from another world that Hec had left behind, and gladly.

He went through to the lounge and flipped on *Play School*. He took a guess at the arch window and jagged it as always. That happened a lot lately. It was as if by drawing away from the cluttered nation of words he had unlocked a part of his brain that just *knew*. He turned the sound down and provided his own commentary.

Today we are visiting a factory where they take your dreams and crush them into something small. It starts when you are a child and everything seems good but, sooner or later, all those hopes are turned into something ugly. That is called recycling. See the dull, angry people pushing the old dreams into boxes? Look at their faces. Do they look happy? It looks dangerous that machine, doesn't it? Look at the wheels and teeth. Whomp! Whomp! Whomp! It is mashing up those dreams. And now it is time to go home. Do they look happy? Look closely. They are smiling. Are they happy or are they just pretending?

Hec turned the volume back up. He liked this presenter. Liked her soft voice hiking up to the end of the sentence. And best of all, when he was sick of her, there was always the off button.

Powderfinger was in the CD player. He turned it on and cranked it. So loud that pictures rattled on the walls. The one of him and Mum on the beach at St Kilda somewhere between the syringes and sea. Him all ice-creamed up. Him, face dusted with sand. Him, two-teeth-gone smile. Mum, sea goddess, a brittle star. Next track. Slowly the music built. Bernard Fanning's voice came off the tremble, the acoustic guitar climbed, drums and cymbals began a wall. The pier was smoky haze and beyond it, out of sight (but not mind) was the bridge. Never out of mind. Hec knew that control was slipping through his hands and that everything,

everything, everything was not turning out like he had planned. He hid his face in his hands, but the music found him there.

e

Dad came home early as promised, with pizza. They ate straight from the box, long strings of mozzarella looping from their chins.

'So, Hec, like I said last night, I need to talk to you about something. Something I have been giving a lot of thought to lately. Hec it's been nearly a year.'

Ten months four days. Not nearly a year. Not even close. I get to decide how long it has been.

'We don't have to forget, but we do need to move forward.'

We. You mean me; you're not talking about yourself. But you're as stuck as I am, Dad. Admit it, will you! Just admit it.

'One thing you need to do is go back to school.'

Hec dropped his pizza back in the box. The anchovies stung his tongue.

'If not school, then something else. A job.' Dad took a swig of water. 'Don't fight me on this one, Hec, it's non-negotiable. You have to do something. It's not healthy to just do nothing. You will end up turning in on yourself and causing even more pain.'

I have turned in on myself, Dad, haven't you been paying attention? It is just me and the pain. The pain and me.

'You used to want to be a writer. That was important to you. I don't know if it is anymore, but maybe just maybe you can work towards that.'

He's getting me a job on a newspaper. He has contacts. It wouldn't be the worst.

'You are going to need to go back to school eventually, but

I have talked to Mr Jard and he has agreed that for this year you can take the time to work and sort things out. There will be a place for you back at school when you're ready. It's a pretty generous offer, considering.'

Probably just start making coffees and emptying bins, but eventually, maybe they'd get me to write. They'd see stuff that I'd just left lying around, brilliant stuff, but casual. They'd see it and realise, Hey, this kid can write. *And then I'd get a computer and some articles to research, maybe then a by-line, but not too quickly so the older guys weren't jealous . . .*

'Work is good for you, Hec. And work can give you things to write about. Life experience, Hec. Nothing beats it.'

Life experience?

'I know lots of people your age don't want to do certain jobs. I don't know, maybe they think it's beneath them. But it's character building.'

Character building?

'All I'm saying is, give it a go. You need to do something.' He looked at Hec sideways, folding his pizza into a sandwich. 'It will be good for you.'

Well what is it? The newspaper. It has to be. Something good has to happen. It can't be this shit forever.

'My friend Merrick Hope. Well he's an old school mate actually; haven't seen him in years, but I bumped into him a couple of weeks back and he said he was one short at work.'

Merrick, what kind of name is that?

'Look it's a start, that's all I'm saying. It's not forever and it will give you something to do and somewhere to go. We all need something to do. We might say we hate work but we all *need* it.'

Cut to it, Dad.

'Okay. I guess you want to know what it is. The job, I mean.'

Are you sure you don't want to go to an ad break just to up the suspense a little?

'Merrick...well...he runs a business that makes candles.'

Hec peered out from the bars of his fingers. *He's a hippie, isn't he? Kaftan, headband, clove oil, patchouli – it will be like period six English all day.*

'It's a factory. A candle factory. They make candles there. You know, wicks, wax, that sort of thing. I mean I haven't actually been there, but Merrick's a good guy. Well he was in Grade Six and I can't imagine too much has changed.'

Grade Six, Dad. A factory? What are you thinking?

It was not easy to get to the bridge at night, without a car. Hec knew where he was going though and he was determined. The bus ran from the city through West Melbourne and down to the industrial estate. It would ferry workers at the start and end of long shifts. It turned at the end of Lorimer Street where the West Gate Bridge hung like a concrete bird over the sky.

Hec got off the bus and watched it cruise up past Pier 35 and desert him. It was the last bus of the day and, with it gone, he would be making the long trip back to the city on foot.

This was not an area where Hec should be at night. But it used to be worse – hard drinkers murdering mates, shootings and concrete boots – or so Dad had told him. He wondered if it was his way of talking it up, creating an aura of menace where there was only hard sand and mutilated seabirds wearing yards of nylon fishing line. Still, he was nervous. It was the first time he had been there by himself.

The lights were winking at him from Spotswood and, as tugs bruised their way back up the river, he ambled between the she-oaks and down to the pontoon. The smell of wild turnip rose from his feet. Then the overtone of oil, dark musk, from the refinery. Finally the sour-packed smell of river sand sat too long. These were the three smells that were this place.

It was not yet the sea, but its water was milky green like a lime spider had been poured into the narrow neck before Hobsons Bay. It was a river tamed, bulked with containers, nudged by huge refinery tanks, cobbled with rough heads of bluestone. The Maribyrnong and the Yarra met up at Coode Island and they brought with them tennis balls, plastic bottles and palm fronds. He knew on the thin ribbon of shore he would find syringes, strewn like still lifes among single shoes, rubber kitchen gloves and old pool noodles. As a kid he loved to beachcomb along this stretch with his Dad bloodhounding behind, warning him not to touch, not that, or that. Now he could touch anything he wanted to, but the hand of fear was on him.

To his left, the bike path ran downriver, past a yellow sign that said 'Beware' above a snakelike squiggle, onto the stinking ponds of West Gate Park. Hec had never believed that there were snakes here, so close to the city. But many things about the bridge surprised him. It cloaked its secrets well.

During the day, the West Gate Punt ran from spring to autumn carrying cyclists across the river to Williamstown. At night the pontoon was usually abandoned, but there was a hunched figure at the far end. Hec walked down the wooden walkway and across the aluminium ramp that connected the floating pier to dry land. Immediately he could feel the water buckling underneath him. Above him, the West Gate Bridge hummed like a substation. He could see its sleek underbelly, its scaled gut hanging over the river. *Beware*. He kept walking, but he couldn't take his eyes from the bridge, the way it flung itself at the far bank, landing among a nest of pylons and black wires. His feet scuffed as he hit the pontoon proper; the bridge swayed. The lights were brighter near Scienceworks, pulsing into the dull river. And still the bridge droned out its dirge. It looked benign, but he knew it was a rogue tumour waiting to erupt into a new life. His dad had told him of when it had fallen while they were building it, killing, maiming, changing. How it had pushed up the mud, slinging it at houses, burying people. Still Dad continued his belief in engineers, like they were gods and it was his faith. Blind faith.

Hec knew that things fell all the time. You couldn't tell by looking at them. The cracks were so small, naked to the human eye. Things fell and as they dropped, they dragged everything with them. It was something to do with physics, Hec was sure; physics and luck, or lack of it.

Hec felt small under the bridge. He always had. It made no difference how much older he got or what he managed to do, the bridge could take his breath away, pin him like an insect, just by being there. He traced an imaginary line from the bridge to the water. It wasn't a graceful arc, just a straight drop. A drop with no style, just economy, ending in the plate glass of the river. Hec moved forwards, keeping his eye on the bridge and the river, trying to align them in his mind to that exact spot where he and Dad would stand before it all became so tainted.

'Watchit, ya *eejit!*'

Hec's knees had hit something soft and his body tricked itself into continuing when plainly it should have stopped. He ended up on top of a fisherman, tangled in him, sprawled over his back as the man bent over his bait bucket.

'Were ye no lookin where yer goin?'

Hec scrambled to his feet and held up his hands in surrender. He wasn't sure what the old man had said, but he seemed pissed off.

The man rotated his shoulder under a clawed hand. He looked at Hec and his face softened. 'Aw, yer awright, son, don't mind me I'm just a *crabbit* old man,' he said and continued to bait up. He whirled his line at the water then dropped the spool into the bucket. They both watched the ripples fanning outwards and dying. There was a brief silence between them, the only noise from a boisterous tug moving upstream and the deadly hum of the bridge.

The fisherman shook his head and said, 'Wanna know somethin?'

Hec didn't, but he nodded politely.

'I've been comin here for near on thirty years. Thirty years. Long time, eh? One thing that's stayed the same is this water. Keeps on draining into the bay no matter what they do to it.'

The old guy was creepy, the yellow light that crumbled off the refinery made him more so. His eyes were knots of darkness under his wiry brow and, as he spoke, he rubbed his hands together so they made a noise like wind sneaking through dried thistle stalks.

'I first laid my eyes on the bay in nineteen sixty-six. I was old even then. See these hands, boatbuilder's hands – all scar and weld burn. This one above my eye. Some mental chibbed me with a spanner.'

He rubbed the pucker of the scar with his pinkie.

'Well shot of the place. A dump. No like here. Raw beauty.'

He swept his arm across from Spotswood to Coode Island, including the umbilicus of the bridge.

'You look familiar, sonny-boy. Do I know you?'

It seemed more an accusation than a question. Hec quickly shook his head.

The man sandpapered the back of his hand with his stubbled chin and even in the poor light, Hec could make out his chipped teeth and the terrible mess of his nose.

'You drink?'

Hec shook his head again.

'Good lad. Shockin habit.' He took a long swallow and winced. 'See that bridge?' He pointed his bottle neck at the West Gate. 'I built that.' He laughed at Hec's expression. 'No by myself. I mean I had help in the matter.'

He coughed and leant against the railing of the pontoon. The water sucked and swirled underneath.

'There were a lot of men, good men, on that bridge. I left all my folk behind in Scotland. We were like a family, us bridge-builders. Believe me, sonny, it's a good thing to belong.

'There was a young guy, a Croat called Stanko. When the bridge fell, I watched him go.'

The fisho took another long swig at his bottle.

'You know what a slab of concrete does when it hits the ground?' The man dropped his flat palm onto the railing. 'It makes a bloody big mess that's what. The folks round here were pickin mud off their curtains fer weeks. As we were diggin our mates outta the shit.'

He hadn't noticed his handline was quivering in the bucket.

'But I loved that job. Everyone tellin me how I shoulda given it up after that. How could I?'

The spool was rattling now, jumping to the lip of the bucket.

'That's what I knew – steel and mates. And with my mates gone, all I had left was the steel.'

The spool shot from the bucket, bounced over the pontoon and to the rail, it was ready to hop over and disappear into the river when the old fisho's foot came down, stopping it dead. He reached down slowly, keeping his eyes on Hec's and smiling. Slowly, he reeled it in, the line biting into his fingers, zipping through the grey-black water.

'This one's a wee stoater.' He pulled with one hand, freeing up line then spooling on with the other. It was a battle. The strain was on his face as he drew the fish in from deep water. His brows were waves, his eyes whirlpools.

'He's looking fer snags, anything – old wheels, bikes, washin machines, skeletons – the river's full of them, and he knows it.'

He dragged at the line until Hec saw a flash of white in the water. He had never been a fisherman, but he could not take his eyes from what was happening. It was a battle between land and sea and it looked as if either could win. Hec closed his eyes and hoped for the fish. Surely this man would never eat something that came from this polluted water. It would be just another waste of life.

Hec caught a flash of it as it neared the surface. He gasped. For all the world it looked like the slender body of a child. He shook his head free of the thought. It came up again, further out, shattering the surface of the water, grunting like a pig. The old fisho was panting. There was whisky leaking from his skin, smoke seeping from his chest.

After fifteen minutes, the fish rolled its glossy belly to the sodium suns that illuminated the bridge. It grunted again, deep belly burps, as it drew alongside the pontoon. The old man reached down and, grabbing it by the gills, pulled it up beside him. The fish was nearly as tall as him, dark-brown flanks in the light of the lamps with dappled purple along its back. He slammed it onto the worn boards. It lay there panting for a moment, its gills clutching at the thin, thin air.

Hec placed a hand on the heaving fish. It felt warm. How could that be?

'King Mulloway, sonny-boy. Knew it.'

The fisho gathered his knife in his scarred hand and pinned the giant fish to the boards. When the blade slipped in, the fish shuddered violently. Hec wanted to be sick. It had looked like a child. A strong smell pulsed from the fish – pungent kerosene or ammonia, piss from a copper pot.

'Others call them jewfish, but I like to think of 'em as Jewelfish. Know why?' The deep purple was draining from its skin, the belly still silvery-white.

'Let's have a wee peek, shall we.' The fisho's knife went in deep, up behind the eyes. The old man dug around and flipped something onto the pontoon. 'Jewels, sonny-boy. One fer you and one fer me.' He picked up the small bloody bag that had come from the fish and forced two tear-shaped pearls from it.

The man pressed the jewel into Hec's palm. Hec looked down at the mess on the pontoon. When the fish had come from the water it had been so vital. There was strength in its tail and the red slashes of its gills. Now, it was an empty sack. Its eyes were dull. It had shed scales over the splintered planks.

'Hey, where you goin? We were just gettin started. Yer no cryin over a bloody fish are you? These bastards fed off my mates. You get it? They live on the dead!'

Hec backed up the walkway and onto the path. Past the she-oaks – whispering to him in the dark. He could see the man's eyes, feel his clawed hand kneading into his. He turned and ran.

'We'll be seein each other!' the man shouted after him.

He was past Pier 35 when he stopped. It was a long way back to the city and he couldn't run the whole length of Lorimer Street. He hoped the trams would still be running. The fear was still inside him and he half considered calling Dad. But it would have meant a total surrender. No, he would walk home just to scare his old man a little, to prove to him that he could do it, that he could be alone in this world without him. It was his choice to come home. And his choice to take that stinking nuff-nuff job at the candle factory.

The walk along Lorimer Street and back into the heart of the city was tiring and Hec's calves ached. When he boarded the last tram it felt good to rest his legs. He thought back on the night. He felt like he had won a small victory.

He had been sitting on the tram for fifteen minutes when he felt the sharpness in his jacket. He reached inside and pulled out the jewel. He held it to the light and it seemed to glow. It was a tear, a drop of sadness from inside the fish; a fish that had swallowed the bones of those who fell from the bridge and with them their sorrow. And then it had swallowed the fisho's hook.

That old fisho. He was weird. And he stank of rollies and whisky and bait. He was wrong. They would never see each other again. Not if Hec had anything to do with it.

THE TRAIN SHRIEKED INTO DANDENONG station and Hec crossed the platform and turned left into Little India. He pulled the scrap of paper with directions from his pocket. Dad's stencil-sharp lettering, his ruler-edge streets, the ladder of rail tracks. Beyond the boundaries of the map, a wino scummed fags and change, a teenage girl bought a hit from a guy in a Metallica shirt. Hec turned the paper over and noticed his dad had written something on the back, but changed his mind and scrubbed it out. He held it up to the light, but the blue frenzy of biro lines was too thick and there was no way of knowing what Dad had thought he needed to say.

Polynesian girls in butt-huggers and hip-hop hats sat staring at the concrete in front of the Alfy Travel Centre. Tall Africans in shirts and dark trousers with skin like ripe eggplant loafed outside of Heritage India – its chaos of bright saris not even worth their cool stares.

Hec walked without catching anyone's eyes, glancing up to get bearings – Café Lahore, Victoria Bitter, Tattoo

City, African and Australian Grocery Store, Club X Adult Megamart, Najafi Carpets, Balkh Bakery, African Braids and Beauty, Greenleaf Hydroponics. Each corner clustered with languages, people swapping fistfuls of DVDs, lowered cars rumbling by.

Past a wasteground of shattered glass and fists of broken concrete, the laneway fed into a courtyard in front of the factory. A guy sat on a low step, arms on his knees, head slumped. Three kids, the youngest only just old enough to walk, smashed bottles with stones nearby.

The building was red brick, knackered with soot and the jumpy lyrics of tags. No *Brayden loves Kayla* here, no *4 eva*. Just hard-arse ghetto tags imported from rap video clips. It was the only factory in an area of mean houses, derelict shops with papered windows and migration agents' offices. The sign above the front door was in big boxy letters: 'Hope Candle Works est. 1966'. And below it in tricky curled writing: '*Light is Hope*'.

Hec watched the workers arrive in torn tracksuits and velour twin-sets, clutching plastic bags and cans of drink. At 7.29 a.m. Hec took a deep breath and walked towards his brilliant new life.

Inside the door, past the time clock and a wall of neatly pocketed cards, the air was greasy with wax. Machinery shouted. Radios were blaring on different stations. The piercing sound of high flute knocked against Farnesy and Barnesy. Ragged squares of insulation foil hung like skin from the roof. Hec focussed on the door marked 'Office' – twenty long steps ahead.

'Watch where you're goin, dick'ead.' The man wore scuffed boots and a hairnet; he had dabs of shaving cream on the lobes of his ears. As he trundled a trolley-load of candles into the gloom, Hec heard him mutter, 'Another half-baked lamb to the slaughter.'

Hec made it to the office door and knocked.

'Come in.'

It was a small office, tiny, as if it had been added as an afterthought. The main island of the desk was surrounded by atolls of paperwork. Hec saw a lot of red reminder notices.

The man at the desk looked up from his computer, rubbed his eyes and offered Hec his hand. It was covered in soft, pink scar tissue and felt smooth and slightly cool.

'Merrick Hope,' he said. 'You must be Hector. Your dad told me a lot about you.'

Hec stared hard at his new boots.

'He mentioned you didn't talk a lot. Well this place might suit you fine. There are some here who don't speak too much either. Oh yeah, I remember your dad also said to call you Hec. Well, Hec, welcome to Hope Candle Works. Want a cup of java?'

Java? Hec shook his head.

'Well then I guess we'll jump straight into it. No big induction processes, we'll just toss you straight onto the floor and let you work with the guys. I'll set you up with one of our more experienced operators first. Come on out.'

Back in the factory Hec knew that all eyes were on him. He felt the noise pushing at his stomach, his chest tightened, his toes curled until their knuckles pained under the steel caps.

'Mr Hope?' It was the guy with the shaving-cream ears.

'Splinter?' said Merrick Hope.

'You gotta get these bloody reffos to pick up their act. I'm telling ya, they'll be the end of this place. All your old man worked for up the shitter. For what? Reckon these idiots'll give a backward glance?'

'Splinter, what exactly is the problem?' said Merrick.

'I'm tellin ya, Mr Hope, it's them. They's the problem. They don't wanna work hard. Always some bloody thing, prayer time or bloody "not-eaty-time" or "my-father-is-so-sicky-time". I tell ya, I'm the one who's bloody sick of it. They shit me to bloody tears. It's gonna be them or me one day, Mr Hope.'

'Splinter, this is Hec. Hec, this is Splinter.'

Hec nodded at him with what he hoped was just the right mix of cool and polite.

Splinter shook his head and said, 'Yeah, we met. And another thing this cheap-arse slack wax.' He toed the bag on his trolley: *Palm Wax Product of Indonesia*. 'It's no bloody good. Dangerous, usin crap like this. I'm tellin you we'll all be blown to Kingdom Come if we keep on with it.'

Merrick's mobile rang and he answered. Splinter and Hec were left standing with nothing to say. Where Splinter's hands poked from the sleeves of his coat there were faded blue tatts. He was not tall and not short but, as Hec's mum used to say, 'it would take two of him to make a shadow.' As Hec watched, he did something so bizarre that Hec was sure he had imagined it. He licked the palms of his hands, one-two, quickly, and shoved them in his pockets, then turned to go.

'Splinter!' called Merrick after him. He held his hand over the phone. 'I'm a bit busy, mate. Could you show Hec around; introduce him to the crew? Cheers.' He went back to his call, giving Hec a small wave and a smile.

'Busy. Doesn't know the bloody meanin of the word. Wouldn't know busy if it ran up his arse and made a nest. Never been busy a day in his life.' Splinter moaned his way to a room beside the office. 'First things first,' he said as he opened the door. 'Get ourselves a nice cup of Inner-national Roast.' He set up two mugs, spooned coffee and three sugars in both and topped them with water from an urn. He pulled a seat from under a nearby table, drew his magazine from his pocket and sat down.

'No point in introducin you to any of them out there cause half of them don't even *speaka de lingo*. Dumb as dogshit they are – shitkickers ev'ry one. That bloody Merrick Hope is the problem. Picks em up like strays. *No writee, no readee, please givee me number one job*. Bloody disgrace. They just come here to get rich and bring more and more of em over. Once they've drained the joint dry they's off like a rat up a bloody drainpipe back to Chingchongchoochooland or wherever the hell it is they come from. Government don't even have the guts to stop them. If I was Prime Minister I'd put them all back in their leaky bloody boats and push them back to where they damn well came from. It's gettin to where you can't even walk down the street without every second person bein from somewhere else. Can't get any decent food. Can't get understood. We went to war against half these buggers and now they's over here messin up the place, turnin it like their own countries. It's gettin to the point where I'm shamed to say I'm an Aussie. I don't even know what that means anymore.' Splinter stopped to take a sip of his coffee. His ears and nose were shot with tiny, exploded veins – a wiring diagram for a time bomb. Hec pointed his lips at his cup and felt the sugar lusting after his teeth.

'Another thing,' Splinter continued, 'They don't have no respect for life. It's cheap where they come from, you see. They deal the drugs, kill our kids with their heroin and their estaksy. They juss don't give a monkey's.' He pulled his seat closer. 'Most of them are criminals. Ninety-nine point nine nine pressent. The other pressent is just plain ignorant and stupid. Been proved scientifically that they's juss not as smart as us. Saw a thing on TV about it, I shit you not. Filled one of our skulls with dried peas and then tried to fit them in theirs. Half the brain capacity, see. Another thing is them diseases. Not natural ones like colds and mumps and such, weird Asian ones that we can't deal with.'

'So let's establish the rules here an now, matey. It's *us* and *them*. You are with me and we are against *them*. No middle ground here.'

Hec didn't know what he was supposed to do. Splinter seemed dangerous. And if he aligned himself with him then he would be against all the others. It seemed like an impossible game to win. Maybe he could just play it like he did at school and exist outside the Loop. The Loop was the problem, being in it, being out of it. If you ignored the Loop it didn't make it go away, but it mattered less. Hec always thought that those inside the Loop were just as trapped as those outside it. But what was the Loop here? Did it lie with Splinter or with the misfit nuff-nuffs on the factory floor? Could a man like Splinter form a Loop? Could a Loop just be one person? Splinter was trying to buddy-up with Hec because he was Anglo – a *skip*.

'Spose we should strike a blow. Don't want Mr Hope givin away our jobs to some queue-jumpin jungle-bunny, do we?'

They can have it, thought Hec. But he followed Splinter back into the factory.

'You can help me unload,' he said, licking the palms of his hands quickly, like a cat cleaning its paws.

The container truck pulled up to the loading bay – its rear doors level with the concrete ramp. A guy swung down from the door and lit a cigarette. He nodded at Splinter.

'Wax and plenny of it,' he said, smoke draining from his nose.

Splinter grabbed a low trolley. 'This here is a pallet jack. And you is the monkey that's gunna operate it. Pump here and it goes up, pull this and it goes down. Even a halfwit like you should manage that much.'

He thrust the handle at Hec. He clipped the seal off the container doors and pocketed it. Then he swung open the container. Hec could feel the vacuum release.

He knew these containers were airtight. He'd watched footage of a solo yachtie who had hit one in the middle of the Pacific Ocean. It had been floating just below the surface. Mum had whispered, *Like an iceberg,* as if it was a secret. But she was wrong. Icebergs were one third above water. At least you could see them coming.

The air was stale, damp, and smelled like plastic bags. There were pallets of wax inside. *Product of Indonesia* – two side by side – three rows deep leading into the gullet of the container. Splinter pushed a large dead cockroach with his foot. 'Get spiders sometime. They spray em dead, but you godda wonder.' He wondered for a moment, then licked his palms.

'Anyways, lookin at it's not gunna get it out, is it?'

The truckie leaned on the door. 'Sign this will ya, mate. I'm dyin for a slash. Where's the pisser round here?'

Splinter signed his papers and pointed out the toilet. 'Come on, Knackers!' he screamed at Hec. 'We haven't got all bloody day. And you slower'n a wet weekend.'

Hec wheeled the trolley and tried to roll it under the first pallet. It jammed.

'Give it some wally! You young blokes've got friggin water instead of blood. Put your back into it.' Splinter's voice echoed inside the truck.

Hec pulled back and tried again, this time harder. It clunked under the pallet and he pumped the handle until it lifted off the ground. As he rolled it back, it jammed against the other pallet.

'Do they teach you nuffin at school!' Splinter screamed.

Yes – irregular verbs, surds, post-modernism.

'Straight, idiot. Keep it straight.'

Hec tried to roll it back to have another go, but it was jammed solid. As he pulled it again, the corner pierced the shrink-wrap on another pallet and wax began to leak.

The truckie peered in. 'Looks like you got yourselves a bleeder.'

'I ain't got nuffin. Nuffin to do with me,' said Splinter. Licking the blame from his hands.

Hec placed his hand over the wound. The wax was cool. There was a river of it on the floor of the truck.

'Here, try this.' The truckie handed Hec a tape gun. 'Wait a sec, what is that?' Below Hec's fingers the corner of a plastic bag nosed-out among the yellow beads.

Splinter's mangy head rode into view. 'Whas goin awn?

What is that? No don't take yer hand away, ya droppie. I'll get Mr Hope.'

'And I'd better smoke this outside. Don't want us all goin up in flames, do we.' The truckie jumped back into the loading bay.

Hec was left trying to stop the flood of palm wax.

Eventually, Merrick stepped into the back of the truck.

'Let me at it, Hec,' he said.

As Hec removed his hand, Merrick quickly tweaked the plastic bag out and taped the hole with the tape gun.

'It's the drugs,' said Splinter. 'I knew it. Bloody chongers are tryin to kill us all.'

'Don't be so dramatic, Splinter,' said Merrick, flicking the bag of white powder with his fingers. 'It's just a sample. A new wax additive. No drugs. No conspiracy. Unload the rest and try not to break any more bags.' Merrick slipped the packet into his pocket.

Splinter followed him out of the truck. 'I arsked'im to be careful, Mr Hope. Showed'im. But they know it all...'

The truckie took the trolley jack. 'Edge it out like this,' he said, swaying the handle from side to side, easing it from its slot. 'Not much room to play with. Not really your fault, mate.'

Splinter exploded back in. 'Course it's his fault. He's a bloody retard. Give it here.' Splinter took the truck out into the wide space of the loading bay and parked it near a rack. He pulled the trolley clear and pushed it towards Hec. 'Next pallet, ya peanut!'

e

The buzzer went at ten and they all crammed into the lunchroom. It was like someone had shaken the planet and the people of the world had fallen into Hope Candle Works.

Men with skin like a moonless night, a woman with eyes as soft and narrow as buttonholes. Containers of noodles and carefully wrapped bread spilled onto the tables and chatter dodged and swung and gathered in tangled piles of accented English. Splinter pulled Hec to a table where a young guy was sitting alone. Splinter growled, 'Geddup.'

The guy looked up at him.

'Gawn! Skedaddle!' His face was millimetres from the young guy's. 'Move yer sorry black arse.' There was still no movement. Everyone was watching, not breathing.

'Ged... up!'

The guy held Splinter's gaze, but stayed seated. Like he didn't care, or he had a death wish. Splinter grabbed the back of his chair and rocked it back. The young guy grabbed for the table with his hand, but was too far past the tipping point. He slammed hard against the wall and fell onto the floor. For a moment he lay there, staring at Splinter whose eyes were crazy with pit bull aggression. Then in one quick movement the boy leapt to his feet and faced Splinter, head cocked slightly to one side.

Splinter snarled at him, lips bared, showing his troubled gums. He said slowly, 'This... is... *my*... chair.' Splinter put his hand on the table. 'My table.' He swept his hand around the room and glared at everyone with furious eyes. 'This is *my* country.' Licked his palms. 'MOINE!' he growled. No one challenged him. Beside him, Hec stood like a stringless puppet.

An older man stepped between Splinter and the young guy. He was crusty, worn, his face a puzzle of unconnected pieces.

'Meestarr Spleentarr. This boy crazymad. He my niece,

thees one, I his ankle. Bat he too crazymad.' He did a little dance, waggling his head from side to side. Then he
grabbed the boy by the shoulder and walked him to the
other side of the room, spitting words in his ear.

Splinter clawed Hec's shirt. 'Siddown for godsake, makin
a bloody testicle of yersel,' he said. Hec registered the other
men looking at him and Splinter, now the Loop of Two.

Hec sat beside him. Splinter's lips were torn into a nasty
sneer as he said, 'He's the worst of the worst. Gawn in the
head. Won't say boo to a goose. He's dumb or sumpin.
Sandwich short of a picnic. Bloody weeeeird.' He circled
his temple with his fingers and then licked his palms quickly.
'You godda show them who the bloody boss is. They godda
learn. They's like dogs in that respect. And that one is the
dregs. He's the dog's dog. Even his own kind don't want
him. The old dickhead that stepped in; he's the only one
who even pretends to know him. Did you hear him – He's
my *niece*. I'm his bloody *ankle*. A monkey's ankle! Ha!
What a dipshit.'

Hec nibbled one of the sandwiches his dad had made:
egg and lettuce, crusts sheared, butter right to the edges.
Splinter struggled over Australia's Largest Crossword. Hec
caught a glimpse of the simple clues and the words Splinter
had crowbarred into the spaces. Some of them were too
long, but he just added an extra box or two. When they
were too short, he blacked out a space. There they sat like
rotten teeth.

Try this one, Splinter, he wanted to shout. *Fear or hatred
of foreigners, ten letters. Tick…tick…tick…tick… Give
up? Xenophobia.*

At the other tables people were laughing and sharing food,

but Hec sat silent with Splinter and just wished it was all over.

When the bell went Splinter said, 'Smoko's never long enough. Reckon they speed up the clock for smoko and lunch, wind it down for work.'

Hec looked up and saw Hope at the door.

'We was just gettin back to it, Mr Hope. Hec here was just sayin how fifteen minutes is not really long enough to have a bite to eat and drink a cuppa.'

'Hec, I'd like you to work with Sami up until lunch.'

'But—' started Splinter.

'You've finished unloading, Splinter. I want Hec to get an idea of the whole operation.'

Splinter pocketed his *People* magazine and took his scowling brow out the door.

e

Sami's hands were quick as they threaded in the wicks from a bank of spools under the machine. His fingers were the colour of wattle bark with shell-pink nails a surprise at the tips. He bent down and fed a wick through the hole in one of the metal cylinders, pulling it up and tying it off before starting again. It was a long, boring job, but he was concentrating hard. There were two hundred and forty wicks and two hundred and forty cylinders. Hec had time to count. There was little else to do. How could anyone do this day after day with the burnt oil smell of wax stripping the hairs from their nose?

Finally, the job was finished and Sami stood up and smiled. He walked over to a huge vat of melted wax and drained some into a bucket. This part of the job looked like it needed speed, as much as the threading needed patience. He strode back to the machine and quickly ran the bucket of sloppy wax into a chute. It glided around the wicks, filling the metal tubes from the top.

'Now we arr doing eet again,' said Sami and moved to another machine. After a bank of three machines had been threaded and poured he returned to the first one. He turned an old wheel on the side and the mould dropped to reveal slim white candles. Sami ran a knife carefully under the bottoms of the candles, separating the wicks. As he went, he grabbed them in bundles and slipped them into boxes.

Sami worked hard without talking. Most of the time Hec was looking at the back of his head while he threaded wicks or packed the candles into boxes. His hair was tight and short, a field of burnt stubble with furrows of pink scars parting it from crown to brow. How and where had he got such scars? It looked like someone had attacked him with a fork.

The work could have been done by machines. Should have been done by machines. It amazed Hec that humans would be allowed to do jobs that were so mind-numbingly tedious. He fought off fatigue, blinked away boredom and tried to keep his mind focussed on the job. Not that there was anything to do except watch Sami's slow, precise movements as he built candles from wax and cotton. The candle factory's motto was 'Light is Hope'. What light was Sami's job shining into his life?

They worked constantly, building a rhythm that was only interrupted by the bell. Then they washed their hands and crowded into the lunchroom.

Splinter was already there. He waved Hec over, pulled out

a seat and patted it. But Hec dodged his stare and grabbed a seat beside Sami, his heart hammering a bass beat in his chest. He unwrapped another sandwich and took a bite, feeling the crunch of eggshell in the sudden dryness of his mouth.

The man on Hec's right was African, like Sami. And like Sami, he had scars. A thick one the side of a lemon wedge across his cheek, a spray of circular ones on his forearm.

'Waas the matta. You look like you naiver seen a blaak maan.'

Hec looked away. Of course, he had. Near the commission flats in Carlton. Sometimes on the tram.

'You well be shy boy, you in the minoreetee heeyaar.'

Sami looked up from the bowl of Froot Loops he was pouring. 'Mabor, geev the boy a break.'

Hector looked at Sami and smiled in appreciation.

'Eets okay. Mabor is jus grumpee because he haav to work wid Spleentaar.'

A small man at the end of the table said, 'And Splinnar, he grumpy wiv world.'

'You gawt that right, Tran,' said Mabor, shaking his head.

'You wan some Froot Loop?' asked Sami, shaking the box.

Hec held up his sandwich.

The woman sitting opposite said, 'Sami is crazy for Froot Loop. He looooooove Froot Loop.'

'And why naat, Sheilaa. What is naat to love about Froot Loop. You have froot and milk and loops in one bowl. Eet is the best. We naiver have these in Sudan. Only millet porridge and bullets.'

'And look whaat these bullet do to your teeth.' Mabor opened his mouth to show a bottom row of missing teeth.

'He is lying to you, you know,' said Sami. 'They knock teeth out with a fishing spear when he was becoming a maan. Lucky I too young. Then the waar and we both leave. Now the girls think he is ugly with his scaar and his no teeth.'

'Poor Mabor. He is cute to me,' said Sheila.

'I am cute,' admitted Mabor.

'She is just feeling sorree for you, Mabor.' Sami smiled a Froot Loop smile.

'I feel sorry for *him*,' said Sheila pointing her chin at the young guy that had stood up to Splinter at smoko.

Sami shrugged and said to Hec, 'He naiver taalks. I think he has seen too much. Many of us seen too much. I am walking from Sudan to Kenya – two yaars. Then four yaars in a camp – vairy baad. My family was killed in the waar. See these scaar.' He showed Hec his forearms. 'And these.' His scalp crossed with a nest of thin pink lines. 'Sometimes we see too much and we caan never get baack what we once waas. Maybe that is his story. He is a refugee like me, but he come baack door. Means that he is only waiting. Mabe he don't even haave Tee Pee Vee. We got full visa Pee Pee Vee. Permanent protection.'

'Teepeevee is short visa,' added Sheila. 'Temporary Protection. Means they can be sent home any time. It is very hard.'

The bell rang again, like school, signalling to the animals to move to the next, greener, pasture. Only there was no green pasture here – just the same dirty weeds over and over again until death by boredom, or the end of the day. There was no way Hec could last.

He spent the next few hours working with Sami and when the bell rang again he was first out the door. It was chucking it down outside, so he bolted to the station, just making the city-bound train. The blood rushed into him as he left the factory behind. School didn't seem so bad compared to work.

The suburbs were sucked of colour; rain angling onto terracotta tiles. Clouds cushioned the sky. Cats sat under eaves licking their paws. Hec blasted through in his bubble with music throbbing deep inside his head. His thoughts were pulled apart by REM's *Night Swimming* – Mum's gold track. Sometimes in the dark, she used to stand on the back porch, swaying to the music, the moon full-bellied over the tin roofs and peppermint gums. Sometimes she would sing. And sometimes she would cry.

From the barricade of the couch, Hec watched the pulp hour on TV. Somewhere in outback Woopwoop the residents were *up in arms*. Half the town wanted the refugees out, half wanted them to stay. The manager at the cotton mill wanted to keep his workers. 'They work hard, they don't drink, they turn up on time. They're good blokes.' The locals at the pub slurred their names over beers. The camera scanned the country – broken trees, a true-blue sky, yellow stubble drying to brown in the fields.

'They're diff'rent, that's all.' *Mother of three.*

'They deserve a go, like the rest of us. Not many of us are from here anyway. Most of us arrived by boat; just depends how far back you wanna go.' *Farmer on a tractor.*

'You just don't know what they're hiding behind those burqas. I heard they use them for terrorist attacks back home.' *Old lady clutching her dog.*

Then the good, honest face of the presenter, one you can

trust – broad, a bit fat from beer and potatoes. 'Hmm, a tough issue for tough times. We'll keep you in touch with that one.

'Next up: benefit cheats – are your tax dollars giving them a free ride? Find out after the break.'

Hec switched off and unwrapped himself from the couch. He opened the double doors and stood on the back porch. The rain had eased, but the sky was still a terrible grey. When dark stole the rooftops he would go inside with the memory of his mum lodged between his ribs. But for now he would just stand and sip the wet air.

Dad's car in the driveway tore him from the moment. His keys rattled in the front door and Hec heard him shuffle through the kitchen and toss them in a bowl. And then he was there, just a cut-out with a briefcase, framed by the doorway.

'You want some lights on?' He flicked the switch.

'How was your day? Have you eaten?'

Hec heard the fridge door open.

'Fancy ordering out?'

The fridge door creaked shut. 'Let's celebrate you starting your new job?'

Hec walked into the lounge room.

'Thai? Indian? Vietnamese?'

Any Sudanese? Apparently Froot Loops are a delicacy in new Khartoum. There was definitely no mention of Froot Loops when Hec had looked up Sudan on the internet. Instead – years of civil war, ethnic cleansing, poverty, nineteen major ethnic groups, over one hundred languages, snail fever (whatever that was), capital Khartoum, White Nile, Blue Nile (the only river Hec had ever known was brown). Even the internet couldn't link Froot Loops and the Sudan.

'How about Chinese?'

Kinda suburban, Dad.

'Why the face? What's wrong with Chinese?'

They all became Thai and Malaysian ten years back.

'What about Thai then?'

Hec nodded.

'Your shout?'

Yeah, right.

'My shout again then.'

Dad lit candles. They got out the best bowls and plates. It was Mum's thing and it felt weird doing it for the first time without her.

The food was good – Pad Thai, red veg curry, steamed jasmine rice. Coriander, lime leaves and lots of chilli; Hec's tongue became a live animal in his mouth. They ate with the thin Japanese chopsticks Mum had bought for sashimi. The noodles slipped and fell, snow peas dodged, chunks of tofu disintegrated at their touch. This was so typical of Dad, mixing everything up and making things harder than they needed to be.

'So how was it?' he asked.

Hec leaned back in his chair and rubbed his stomach.

'The job, you idiot.'

He shrugged.

'Rome wasn't built in a day.'

Rome?

'Never mind. Here, have a fortune cookie.' Dad threw one at Hec.

They're Chinese, aren't they?

'I know. Fortune cookies are Chinese, but so was this restaurant ten years ago. Old stock.'

Hec crunched open his cookie then unfolded the square of cheap paper. *Every great journey begins with one step.*

Dad looked at it, and laughed, and opened his. *Spend time on the important things. The rest will take care of itself.*

Hec mimed throwing the dishes at the wall.

'Nice try. I guess if we broke them it would be very Zen. Or maybe very Greek.'

Hec washed, Dad dried.

'So, did you make any new friends?'

It's not kindie.

Dad shook his head. 'It would be so much easier if you talked to me, Hec. I know you can.'

Hec dropped the stainless steel scourer into the sink. It sank slowly, little wiry hairs disappearing into the foam. He nodded to the chalkboard.

It read:

I am working with a racist
and assorted nuff-nuffs.

I think school was better.

Dad put the tea towel over his shoulder. 'If you want to go back, Hec, I can probably still arrange it. But I think you should give the factory more of a go. Those nuff-nuffs as you call them are mostly refugees. I talked to Merrick. Walk a mile in their shoes before you judge them. And as for the racist, challenge his views. It's just ignorance.'

Hec snorted.

'I know it's hard. But sooner or later you have to stand up for something. Fence-sitting can seem safe, but one day you'll end up with splinters up your arse.'

How true.

3

THE NIGHT THREW ECHOES ALONG the street. They bumped between the narrow houses and eased under the broken sash of Hec's window. His restlessness had tied his sheets into wet knots on his bed. Sleep wouldn't come.

His body felt alive with electricity. It was an effort to lie still and, when he did, his mind took over the movement. He thought of the fish that the old guy had caught under the West Gate – how it had shaken its life onto the dark pontoon. The pearly jewel from behind its eyes was on the windowsill catching the light of the faraway moon. It was how Mum had cleansed her crystals, but Hec doubted that it could purify the sourness she had tainted his life with.

Eventually, he got up and wandered into the kitchen. Dad was asleep; he could hear heavy breath filling his bedroom. Hec turned the tap on and pushed his lips to the spout to drink. When he was eight, he had lost the corner of his front tooth drinking this way.

As he turned his head, he saw a moth beating itself on the window. Its eyes were tiny fires, wings a tissue-paper blur.

They came from the high country, these moths, and would make the trip to the coast to breed and then to die. Dad had told him how they navigated by the moon but the bright lights of the city tricked them and they would end their lives here; sidelined forever. Hec let the water fill his mouth and drain into the sink. He was mesmerised by the moth. It started down at the bottom of the window and fluttered its way to the top, then dropped and started again. If he left the light on, it would have tired itself by the morning and he would find it dead on the ground outside. He went over and flicked the switch. The house sucked in the darkness.

Suddenly he had the urge to be somewhere else. He went to his room, pulled on some clothes, and slipped quietly out of the house. The fish-jewel was in his pocket, a talisman; he could feel it jab his leg as he mounted his bike and pedalled towards the bay. Acland Street was quiet, just a couple of kerb-crawlers, and some junkies looking for a place to hit up. He pulled onto the kerb and sat in the shadows as a police car drifted by. He hadn't brought a helmet and his bike had no lights. All he needed was to be taken back home in disgrace.

When they had gone, he pedalled hard until he hit the Esplanade. The pier cast nets of light onto the calm water. He could see the huddles of fishermen, the red glow of their smokes as he rode further along the bay.

Down Beaconsfield Parade, the bay licking sand off the beach, low tide; Hec could smell the seaweed, a salty tang. It surprised him, here, so close to the city. It was a smell that didn't belong. The rhythm of his pedals relaxed him, the cat's eyes, the white lines and streetlights rolled by. He was alone. The breeze riffled through his hair.

The *Spirit of Tasmania* was berthed at Station Pier, preparing for the trip through the Heads and into the moody waters of Bass Strait. Hec stopped for a moment to look at it. He could feel the restlessness in the great boat, the groans that it occasionally let out, the way it rubbed itself against the pier like an animal scratching an itch. Shutting his eyes, he imagined a huge open-sea swell. The boat muscling into it, feeling its power against the ocean. This was where it belonged; the land was only a resting place before the real business.

Hec pedalled along Beach Street, swung onto the Boulevard and into Todd Road. The moon hung above like a round of soured cheese. He could see gulls in the lights, turning in the updrafts, ignoring the curfew. The bridge looked low to the ground here, the most unflattering view. It seemed as if you could easily step off it and land gently on the grass. But Hec knew better.

As he cruised through the reserve, the stinking mud from the shallow ponds poured into his nose. The bridge was carrying trucks and cars even at this time of the morning and it reminded him of a bass guitar, just one low chord, left long.

It didn't surprise him that the fisherman was there on the pontoon. It was almost as if he had known; like guessing the right window in *Play School*.

The man's fingers were grubby yellow under his small lamp, too thick to bait the hook. It was like watching a seal trying to thread a needle. In frustration, Hec grabbed the hook and bait from the man. He did not say a word and the man didn't complain. Hec had never fished in his life. Never baited a hook. But he knew what was needed. He slipped the barb through the soft pipi and slid it up the shank in one fluid movement.

Silently, the man took the baited hook and, swinging the line, let it sail into the dark. Hec heard the soft plop as it entered the water. With this done, he dragged a bag of White Ox from his pocket and rolled a smoke, still not speaking. He lit up and, turning his head to the bridge, blew smoke straight at it.

'My family were fishermen.' He took a drag again and released it through his nose. The tobacco was strong and Hec stifled a cough.

'Hard life. I'm talkin way way back when they were cleared from the land. Some left forever – Canada, America, New Zealand, here.

'You see, there was more money in sheep per acre than in people. So the crofters – tenant farmers – were booted off. Even though they had been there fer ages.

'My people went to live on the coast. Up north. It's no a friendly coast like here, mind, just salty cliffs, heather, bare rock. They had to farm a wee patch of dead ground. Eatin kale, dock when things got real tough. Had to rope the wee ones to the house so they did'nae fall.'

The old guy was like a train when he talked, words clack-clacking from the back of his throat, hitting the air between them.

'They would fish as well. Four or five to a boat, push out from the cliffs in good weather to get at the shoals of saithe and mackerel that came up the coast. When the wee ones grew, the boys would take their place in the boat. Fishin with lines, mind. *Darras* we called them. Wooden spools with six feathered hooks. You'd just pull them up, three or four fish to a line. It wasn't sport, mind, it was food. The bottom of the boat would run red with blood. Fish flappin themselves dead.

'One day they went out. All the boys bar the wee-est. It was calm, but they knew a storm was brewin. They could see the cows lyin in the fields, a bad sign. The father, my great grandfather, said to turn to home. But they were onto a good shoal. Left the run a wee bit late.

'Great grandmother took the two kids down to Glasgow after they went under. Took in washin.'

The old man spat his fag at the river. 'I grew up on the Clyde. The dirtiest river in the dirtiest town. We had nothin. My old man was a boatbuilder and I followed him. But then the yards closed. No profit, y'see. Same old story. And Glasgow became a wasteground. And I left. Nigh on forty years ago.'

He coughed and pulled a bottle from his bag. 'Well, that's my story, fer what it's worth.' He looked at Hec. 'So what's your story, sonny-boy? Where your people from?'

Hec looked up at the bridge. He knew so little about his family. His grandparents were dead before he was born. His mum hadn't really talked about them and his dad even less.

'You have to know where your people come from. That way you know where you're goin. That's what make us.'

Bullshit.

'You keep that jewel from the fish?'

Hec felt in his pocket for the tear-shaped pearl. It was there. But he shook his head. The man looked injured.

'You should be goin. Yer mum will be worryin herself silly about you.'

Hec picked up his bike and wheeled it back off the pontoon.

The man called after him. 'You keep that hoodjimaquiff, mind. It might just have some power in it yet.' He pointed his crooked old finger at the humming bridge. 'Maybe it holds the screams of those that went down.'

4

HEC WAS SET TO WORK with Silent Boy. Two mutes quick-fingering candles into boxes. Ten to a box, twenty boxes to a carton, a hundred cartons to a pallet, ten pallets to a day. Hec had never known boredom like it. He felt it swelling, minutes drawing themselves long and fatty, like stringy mutton inside him. It was suffocating to think of this stretching for years and decades if he didn't take the path back to school.

But then there was the rhythm and it lulled him. He began to drift, even as his fingers pushed the candles into boxes.

Bells came and went, smokos, lunchtimes. A week was swallowed. He watched Silent Boy opposite him and wondered what his story was. He had tried to listen as the boy's uncle talked to him at lunch, but he could only guess at the meaning, from the way in which the foreign words were presented through bared teeth; in dolorous growls from the back of the older man's throat, punctuated by sprays of rice and onion. Hec saw the power in silence. In holding back. He remembered an old saying: *It is better to remain silent*

and appear stupid than to speak and show your stupidity.
With silence, no one could use words against you.

At ten to three on a long Friday, the hour when mind-drift
tightened its grip, Silent Boy got the whisper. He jumped
quickly from his workstation and evaporated out the back.
When Hec looked around he noticed gaps in the line, faces
missing. Merrick appeared with two men in suits. They
stopped to question some of the workers – Sami, Sheila,
Mabor. They all shook their heads, stared at their toes. The
line slowed. Everyone was watching. Hec could feel the
walls of the factory suck in as it held its breath. Tran whis-
tled in his ear, 'Immigration.'

One of the men caught Hec's eye. He was a jowly sort of
bloke with thin red hair and flaky skin – a fantapants. The
man held Hec's gaze, not blinking, not smiling. The other guy
grabbed him by the crook of his elbow and said something
to him, smiling. Fantapants broke off and laughed. Then the
two men shook their heads at Merrick Hope and left.

At the end of the day, Merrick called Hec into the office.
Silent Boy and his uncle were there, the boy scuffing his
shoes on the floor while the uncle gave his stained teeth
an airing.

'Hec, come in and sit down.'

Hec shuffled further into the room, but stayed standing.
Merrick got up from behind his desk, walked around and
sat on it. The office wasn't big and the effect was alarming.
Suddenly they were all very close to each other and Hec

felt unsafe. The uncle licked his teeth and Hec noticed his tongue was forked. Silent Boy was scuffing his shoes, sending little jolts of noise into the room. The door swung itself shut and Hec jumped.

'It's okay, mate. There's no trouble or anything,' Merrick said. 'I mean, your work's good. You get along. You're a bit on the quiet side, but we're used to that around here aren't we?'

The uncle chuckled. He kicked at Silent Boy's feet and the scuffing stopped.

'It's just...' Merrick pinched the bridge of his nose. 'We have a little problem. Well, not so much of a problem, really, more like an opportunity. You see, Massoud here and his nephew need a place to stay for a while.'

The uncle drew closer to Hec and he could smell the sourness on him. One of his pupils was a full-stop. The other – a bullet-hole.

'I mean I'm going to have a word to your dad and everything, but I wanted to clear it with you first.'

The uncle shut his lips and nodded at Merrick.

'You can think of it as an educational experience. It's not every day that you get someone from another country come and live with you. And they'll be no trouble.'

'Naw trawble,' gurgled Uncle Massoud.

'They'll pay your dad board and help around the house.'

'Helup, yas.'

Hec looked at Silent Boy, but his chin was buried in his chest.

'So can I take that as a yes, then?' asked Merrick.

'Yas!' said Uncle Massoud, a little too loudly.

It really made no difference what Hec said, his dad would have the last word.

'Okay, that's all settled then. I'll call your dad and set it up, let him know you're on board.'

'Awnbawrd?'

'You'd better get going or you'll miss your train. I'll see you tomorrow.'

The chalkboard read:

Massoud and nephew moving in. Keep house clean.

And with that the deal was done.

They got his mum's old room, the one she used to paint in. The one that leaked music into the garden through the old, warped French doors. They slept on thin cotton mattresses that they rolled up each morning, balancing their plastic bags of stuff on top.

Silent Boy found the typewriter on the first Sunday morning. Hec woke to the pecking of keys on paper. He sat and listened to it for a while then rolled over and covered his head with a pillow. Still the noise kept coming. Hec could feel the weight of the words, the syntax crash like cymbals. What was worse was the noise between, the aching silence before the next letter. Hec couldn't see the point in typewriters. There was simply too much at stake. You had to get it right first time or there were pools of Wite-Out involved.

When he was ten, he had begged his mum for the old machine. It had been his grandfather's and Hec had loved its solidity, its permanence. It had lived on his desk until he had jammed the keys. But the romance of the machine gave way to the ease of the computer, the ability to cut and paste, to rewrite. Mum eventually rescued it from the floor and carried it back to her room.

He had not heard the sound for years, but he immediately knew it. It sliced the air – *shik . . . shik . . . shik . . . shik-shik*. He hauled himself out of bed, he turned on some music. But the noise worked its way between the key changes, the gaps between the songs were trashy with it. For a mute, Silent Boy knew how to make himself heard.

Hec got up. It was a cold morning and he could feel the breath of winter easing up between the floorboards. Pulling on a jumper, he walked to the doorway of Silent Boy's room and watched. He was sitting at the desk with his back to the door. Hec could just make out the high pass of his cheekbone in profile. He typed two-fingered, dashing them on the keys. There was already a small stack of paper beside him. How long had he been at it? Why did this story come in such a rush? When Hec wrote a creative piece for English it would come in fits and starts, like an old car working its way up a hill.

Uncle Massoud slept noisily on the floor, unaware of the story unfolding around him. His lips were open and his slit tongue lolled from his mouth. There was a huge patch of drool on the pillow.

As Hec turned to go, the door creaked away from him. Silent Boy looked up, his eyes wide. Hec smiled and shrugged, pursed his finger and thumb together and pushed them to his lips. *Breakfast?*

Silent Boy nodded. He got up and hid the typewriter

back in the desk drawer. The typed papers went inside his pillowcase.

They sat in the kitchen. Hec felt comfortable with Silent Boy. You could hear the crunching of Froot Loops, the snap of fat Saturday news hitting doorsteps along the street, Dad calling out in his sleep, pigeons playing woodwind on the telephone wires. Even when there was silence, there wasn't. People who talked didn't understand. They didn't listen, except to their own breathless hunger. Their need for words.

'*Salam.*' Uncle Massoud was awake. 'Good maarning.'

Hec nodded to him.

'Brakefass? Gooood.' Massoud rubbed his belly, but instead of sitting down he went to the bathroom. Hec never saw the man eat. He saw the remains of his odd hour snacks – the wasted food left to harden until the morning, the plates he made Silent Boy wash and dry. He was an odd man. There was something not right in the way he treated his nephew.

Massoud was twenty minutes in the bathroom, but showed no signs of being any cleaner. He seemed sleepy and happy.

'I see Meestar Merrick,' he said, leaning on Hec's chair back with his scarred paws.

Hec nodded even though he thought it strange that Massoud would have business with Merrick on a Saturday. Massoud showed no sign of going and Hec felt uncomfortable with him lolling behind him. Silent Boy kept his head down, herding his Froot Loops into his mouth with his spoon. Hec needed to break the spell. He touched Silent Boy on the arm and nodded to the door. They got up together and went out into the static morning.

It was a good day for walking as they turned out of Acland Street and onto the Esplanade. The Espy was nursing a hangover, its mouth open to the street, belching the syrupy last-drinks memory from the back of its throat. Kitesurfers were already at it, pulling themselves free and landing to camera clicks from the pier. Silent Boy watched the bay, a mistrustful knot between his eyes. Hec tried to read his thoughts, but all he could retrieve was the buzz and beep of traffic searching for espresso and the biggest Big Breakfast.

It took them more than an hour, but they made it, crossing the sour swamp of West Gate Park as the sun was eclipsed by the bridge.

Mum would often tell Hector that Melbourne didn't have the Harbour, the Opera House or even a coathanger bridge. It didn't have the ferries, or surf smacking up close to the city, or a zoo that climbs from the water like a sundrunk iguana. But it wasn't second-best to Sydney. It had its cafes, it had European styling, the upside-down river, museums and the wickerwork cone of the Arts Centre. It had gardens, the clocks at Flinders Street, meals for five bucks at the Hare Krishna joint on Swanston Street. It had sushi and gnocchi and fish and chips and live bands on a Sunday afternoon. But Hec chose to show Silent Boy the bridge.

And it was as if Silent Boy understood because he lay on the pontoon, his stomach flat on the grey hardwood, and touched the water. Where his fingers broached the surface, rings formed and radiated like shockwaves. His lips moved, but only silence poured from them. Hec watched as he brought his fingers to his lips and, as he sat up, to his heart.

Hec could smell the old man coming before he could see him. It was the smell of someone who'd lived too long in his body. An argument between stale fish and whisky, and a backnote of King Mulloway about him. And he came in his tangle of greasy clothes, whiskers tucked into the creases in his face, a small stool looped over his shoulder. He came with his bucket and his bag and the curve of a knife slipped between his red flanny and his waistband.

'Back again,' he said and unfolded his stool on the pontoon. He brought out his bottle and took a quick drink. 'Who's yer mate?'

Hec simply raised his chin towards Silent Boy.

'Yer a good match you two. Dumb and dumber. I guess it's all up to me again, is it? Good job I got words enough fer all of us.

'So what ye doin down this way? You two boys got nowheres better t'be?'

He shook his head. 'It's like talkin to a brick wall...two brick walls even.' The fisho pointed at Silent Boy. 'You don't look like you're from aroun here.' He shrugged. 'Then who does these days, eh? Used to be that everyone was the same. But times change and if we don't, then we get left behind.

'Did I ever tell you about Stanko? Mate of mine. Croat bloke straight from the Balkans. That bloke had more life in his left toe than the two of youse put together. He would sing all day, top of his voice, all them terrible gypsy songs. We'd pelt him with rivets, but would he shut up, would he hell. He sang like the whole world was in those songs.

'He got married one June, the *eejit*. Hailstones the size of gobstoppers for confetti. I was best man. Gave a speech and all. Mind, I was a bit pished and they couldn't understand a word. But Stanko slapped my back and said he loved me.'

The old man looked out at the river. At the swirls of oil like knots on a tabletop.

'They had a wee-one in the summer. She was a beauty. Just can't remember her name.'

He scrunched his eyes as if he was trying to look into the past and it was causing him pain.

'Why can't I remember her name?'

Shaking his head, he pulled out his White Ox and rolled himself a smoke. As he tucked it in the corner of his mouth, he patted his pockets for matches. Hec and Silent Boy waited for the story to continue, but it wouldn't be rushed. The old man drew deeply on his fag and released the smoke through his nose. He wiped the corners of his eyes with his thumb.

'You see, mates are important. Next to family, the most important thing. I knew Stanko four years before the big drop. Would have protected him with my life.

'I came here fishin after that. Every Sunday. Like my own private religion. About a year in, I caught a big bugger of a fish. A stoater. As big as one of them wrinkly dogs. You know the ones. Shar Peis, they call them. Big as that and twice as bloody ugly.

'I opened him up. Stinkin, he was. Stuffed with mud and weed. But I saw somethin shiny in it.' He looked at the boys through his cigarette smoke. 'Know what it was?'

He waited for a response. His boxer's head tilted as if to let water from its ear.

'Stanko's wedding ring.' He raised his eyebrows at the boys. 'No finger, ye ken. But it was his ring awright. No bullshit. Couldn't believe it. Took it to his wife, but she shouted at me to bugger off. Said I was mad. Mad, me? She was the one shoutin.'

The old man rubbed at the boards with his toe. When he looked up, his eyes were moist.

'You'd think a big thing like that would go down quick, eh?' He pointed his wet fag at the bridge. 'It dropped like a shot beast. Its knees buckled and crumpled into the water. I had walked back to get lunch from my car. That saved me. I wished for years that I had gone down with it. *Survivor guilt* they called it. Like by putting a name on it somehow it'll be awright.

'You mates need to take care of each other.'

Hec looked at Silent Boy. Was he really a mate? They hardly knew each other.

'Now, you *eejits* can leave me alone to catch some fish.'

He bent over his bait bucket, dropping fag ash into his pipis. Hec and Silent Boy just stood there, waiting, as if the mad old man would give them the wisdom to fix all that was wrong.

'Gawn. Piss off. I need to fish and you *teuchters* will scare them.'

He shoved Hec gently on the shoulder and turned Silent Boy around and faced him to the shore. They took the first steps and the fisherman called after them.

'Take care of each other, mind.'

IT WAS NINE-THIRTY AT NIGHT when they got out at the station. Hec's heart was leaping about like a mouse in a bucket. It had been raining all day and the streets were slick and dangerous.

Hec didn't understand what was going on. He had gone to sleep early. There was work the next day. But Silent Boy had woken him and showed him Uncle Massoud's empty bed. Hec shrugged, but Silent Boy dragged him to the station and onto a train.

They stood in front of the candle factory. Its sooty face sneered at them in the blue dark. Silent Boy led Hec by the hand, round the lumpy courtyard and to the rear of the factory where the loading bay was.

The gate was wide open and there was a forty-foot container at the loading bay. Silent Boy put his finger to his lips. Hec could feel a bubble of laughter well in his stomach. It was like telling a blind man not to look or a deaf man not to listen. But then he saw Uncle Massoud and Merrick Hope at the rear of the container.

Merrick had a pair of boltcutters. Silent Boy and Hec crept along the loading bay wall until they were hidden behind the rubbish skip. Merrick snipped off the customs tags and Massoud swung the handles over. Even with the door obscuring their vision, Hec could tell it didn't release its vacuum as it was supposed to.

Hec knew it was drugs. Splinter would be ecstatic – all his paranoid conspiracy theories come true. The bag of white powder they had found on his first day wasn't a wax additive sample after all.

Then he heard Massoud saying something in Dari.

Hec looked at Silent Boy who nodded. *What is going on?* Hec shouted with his eyes. Silent Boy pointed back at the container.

In the gap between the door and the floor, Hec could see feet, shuffling. He counted ten pairs of sandals, one walking stick, a child's bare toes. Then the door swung closed again and the light from the loading bay exhaled into the night.

So it wasn't drugs. It was a group of tired people. Their clothes were dirty, long shirts stained with oil. They wore baggy pants, the child was dressed in a long tunic and a headscarf. Her eyes were dark and narrow, they flitted around the men as they talked; her small hand was held by a boy Hec's age.

A van pulled up at the loading bay and Hec and Silent Boy drew further into the shadows. A guy got out and stretched. It was the immigration guy, Fantapants from the raid at the factory.

'Got a load for me, Merrick?' he said.

'This is the first and last, Rudman,' Merrick replied to Fantapants.

'Ah, if only life were that simple, eh, Merrick? If only.'

'With the factory back on track, I'm out.'

'Yeah, well.' Rudman scratched his chin. 'Thing is you're involved now. You're an integral part of the operation. You and good old Massoud here.' He slapped Massoud on the shoulder and the man grinned until his small eye completely disappeared.

'No, that's it. It's over. Once was enough. It's too dangerous.'

'What I'm thinking, and tell me if I am off the mark here, is that it would be dangerous for you *not* to be involved. The way I see it is that if we are no longer business partners then it might be beneficial for me to have a chat to my mates in customs, so that they priority search *all* your containers. Stop the flow of illegal wax. It's a terrible thing, these cheap imports.'

He put his arm around Merrick and softened his voice.

'Let's look at the whole thing another way. I'm a glass-half-full sort of guy and I think you are too, Merrick. You are helping these poor people to a better life. It's way too risky for them to come by boat now. The patrols are on the lookout. But this way, well they're hidden aren't they? And you, you are doing a humanitarian service. You're a modern-day Oskar Schindler.'

'And what if someone dies?'

'Merrick, *Merrick*. Be rational, mate, how are they going to die? Massoud here has taken care of everything. The team in Jakarta give them food and water, plastic tubs to crap in. They drill vents and give them battery fans. We are not heartless men, Merrick. Look at these people, we are helping them.'

'I just want out that's all.'

Rudman coughed. He grabbed the little girl from the boy's hand. Held her up in front of Merrick by her arms. She began to weep.

'Look at her, Merrick. Look into her eyes and tell her you don't care.'

'It's not that I don't care—'

'Shhh, now.' His face was next to the girl's, but he was talking to Merrick. 'This conversation is over. We're not having it.' Rudman dropped the girl and she ran back to the boy.

The group of Afghans were starting to get nervous. Massoud muttered quietly to them, patted them on their arms.

'They needs to go,' he said.

'They do,' said Merrick. 'But this is the last time, okay.'

Rudman opened up the back of the van and ushered the group inside. He shut the door behind them.

'Not the last time. Not,' he said.

'You can't make me do this,' Merrick shouted as Rudman got into the van.

But all he got in reply was a wave from the window as the van turned the corner.

Back at home, Hec and Silent Boy sat at the kitchen table and drank glasses of warm milk laced with a spoon of Blue Box honey. It was what Hec's mum used to make him when he couldn't sleep. She believed it calmed the mind.

Hec didn't know what to do. His dad would never believe him. It was easy for Merrick to lie. He had words. If he went to the police, then Silent Boy would get caught up in the whole mess. They'd nab him for sure and send him back. And hadn't the fisho told them to take care of each other? Why did he feel compelled to listen to a drunk old man?

The best thing to do was just stay out of it. No one was getting hurt and as Rudman had said, the Afghans were getting what they wanted. Then why did Hec feel so bad? Why did he feel responsible? It was ridiculous. And complicated.

Silent Boy had begun to sit with the others. Uncle Massoud still sat alone, his head bent low over a plate of rice and meat. Splinter skulked in the corner, seething, muttering curses, licking his palms.

Work had set into a rhythm for Hec. The early morning, before smoko, was a fog of noise, the tang of wax smoke, a greasy pall that clung to the skin and hair. Mid morning to lunch was quick and happy. Lunch to the late bell dragged itself, lead-eyed, round the clock. Smoko was for gossip. Lunch for philosophy.

Silent Boy and Hec shared *naan* and *kabob* leftovers from the previous night's dinner. Silent Boy took the flask of *chay* to fill at the urn. Hec loved this green tea, the way the leaves flurried, a storm in his teacup. He drank it all the time now. It had become his and Silent Boy's ritual. A glass of warm milk and honey in the morning then green tea throughout the day.

Splinter approached them as Silent Boy filled the flask.

'Get a wiggle on, dumbarse,' he spat.

The room tensed, but Silent Boy kept his cool. He peered into the neck of the flask to check its progress.

'You listenin?' Splinter turned his mutton-cube head under

Silent Boy's. Leered up through the steam at him. 'Listen, ya little goat-shagger, I need some water for me coffee and you need to let me at it.'

Silent Boy moved to one side and Splinter, taking this as his cue to move in, pushed his cup under the spout. Silent Boy pushed back and the water coursed over Splinter's hand.

Splinter dropped the cup and screamed. Mabor got up from his seat, but Sheila put her hand on his arm.

'You bloody little reffo dipshit. See what ya done. Time you was put in your place.' He turned on the room. 'All of youse.' He punched Silent Boy hard in the mouth. But Silent Boy didn't go down. Blood trickled from his lip. Uncle Massoud shouted something, but he stayed where he was.

Tran screamed, 'Fall down. Why you not fall down? You mad?'

'He's mad awright. And I'm goin slap some sense into him.' Splinter licked his palms slowly and clenched his fists.

Everyone was frozen. Hec stood up. *Take care of each other*, the fisho had said. Hec could feel the fish-jewel in his pocket, the sharp point pressed into his skin. The distance between him and Splinter seemed great. He crossed it in slow motion, blood singing in his ears. *Take care*. He put his hand on Splinter's arm and as he did so, he knew it was a mistake. It was like trying to reason with fire.

He didn't feel the punch. But he remembered later how it had sounded as it broke bone. He remembered the lights turning like time-lapse stars above him and how cool the lino felt against his cheek. Then he remembered falling into mineshaft black with his body relaxed and every muscle turned to fluid and his smile stretched out like wings, his feet pointed up, the wind stealing his hair, eyes like sideshow carnival lights, kids popping ping-pong balls into his open mouth and no sound escaping ever... ever.

Splinter got fired. And Hec got a week off work, and soft food. He had jumped off the fence and got rid of the splinter from his arse too. But he was no hero.

When he returned to work, everyone ignored him. Why? Because he had done what they feared to do? Because they were ashamed of their cowardice?

Mabor finally talked to him. They were setting up the wicks. 'You think you done big hero thing. You done one maan. Tousand more behind him. Ten tousand. You naiver win.'

Then it is better to do nothing? Hec thought. *To live in fear? I don't think so.*

'It is easy for you, Hec,' Mabor said as his wattle-bark fingers worked the spools. 'You are the right skin colour. You have the right eyes and naime. And still you lose. Whaat hope for us?'

But after it had all settled down Sheila pulled him aside and whispered to him, 'You was brave, Hec. Stupit, but brave. You help you friend.' She smiled at him. 'When I come from Cambodia everyone say, *Go back to China.*' She shook her head, so her ponytail swung from side to side. 'I'm not from China,' she said. 'I wish I had friend like you.'

6

ANOTHER TWO WEEKS PASSED BEFORE Hec and Silent Boy made the next night trip through the suburbs. Uncle Massoud had been missing from his bed again. That was how they knew something was going down. It was later this time, almost ten and Hec knew they needed to make the last train home, just after eleven.

They saw the same people. The tramp carrying his bag of bags and a blanket, dozing his way in and out of the city. The afternoon shift-worker coming home with weariness tucked in the corners of his eyes and his blue pants strung with typesetter's ink. The call-centre girl playing Tetris on her phone, the hem of her dress dipped in mud.

And at Dandenong, the threat of the late-night crowd. The static of their pants crackling as they rolled down the street. Hoodies and hoons, lowered cars with the tub-thump of their subwoofers denting the air. And at the Hope Candle Works the smeared charcoal facade. The yellow mouth of the loading bay.

Hec leaned against the skip and felt the metal chill his

back. It was turning to winter and the news was full of boat arrivals. They were housing them offshore, cutting islands loose from the mainland, changing borders. Hec didn't know what it all meant, but he saw the new faces at the factory. How they looked into space without focussing; how they talked in whispers.

They got into position behind the skip. The container wasn't there yet, but Hec and Silent Boy could see Merrick and Massoud leaning on opposite sides of the doorway, waiting.

After a while, the van arrived and Rudman jumped out. With one hand on the loading bay, he vaulted up beside the two other men.

'They not here yet?' he asked, dusting his hands together.

'Maybe they're not going to show,' said Merrick.

'Glass-half-emp-ty, Mer-rick.' Rudman slapped him gently on the cheek on each syllable. 'I had word from the port, they loaded up an hour ago.

'In other glass-half-full news: there's a big Taliban offensive now spring has arrived in Afghanistan. "The fighting season" they called it; I love that – it's like when fruit comes back onto the shelves. We need to prepare for an increase in business.'

Merrick jiggled a pair of boltcutters against his leg. 'Not happening,' he said.

'Here the truck,' said Massoud.

The truck beep-beeped its way down the alley to the loading bay. It stopped, releasing air. Slowly the door opened.

'Haz,' said Rudman to the man.

Haz nodded around the group until he got to Massoud. 'I know this bloke,' he said slowly. 'Name's Saladeen, right? You had a young fella with you last time we met.'

'Massoud,' said Uncle Massoud and stuck out his hand.

'Right you are then,' Haz said. 'Massoud it is.' He turned to the container. 'I'll unhitch her and get gawn. Got to get back to Adelaide with a load tonight. A nice little turnaround job this one.'

Haz unhooked the trailer. When he was finished he jumped back in his truck. 'Last run for a while,' he shouted over the engine noise. 'I got enough to last me. I'm heading bush.' He waved out the window and was gone.

Merrick exhaled. His breath formed a heavy cloud.

Rudman put a hand on Merrick's shoulder. 'Merrick, you are a valuable part of this organisation. This is only the beginning.'

'Spare me the pep-talk, Rudman.'

Merrick snipped the seal and opened the doors. A group of people surged out. There was shouting. Hec could see bodies falling to the ground in the gap below the door. The noise got louder and louder.

Suddenly there was a gunshot and everything fell silent. Rudman lowered the pistol and clipped the door against the container. The group was revealed to Hec and Silent Boy. Some were lying, others standing. They were Afghans: the older men with beards, young guys wearing jeans, a few women and children. Near the edge of the group a woman sat, her head bent over a small bundle in her arms. She was crying.

Rudman scratched his chin. 'What's their problem, Massoud?'

Massoud questioned the men. They rattled agitated answers at him.

'This woman baby die two days before. Not too much water for all.'

Rudman looked at each of them. 'Tell them it is not our

fault. That we pay the people in Jakarta to provide food and water. What they do with the money is their business.'

'I not can tell them.'

'Why?'

'They will kill me then they will kill you.'

'I have the gun, Massoud. Tell them to be reasonable.'

Massoud told the group and the men pulled at their beards and shouted. Rudman shot one of them in the foot. He fell to the ground. The others stared at him in disbelief. The children started to cry.

'I'm not a violent man, people,' Rudman touched his nose with the barrel of the pistol. 'But you are pushing me beyond my limits. Take the baby away, Massoud.'

'Na, Meesta Rudman. Baby is dead. Is not allowed.'

'Get the baby or I will shoot *you*!' screamed Rudman.

'This is crazy,' hissed Merrick.

'You want to take care of this, Hope?' Rudman asked.

Merrick hung his head.

'Then shut up.' He pointed the pistol back at Massoud. 'Do it or I'll pop a piece of lead in your ugly hide. And when I do I will get a bravery award for exposing a terrible smuggling ring and its evil mastermind.'

Slowly Massoud walked to the woman. He bent down and grasped the small bundle of cloth. The mother wailed and held on. The men gritted their teeth and spat curses at Massoud. He gripped tighter and pulled the body free.

'Grab a bag from the van, put it in and stash it behind the seat,' said Rudman.

'No!' screamed Merrick. 'It's a baby.'

'It's dead and we need to get rid of it. I don't want it contaminating the rest of the cargo.'

'They're people!'

'They're money. Remember that. Now do it Massoud or I'll shoot you and dump you with the baby.'

Massoud went to the van. With one hand he ruffled open the neck of a garbage bag and dropped the baby inside. Hec and Silent Boy held their breaths. The truck was very near the skip. From where they were crouched Massoud could easily see them. The only thing that protected them was shadow and silence. Massoud pulled the drawstrings of the bag together and knotted them. He swung it into the cab. It landed on the floor with a thud and a groan escaped Hec, like the grunt of the dying Jewelfish.

Hec saw Massoud look towards them, saw his tongue dart out and rip across his lips. He started for the skip.

'What are you doing?' asked Rudman.

'I hear one noise.'

'It's nothing. You're jumping at shadows. We need to get the cargo into the van.'

Hec saw Massoud turn again. It looked as if they would be okay. But something made him stop. Hec pressed the sharp point of the fish-jewel into his palm and wished him away.

'I just check, Meesta Rudman.' And he walked back to the skip.

Silent Boy was behind Hec. Hec knew what he had to do. If he gave himself up then Silent Boy would be okay. It could give him enough time to escape. But before he could react, Silent Boy grabbed him by the shoulder and leapt from their hiding spot. Hec watched as Massoud and Silent Boy's feet met and as they fell together.

'Get up!' yelled Rudman. 'Bring him here, Massoud. This is getting messy.'

Massoud twisted Silent Boy's arm behind him and marched him onto the loading bay.

'Kneel,' ordered Rudman. 'Kneel!' He smashed the pistol butt into the back of Silent Boy's head. Silent Boy fell onto his knees. Rudman walked behind him and placed the muzzle on his skull. He licked his thin lips. The mothers held their children tighter, pulled them into their dresses.

'Naaaaaaaaawww.' The noise rose from deep inside Hec. It tore his throat as it came. It pushed past the silence. It ignored history. His private sadness. What had gone before. He exploded from behind the skip. He saw the gun pointed at him, but he kept coming. As he tried to jump onto the loading bay, Merrick's foot stopped him. It knocked him backwards onto the ground.

Rudman smiled. 'Nice work, Merrick.' He pushed the muzzle hard into Silent Boy's mouth. 'We'll start with this one and finish with his friend. What a sad story. Two mixed up friends. A murder-suicide. The Muslim fundamentalist kills the Aussie kid then tops himself. The media will love it. The tide just keeps turning against these poor boat people. But our business just gets better. That's what I call positive growth.'

The shout came from the top of the container. 'Hey! I got a new endin for you dicks.' Silhouetted against the sodium sky was a man. In one hand he held a bottle. In the other a lighter.

'Warned ya bout that cheap-arse wax didn't I, Hope? No good, I said.' He lit a taper at the neck of the bottle. 'But you never listened to me. Pretendin to be all holy. Ha! Yer a fake.'

'Splinter. Put down the bottle. This wax'll take everything,' said Merrick.

'Everything's already bin taken. I lost my job cause of them two.' He pointed the lighter at Hec and Silent Boy. The taper was still burning. 'Did you stand by me? No. You chose a bunch of reffos and a dumb teenager.'

'Mate. Be calm. This isn't going to solve anything.'

'I am not your *mate*, Hope. Once I coulda been. Once.'

'Maybe we can start again. Maybe you can have your job back. Maybe we *can* be mates.'

'Maybe. Maybe! Things are never going to be the same. And if they can't be the way they were, then they got no right bein at all.' He raised the bottle above his head. He threw it and it landed among the pallets of wax.

Merrick ran to the pallets and dived inside to try to retrieve the bottle. But it had broken and released its petrol. As the flame took, it sucked the air with it and became a living thing. It spread its blue calm over the bags of wax. Over Merrick. He didn't scream. The bags melted. Wax beads poured onto the floor. The tongues of flame licked at them. Consumed them. *Djinns* and wraiths danced to the ceiling. As the heat forced the group off the loading bay, Rudman rounded the Afghans into the van and reversed quickly away.

On the top of the container, Splinter fell to his knees. The fire was spreading towards him. He jumped to the loading bay, running to where they had last seen Merrick.

'Mr Hope!' he shouted. 'I'm sorry Mr Hope.' The heat was vicious. Wings sprouted on his shoulders. Fire swallowed his hair in a rush. Dragged him into its arms. And then he was a shadow. A hole. A memory.

The blackboard read:

It stops now.

It surprised Hec how neat Silent Boy's writing was. How his words curled and sung, how their serifs hung like angels.

Hec opened the door to his mum's old room but Uncle Massoud was in his bed. Silent Boy's mattress was still rolled against the wall. Massoud looked up from his pillow.

'This is secret, *balē?*' he whispered.

Yes, this is secret. Everything is a secret. Everything and always. Hec closed the door and lay on his bed. He held his hook-shaped jewel to the light. The fisho had said that the dead were in that bone.

Dad woke him. It was daylight.

'Hec, there's some guys from immigration want to talk to you. Said they want Massoud, too. That you could explain. What is all this? You need to talk to me, Hec.'

Hec got up and opened the door. Rudman and another officer were standing there. 'You could be in a lot of trouble, Hector. We need Massoud, where is he?'

Hec led them to the bedroom. What did he care if they took Massoud. But the room was empty, the curtains blowing through the French doors.

'Where is he?' asked Rudman's mate.

Hec shrugged. Rudman pushed him up against the wall and whispered in his ear, 'You know silence is a very underrated quality in the young.'

'Let him go,' said Dad from the doorway. 'Let him go, or I'll call the police.'

Rudman held up his hands. 'Just trying to do our jobs. Trying to protect your country from illegals.'

Hec followed them out to the car. Rudman stopped him with a hand on his chest. 'You can't see him you know. He's going back.'

But Hec could see him. Silent Boy looked from the tinted windows. He pushed his hand on the glass and Hec placed his hand on top. And the window grew warm between them.

'He wants you to have this,' said Rudman's mate as he handed Hec a pillowcase of papers.

Rudman said, 'It's a bit of a read. I did a bit of editing on the later stuff. We got a copy. You can keep this one.'

Hec handed the fish-jewel to Rudman. Maybe it did have power, like the old fisho had said. Maybe it was a talisman. Maybe it would keep Silent Boy safe.

Rudman turned the teardrop pearl over in his hand. 'This what he gets for all those words?' he asked. Hec nodded. 'Poor trade,' said Rudman.

Then they slammed their doors and started the car. As they reached the end of the street, rain began to fall. It got heavier and heavier, but Hec just offered his face to the sky and stood still.

His dad yelled from the house, 'Come inside, Hec.' But he couldn't. Eventually the drains blocked and the gutters backed up over the footpaths. And the street became a river and then an inland sea. And still it rained.

And out beneath the bridge, the old fisho crouched at the water's edge. And the drains carried it all to him. He bent to the water and listened.

part three

Across
the
Bridge

IN MY UPSTAIRS ROOM AT the Ariana Guesthouse, I open the journal my father gave me. There is so much blank paper, so many ruled lines. So many rules.

I don't know where I should begin, how to track the years between what happened with Omed and what is happening now. My pen is a crippled limb.

I am twenty-two. I should know these things by now. Even back in high school I learnt the basic rules of journalism – how to tell a story without wasting words. Three years of uni just drummed it home. But I am jammed up here. The words are caught inside me.

The dust has already settled on the page, it makes the pen grab at the paper. I write:

Who: Omed and Hec.
What: The story of two silent boys.
Where: Afghanistan: the most dangerous country on earth.
Why: To find out what happens next.
How:

How? I leave some room and skip to the next page. As I write, the ink spills from one word to the next like blood.

Kabul is full of dust and light. It is a ghazal, played loud from a yellow taxi. Its heat is a burqa. It is a kite. It is a dog-possessed beggar, running on all fours between the traffic. It is a pole of bright balloons sold to passing cars. It is a torn street, a pakul hat, a boiling samovar, a fistful of worn Afghani banknotes, kabob smoke, Mazari melons, car horns, shoeshine boys, kids with burning tins of herbs demanding coins.

And now it is me. Me in the chaikhana, eating naan. Me sweating in the midday heat. Me second day in, another victim of propaganda from the long War on Reason and Tolerance. I am scared of long beards, and scarves wrapped around faces. What are they hiding?

The red and green Farsi script screaming from billboards shouts to me: Fear me! I am the other! I am different! I am dangerous! I am militant!

It's like I have walked into a 3-D movie without the glasses that bring it to life. I am seeing two versions of reality — my own, laid on top of Kabul — and everything feels slightly out of focus.

Under the TV playing an Iranian soap are an old man and his wife. He is in a ragged turban, a white beard, a dirty green shalwar kameez. She is slowly swallowing handfuls of qabli pulao, rice with raisins and grated carrot. Her secrets are swallowed by her burqa, The hem is torn. They are from the Provinces. Him with his plastic bag of pills and herbs, his glass of chay sabz: green tea, sticky with sugar. They are wasting time, waiting for a bus to take them home.

I am back in my hotel room and the power is out. Outside,

*the generators of Kabul kick in. But not here. Faisal is stoned,
lying in the kitchen, on his bed, dreaming of his wife and
kids in the camps in Pakistan. I have renamed this hotel
Fawlty Towers (and sometimes Farty Towels). If Faisal is the
Dari-speaking Basil Fawlty, then Ghulam Ali is the Manuel.
He laughs and smiles when I ask for breakfast, brings tea
when I hope for jam. The only words he knows in English
are, Good maarning, and he uses them often. There are no
Sybil and Polly here; this is a man's place. Its rooms are filled
with Turkish electricians and engineers heading to Kunduz
and Jalalabad on contracts. Testosterone and kabob is on
the menu every day.*

Eventually, the heat forces me from the room. Even with the
windows open there is no oxygen. Dust covers everything.
It is part of the air. In the evenings when the winds come,
you inhale particles of Kabul with every breath. My teeth
crunch as I bring them together. My lungs are muddy.

In the garden, Ghulam greets me.

'Good maarning.' He bows and smiles and shakes his
head from side to side. It is hard not to like him, even in
the heat of late afternoon.

'*Chay*?' I ask, hopefully.

'*Chay sabz*?'

'Yes, *chay sabz*.' Is there any other?

Ghulam smiles and walks backwards from the room, he is
carrying a broken toaster and the cord leaves the room last.

I sit down on the plastic garden chair and look at the
hills. Mud houses hang from the rocky slopes. I have heard
they are getting higher every year as the refugees return. The
government has lost control of the building permits, but the

residents promise to leave when they are asked. It is this politeness that most astounds me. They have to carry water up there every day in goatskin bags and old oil containers. But the kids are on the roofs flying kites. They are just tiny diamonds, fifty metres up.

A girl opens the glass door and comes straight up to my table. 'May I sit here?' she asks. There is a white scarf wrapped around her hair, so light it could be mist.

'Is it ok?' Her hand is on the back of the chair.

'Sure, sure. Sorry, I was just thinking about something.'

'That's ok.' She slips into her seat and smiles.

My mind is spinning its wheels, trying to get traction on a thought. Any thought.

'So what brings you to Kabul?' she asks.

I wish I had a cool answer and was cooler. I wish I really knew why I was here. It is easy to write: *To find out what happens next*, on a fresh page, but what does that mean?

'I'm a writer. Well, I'm a journalist. But I'm here to write. When I say writing what I mean is not-journalism.' Sometimes I think a year of not talking has permanently welded shut my speech-centre.

'Sounds confusing,' she says, her eyebrows the highest arches. 'What are you *writing*?'

'A story.'

'Is it classified or something?'

'Not really.' Do I tell her? If I say it out loud does that make it true? 'It's sort of my story and sort of someone else's. The someone else – he was a refugee and things ended badly for him.'

'They often do.'

And then a tap opens and my story gushes out. 'When

I finished my journalism degree I realised I hadn't believed in or cared about anything I'd written in that three years. That there was only one story worth telling. Instead of getting a job like every other sensible person in my year, I came here.'

'Oh-kay,' she says it slow and I imagine the little hyphen as a bridge between the syllables.

I say, 'The refugee, he was called Omed. *Is* called Omed.'

'That means *hope* in Dari.'

'I didn't know that.'

'And now you do.' She folds her legs under her on the plastic seat.

'He might be dead. I couldn't find out anything from Australia.'

'And why do you need to know?'

I blurt out, 'To find out what happens next.' My journal is on the table between us. I put my hand on top of it in case she is curious. In case she finds out my throwaway lines are carefully scripted inside it.

'To who?' she asks.

'What?'

'To find out what happens next to who?'

Again with the spinning wheels. Can she hear them screeching, the smell of the burning rubber? 'What happened to Omed, I guess. And what happens to me. It's a shared story.'

'Like Hansel and Gretel?'

'Without the forest, the stones, the bread, the birds, the gingerbread house, the witch.'

'So nothing like Hansel and Gretel?'

'Not really, no.' I cough out a nervous laugh.

'Everyone has a secret here,' she says out of nowhere.

'Do you?' I ask.

'Except me. I am an open book.' She opens a small mirror and rubs the dirt from her forehead. 'You're a New Zealander, right?'

'Australian. And you?'

She laughs now, and it sounds like the finches I have seen in wicker cages strung above shops. 'I'm Afghan.'

'Cool.' I wonder about the perfect English; her accent.

She shrugs. 'So where are you going in Afghanistan? Are you waiting for an army embed? The next great war story. Kandahar? Orūzgān?'

'Bamiyan.'

Her eyes ignite. 'Bamiyan is the most beautiful place on earth.'

'That's a big call.'

She smiles and the dimples on her cheeks could hide snipers. 'You wait,' she says.

'I have been. Waiting, I mean. I can't figure out how to get there. I hear it's pretty dangerous. Taliban, bandits.'

'Just don't go through Wardak. It's shorter, but you'll get nabbed for sure. Buy yourself some local clothes and cross the Shibar Pass. It's not too bad. Don't hang around in Ghorband though – the locals aren't so friendly.'

I want to ask her what she considers friendly and what she considers unfriendly. The words *friendly fire* ricochet in my brain for a while. And then *oxymoron* stumbles out, bleeding, clutching its comrade *war on terror*.

'Really, the worst part is the road.'

'Roads are no problem,' I say. Roads I know. Roads I can deal with. 'We have bad roads in Australia too.'

'Maybe not like this one. I am pretty sure this is unique.'

'How do I get a car?' I don't want to treat her like a tour guide, but this isn't Thailand or Vietnam. My guidebook was written in 1970. Forty years on, the situation is what is called *fluid*. Meaning what? That it will cool me and quench my thirst? No, meaning that it keeps changing, that it may rise up and separate my head from my neck.

I say, 'The overland companies want five hundred US or they want to take me there and back in three days in an armoured four-wheel drive.'

'Just go up the street to the bazaar. At the *charahi* – the roundabout – there are *Tunis* that leave every morning. But early, like 4 a.m. Wear your local clothes and keep your mouth shut. You'll be fine.'

It sounds extremely dodgy, like everything about this country. But I keep on asking questions, and not the important ones like: *Will I be kidnapped by militants?* or *Should I buy a gun?*

'What's a *Tunis*?'

'One of those Toyota vans. I think the word is a Dari mangling of TownAce. They'll go anywhere.'

Just walking to the *charahi* would take more guts than I can summon right now. 'I don't know.' In the spaces between the words I am screaming, *I want home! I want off this ride!*

'You'll be cool. I mean it. Look, if you're worried, I'm leaving day after tomorrow and you can tag along with me.'

'You're going to Bamiyan?'

'I have a project starting there.'

'What kind of project?'

'Education. Women and children. I'm trying to get a school up and running in a valley to the west of Bamiyan.'

'That's huge.'

'It's not so big. There are people doing incredible things here. You are lucky to see this place at this time.'

She tilts her head back so I can see the taut lines of her neck. 'Ghulam! Ghulam Ali! *Lotfan, chay sabz!*' she shouts.

'I didn't even get your name,' I say.

'And I didn't get yours.'

'It's Hec.'

'Arezu. My name is Arezu.'

'That's beautiful.' *And that was so creepy.* I feel like an old man in a dirty coat on a commuter train.

'It means *wish.*'

'So what are you wishing for?' *And why am I such a freak?*

'Me? Oh, the usual: world peace, an end to hunger and poverty. A glass of *chay sabz.*'

'Good luck with that last one,' I say. 'So where are your parents from?'

She leans back in her chair. 'My mother, she's Hazara, from Bamiyan Province. My dad's from the US. They met here in the seventies. When the Russians came, they went to the States.'

'So, do you feel American or Afghan?'

'Both, though I wasn't born here. When I graduated from college, I knew I wanted to work in Afghanistan. When the Taliban fell, I decided to come here.'

'That's pretty brave.'

'I'm not brave, not by Afghan standards. I wouldn't have come here under the Taliban. Some people stayed. Some foreign NGO workers, a lot of Afghan people. They are the brave ones.'

'But the locals didn't have a choice, did they?'

'Some went to Pakistan or Iran. Those with more money went further – Norway, America, Australia. Some had no money and so no choice but to stay and suffer. And others stayed because they believed this was their country and they had a right.'

Rights? It is hard to believe they could exist with all this mayhem. 'It must have been hard here under the Taliban.'

She smiles. 'Yes. And the Russians. And the civil war.'

Ghulam Ali eventually brings a flask of tea. Arezu pours us each a cup and we watch the leaves settle.

'So,' she says, 'if we are going to Bamiyan we should get you some travelling clothes.'

I have never been to a tailor. Never had a man run his tape across my shoulders and down my leg. He scribbles my measurements in a columned book. He asks what kind of collar do I want – French or Hindu?

'Hindu,' says Arezu. 'Trust me. And you should have the rounded bottom on the shirt. It is much more elegant than the straight.'

We choose a cloth. Arezu feels the weight of each one between her fingers, holds them to the light. 'If the cloth is too dark,' she says, 'it will be too warm for summer. But if it's too light, it will show the dirt.'

I choose a blue that is like the Kabul sky at dusk. The tailor promises the *shalwar kameez* will be ready tomorrow morning.

'What have you got planned for the rest of the day?' asks Arezu.

'Nothing.'

'Let me show you Kabul then,' she says.

'First of all – life,' she says and we catch a taxi to the bird market at Ka Faroshi. The streets are a mess. The city's walls are scabby with bullet holes. The roads are open sores.

'The mujaheddin fought the Russians for ten years.' Arezu pulls her scarf over her face to filter the dust. 'Then civil war erupted as the warlords squabbled for power. Finally, the Taliban flung rockets and mortars at the city.' She nods to a half-finished apartment block. 'There is a lot of rebuilding. Aid money pouring in from around the world. But for the people of Kabul it can't happen quickly enough. They are sick of this chaos.'

The Ka Faroshi bird market is hidden behind the Pul-e Khishti (Bridge of Brick) Mosque, beside the Kabul River. Arezu crosses the bridge, the tails of her scarf trailing her like smoke. She is hard to keep up with and it is crowded here. Money changers, donkey carts, herds of goats; stalls selling limes, sweet dates covered in flies, plastic tubs, sachets of snake-killer; widows begging, tied to the ground by their blue burqas; Vaseline by the kilo; dried mulberries; juice stalls; goat heads; peeled cow legs on barrows; bright beads in bottles. The noise is a weapon, unconcealed. Whistles and shouts and the crying of animals; the croaking pleas of beggars. We push past concrete blocks and into the market proper.

'The Four Arcades Bazaar used to be here before the British flattened it in 1842,' says Arezu over her shoulder. 'They wanted revenge after us Afghans gave them a thrashing in Jalalabad.'

But life continues with bangles and flyblown meat and cheap Pakistani suits and music and trembling masses of happy children reciting, *Hellohowareyouiamgood*.

Arezu takes a right beside the mosque, down by the hanging carcasses of lambs, their impossibly huge arses flecked with wasps. On the other side – street barbers under tarps, scraping bristles from leather faces. We turn again, between the booksellers, red spines, red-eyed sitting on their worn rugs. And again near the kite sellers, spooling string, cutting struts, folding paper.

And we are a hundred years back. Wickerwork tumbling across the narrow alley. Doves and fighting partridges and canaries managing their cheerful songs. Arezu stops to buy a small brass ring. She laughs, holding the ring up to my ear so I can hear the little bell inside.

'It's for a *kaftar* – a dove. They fly them here in competition. Sometimes the best doves will lure a competitor's bird away from the flock. Then the owner will have to pay for its return.'

Across the way is a *kaftar* shop. The owner is an old man with a grey bib of beard tumbling onto his shirt. Here, the birds are kept in a big caged enclosure in the back. She asks to see a one.

'*Balē. Balē.* That one.'

She claps her hands once in excitement as the bird is brought out. It is brilliant white with a brown throat. Holding it gently on its back, the owner helps her slip the ring onto its leg.

'What are you going to do with it?' I ask.

'You'll see,' she says, paying the man a bundle of filthy notes. She tucks the dove inside the folds of her scarf. 'Come on.'

We walk back down the alley and into the market. At the Pul-e Khishti, she stops. Touching the bird's head lightly to her lips, she flings it into the air above the sickly trickle of the Kabul River. Its wings unfold and it is blinding white against the sky. It turns a circle once, twice, over the river-bed with its throngs of humans, shitting, eating, laughing, singing, dying. It is graceful, a poem with wings. It makes one final turn and heads back towards the bird market.

'It's going back,' I say.

'Yes.'

'A bit of a waste of money, wouldn't you say?'

'No.'

'What was the point?'

'I wanted to see it fly,' she says.

The Landmine Museum is beside Ghazi Stadium. Arezu nods to the stadium. 'They play soccer there now. Back when the Taliban were in power it was used for stonings and executions. They chopped off the hands of thieves.'

Arezu continues, 'In Khandahar in 2000 a team from Pakistan were in the middle of a game when the Taliban marched in and arrested all of them for wearing shorts. They were deported after having their heads shaved as punishment.' She shrugs as if to say, *At least it was only their hair*.

The grounds of the Land Mine Museum are filled with old warplanes and helicopters. One of the choppers is painted with a mural of camels crossing green fields, men dancing with outstretched arms.

'Weird,' I say pointing at the chopper.

'It's an internet cafe. The OMAR institute have an education program here for kids. See that plane.' She points to a bomber with pictures of de-miners at work and a slogan: *Destruction of one landmine is to shut the door of poverty, disability and begging.* 'It's a classroom. They teach schoolkids how to recognise mines, where not to play, what to do if they find a mine.'

We go into the museum. Around the walls are display cabinets filled with munitions. There are mines from every corner of the world. Afghanistan has been the most favoured marketplace for the landmine industry.

'See these cute things,' says Arezu. She points to brightly coloured plastic toys as big as the palm of my hand. 'Butterfly mines. Beautiful name, don't you think? They flutter down from planes and land in village fields. Kids are attracted to bright colours.'

I pull out my journal, flip it open, and write: *It is hard to imagine the shock that a child must feel as a toy removes her arm.*

Arezu holds her finger on the glass of the display case. 'Can we see this one?' she asks as if she wants to try on a ring. The museum guide removes a yellow mine and hands it to her. She passes it to me.

There is something heavy about it that its size doesn't convey. Its plastic fins are attached to a cylinder that holds its payload. It is simple and deadly. Designed by a man who hated life or was so removed from it that he didn't care. I hand it back to our guide. He takes it without emotion and slips it back under glass.

There are Iranian copies of Italian mines, Russian mines like wooden pencil boxes, Chinese and Pakistani mines. Our guide tells us that between the Russians, the mujaheddin and the Taliban, twenty million mines were seeded into Afghan soil.

There is a mujaheddin IED on a table. An Improvised Explosive Device. It is an old pressure cooker, stuffed with twenty-five kilos of explosives, and wrapped in cloth. It was made around 1985 and found and defused nineteen years later by the OMAR mine-clearance team. These things are still being made and buried below roads. Sometimes they find military convoys. Sometimes they do not. Now the bombs come with remote detonators that are triggered by mobile phones. Which is why the foreign armies have jammers that block the signals from phones while they are passing.

'Here's one of my faves,' says Arezu. 'It's a cluster bomb. Made by us, the Guardians of the Free World. They drop it from planes and it opens to release these bomblets. They float down softly on little parachutes. And when they're picked up, when they're shaken. Boom.' Her fingers spring apart in front of my face.

On the wall are photos of kids without limbs, of plastic legs and crutches. I am ashamed of my disgust. Of the revulsion I feel at these withered stumps. The final product of all this technology.

'This is death,' says Arezu, sweeping her arms around the room. I think of the dove, how it circled above the Kabul River.

'Life and death come so close together here. The average age for a man in this country is forty-three.'

'It's depressing,' I say. There seems nothing else to add.

'It is if you let it be. Me, I feel anger. That makes me want to do something.'

'But how can you change a whole country?'

'I can't. But maybe I can change one person's life. Maybe then it is all worthwhile.'

My new *shalwar kameez* is ready in the morning. It is delivered to my room by Ghulam Ali. I try it on and Arezu and I walk down to the tailor, laughing as we go. He is a skilled craftsman and proud of his work. He slips a waistcoat on me while we take a photo. We pose side by side, leaning towards each other like twin towers, like the sides of an arch.

In the afternoon, Arezu takes me to Chicken Street to buy a *pakul* hat and a scarf. This is where the hippies came in the sixties and seventies when the trail was open from Europe to India. It would have been a happier time for Kabul and I picture my Mum as a flowerchild meeting Dad over mint tea and a sheesha pipe. But, of course, it never happened. Mum was fifteen in 1970 and went to Jan Juc for her holidays. Dad would not have been seen dead in flares or a headband.

A bunch of street kids follow us, selling photocopied Taliban books, guides to Kabul and bad maps.

'I wanna be your bodyguard,' says one.

'You're too little,' says Arezu.

'Then you take two. He is my friend and very strong. You take two for one price.'

'I don't think we need a bodyguard,' I say as he holds his tiny biceps up for me to squeeze.

'Sure. Every foreign lady and man need bodyguard. It is the rule. There is danger in Chicken Street. Taliban.'

'Taliban?'

'Sure. Taliban. You work for UN?'

'Nope.'

'UNHCR?'

'Nope.'

'Red Cross?'

'Nope.'

'Whaddyou do in Kabul then?'

'I am a writer.'

'Writer?'

'You know, writer.' I pull out my journal and show him the pages.

He screws up his nose. 'Journaliss?'

He thinks he has me trapped, but I wriggle free. 'No, I write books.'

'Ah, book. You wanna buy book. I sell you Taliban book bess price in Kabul.'

'In here, Hec.' Arezu pulls me into a shop. We take off our shoes.

'I wait for you here, Mister Hec,' says my bodyguard and bookseller, dodging the shopkeeper's stare.

The shop is piled with carpets and jewellery, old muskets and hats. There are three men sitting drinking *chay*, a saucer of boiled sweets between the cups and pot.

'Hello, sir,' says the youngest of the three. 'Can I help you with some hats or carpet today. Some is flying. Same price, you choose.'

'We're just looking.'

'And looking is, of course, free.'

He gets up and whisks the covers from a display cabinet. 'Silver, turquoise, lapis from Badakhshan from mines of Sar-e Sang. Use for Tutankhamen's death mask and for paints in old Europeans. Rubies, diamond. I have all.'

'Coloured glass,' whispers Arezu in my ear.

'Maybe ring for your wife.'

'She's not…'

'Carpet, *kilim* rug.' He rolls out a carpet, displacing his cross-legged friends. 'From Herat this carpet. Fine quality. Number wan.'

'I need a hat.'

'Ah, hat. How many two, three, you take ten, I give you wan free.'

'Just one. For my one head.' I point to my head.

'Wan?' He clucks his tongue at my cheapness. 'Okay, no problem. Mazari bead hat? This one nice design.'

'*Pakul*,' says Arezu.

'*Pakul*?'

'*Pakul*,' I echo. It sounds like a bird at the bottom of a well.

He brings out a stack of *pakul*. 'Number wan quality, seven dollar.' He jams it on my head.

'It doesn't fit.'

'No problem, sir.' He stretches the cap over his knee.

'It's the wrong colour.'

'We have many-many colour. Too many.' He deals *pakul* onto the ground, in suits – oatmeal, camel, brown.

'This one is nice.' Arezu puts it on my head. She nods approvingly.

'And, of course, scarf to stop dust out of noses and mouthess.' He pulls a wad of scarves from behind him, draping them round my neck one by one.

'How much?' I ask.

'How many you want?'

'Just one.'

'Wan?' He looks at me as if I am out of my mind.

'One.'

'Three dollar best quality.'

'Five for the hat and scarf,' says Arezu.

'No profit. How will I eat?' His brow wrinkles with the pressure. 'I give you disgown one dollar.'

'Six.'

'Eight. My final price.'

'Seven.'

'Seven I cannot do. I will be hungry. My wife and children will be hungry. My widow mother will be hungry. Come, eight dollar.' He grabs a plastic bag.

'Come on, let's go.' Arezu gets up.

'But—'

'Come on,' she grabs my elbow and yanks me to my feet.

'It's only one dollar,' I say.

'Wan dollar!' screams the shopkeeper.

Arezu drags me from the shop. The shopkeeper follows. 'Okay, okay. Seven dollar. Okay. Take it.'

I hand over the seven dollars and get my hat and scarf. 'One dollar,' I say to Arezu.

'It's the principle,' she says.

The bodyguards are still waiting. I buy them all a cold drink. It costs me two bucks.

'Let's do coffee,' says Arezu and she takes me to Kabul City Centre. We pass through security, a metal detector and a frisk. There are male and female guards and Arezu is patted down behind a screen. A sign on the wall says 'No guns'.

Inside, the place is glass and mirror, top to bottom. The cafe is on the ground floor and from here the glass elevators carry rich security workers, NGO staff and privileged locals up to the heavenly heights of the Safi Landmark Hotel. Near the stairwell, bearded men touch their foreheads to red carpets while their friends keep watch on Kabul's youngest and brightest, flirting in front of the Mehak Valley Beauty Shop.

We order lattes and a slab of carrot cake to share. On the next table, teenagers sip juice and text their friends. Businessmen do deals. A hawker cruises the cafe selling phone recharge cards. Turbaned men from the provinces ride the escalators.

In my journal, I write: *Like Crown Casino without the gambling.*

'What you writing?' asks Arezu, sipping foam from her upper lip.

I shut the cover. 'This is not Afghanistan,' I say.

'There's more than one Afghanistan,' says Arezu. 'It's more complicated than you think. The foreign media might characterise it as full of fundamentalist crazies, deserts and burqas. Sure, they are all here, but there is a lot more besides.'

Back outside kids roast corn in basins of hot sand. Men sit for hours smashing the husks from almonds and placing them in neat piles. Trucks full of quivering bull carcasses rumble by. Outside it is hot and dusty as it has always been and will always be.

I AM STILL RUBBING KABUL'S crust from my eyes when we catch the *Tunis* out of town. It is light early and the streets are quiet. Dogs stretch and yawn, the pink curves of their tongues roping in the tepid sun. *Naan* shops are open, they seem to never shut, and there are people squatting by the gutters sipping their first cup of *chay*.

Afghans drive on the right-hand side of the road. But it seems more of a suggestion than a rule. Cars fit where they can. Bikes, trucks, taxis, horse carts used as chariots, and pedestrians meander over broken strips of tar and dirt, into chaotic roundabouts, through roadblocks and around whistling traffic police. There are left- and right-hand drive cars, all Toyotas, imported cheap from Pakistan, Iran and Europe.

There are Pakistani trucks by the side of the road out. High-fronted like ancient carts with painted panels of mountains and streams and birds. They are fringed with camel bells. The drivers are asleep inside, feet propped on steering wheels, mouths open.

Melons from Mazar-e Sharif are coming into town by the truckload. Afghans are mad for them. They are sweet and perfumed, crisp between the teeth. They are piled high on trucks. Men lie on top, scarves wrapped round their faces to filter the dust.

As we leave town we cross the Shomali Plain.

'The Russians fought here, then the mujaheddin and Taliban.' Arezu is crunching an apple, the words are juiced-up and slurred. 'It was blown apart. They have grown grapes here for hundreds of years. Some people say Alexander the Great brought them.'

But all the vines here are new. It is not hard to imagine why. Tanks and mortars took care of them along with most of the population.

There are stalls starting to open by the side of the road. Tomatoes, melons and cucumbers, and phone recharge cards. We stop for fuel and Arezu hops out and returns with apricots. She seems to exist on fruit alone. She shares them around the passengers. They are sweeter than any apricot I have ever eaten. The flesh falls from the stone and dissolves in my mouth. The juice runs over my new shirt.

The road is good. Broad and smooth and filled with traffic heading north. Beyond the Salang Tunnel: Mazar-e Sharif, Kunduz, Badakhshan, the 'stans' – Tajikistan, Uzbekistan, Turkmenistan; and off to the far north-east: China. You could go anywhere with a little money and determination, if it wasn't for bandits and the Taliban.

'I don't know what you were talking about with the road. It's fine,' I say to Arezu.

She just smiles at me.

I pull out my journal and hold the pen over the page,

threatening it. But the words stay inside. I write the date and *Kabul to Bamiyan*. And the pen hovers some more.

'Writer's block?' Arezu asks, cheerfully.

'Don't believe in it.'

'Really?'

'Yes,' I say. 'No.'

'Both?'

'I didn't talk for a whole year once.'

'Like a vow of silence.'

'Something like that.'

'How did that feel?' Why didn't she ask me why? That would be my first question.

'It felt like nothing. Like I had nothing to say. Like words were not enough.'

'What did your mother say?'

I look at her for a moment and know I cannot tell her, not yet. In place of the answer comes a huge rush of memory.

'When I was six, I was climbing a tree in a park by the river. The branches swept down to the ground and I just stepped into the sky. I climbed high, higher than I had ever been, until my mum was just a full stop below. And once I was there, I stood upright on my branch and let go with my hands, balancing with the wind rushing past my ears. I remember the sway in the tree, and how I knew that its roots were deep into the soil. And I felt the danger of falling, or flying, and the thrill of it. I felt like I was between two things and I could choose to go either way: climb back down or step off and fly. I was only six, how could I feel that?'

I shake my head free of the memory. 'I don't know what that means,' I say.

Arezu lays her hand on top of mine. 'Perhaps it doesn't mean anything yet,' she says. 'But one day it might.'

e

About an hour into the trip we take an unmarked turn to the left. At first it appears we have driven into a quarry, then it becomes a stream. The *Tunis* lurches and rolls like a drunk.

'Welcome to the real Afghanistan,' says Arezu.

And so we spend the next four hours. First and second gear get a workout as third and fourth lie idle, their teeth still sharp and new, grinning at their poor overworked cousins. We average about twenty k's an hour, the driver stealing time on the rare straight sections and slowing to a crawl to pass trucks and buses above the drop to the Ghorband River. Small boys push donkeys laden with freshly cut grass along the rocky verges. They gulp our dust as we pass. We stop for sheep-jams – twenty or thirty deep across the road, a heaving mass of wool and shit and lanolin. The herdsmen, old men and young boys, beat them with willow sticks until they move enough for us to pass.

At lunch we stop at a *chaikhana* perched above the road. The men eat along a verandah on plastic mats, squatting on the floor with *naan* and *kabob* and tin pots of green tea. Arezu and I are shown a room.

'I can't eat with the men. Not in this town,' she says.

'Where are we?'

'Chahar-deh-e Ghorband.'

'Didn't you say something about not stopping in Ghorband?'

'We'll be okay. What do you want to eat?'

'What are the choices?'

Arezu looks around at the place. '*Pulao* or *kabob*.'

'I'll go *kabob*.'

'Brave man.'

Arezu orders *kabob*, *qabli pulao* and *shorwa* – a thin soup. *Naan* is slapped onto our mat. *Chay sabz* is poured. The food arrives. Arezu turns the *pulao* over with her spoon. 'This is just rice,' she says. '*Zardak*? *Kheshmesh*?' she asks the cook. He shrugs. 'No carrots or raisins in town, I guess,' she says, dabbing *naan* into her *shorwa*.

My *kabob* is cubes of blackened meat alternated with pinches of fat. I pull some from the metal skewer with my *naan*. It is rubbery and tastes earthy. I wash it down with tea. 'What is that?' I ask.

Arezu picks up a skewer and examines it closely. She smells it, pulls a hunk off and chews it. 'Lamb's kidney,' she decides.

'Yummo.' I finish it though. The chef is sharpening his knife on a worn stone. He looks like he doesn't take complaints lightly.

'This is the last Pashtun village before we hit Hazara territory. They are a bit unfriendly here. They don't like outsiders.'

'Nice place to run a business.'

Back in the *Tunis*. Back on the twisted road with our twisted backs. The faces change. They become more Asiatic. Here are the sons and daughters of Genghis Khan. The Hazara. They are threshing wheat stalks, sorting the grain from the chaff with long wooden forks, casting them to the breeze. They are cutting feed for their donkeys and sheep, setting it in piles. They are selling apples in shingle boxes by the road. The children are riding donkeys, their curious eyes following us.

The houses are flat-roofed, winding back into roadless valleys. They hang from rock, small-windowed, low door-ways leading to dark interiors. The light here is blinding. It arcs from hill to hill with welding-rod intensity. The hills are terrifying in their beauty. They are a mass of great seams, fold upon fold, pushed into the sky. They are buckled and spired and pinched upwards by giant hands. I am storing this all, choosing the phrases I will describe it with later when I am able to write them down without tearing great holes in the paper.

We wind up the Shibar Pass. I look in my guidebook and find that Alexander the Great crossed here in the winter of 327 BC, his men dying of the cold far from their Macedonian homes.

Russian tanks lie rusting by the road. The Russians fled Afghanistan in 1989 after ten years of trying to bring the country into line. I imagine young Russian soldiers, stoned on local hashish, twitching the barrels of their Kalashnikovs at shadows. The mujaheddin slipping under cover of night up to their eyries where they pick the infidel invaders off one by one.

After the pass, we plummet into Bamiyan Province. This is where Omed's story began and this is where I have been travelling to since the day I last saw him. My ears pop as we fall and the pressure we are under loosens its grip on us. I wonder where Omed is and think of the possibilities good and bad. What it will feel like to stand in front of him after all this time? What I will say? I practise my lines. *How have you been? What happened to you?* Will he have forgotten all the English he once knew?

The road needles itself through huge turrets of rock. The river is channelled into fields.

'Some people say the Afghans can get water to run uphill,' says Arezu, pointing at a channel disappearing into the hillside.

We stop at an army checkpoint at Shash-pul (Six Bridges). They check our passports and laugh at my *shalwar kameez*. They are bored. It is too safe in this valley for them. There is nothing to do but drink *chay* and stare at the hills. We get out of the car while they smoke, and poke the luggage, and chat to the driver.

Arezu points out a red hill. 'That is Shahr-e Zohak – the City of Zohak.'

'What's Zohak?'

'Not what, who. Zohak was a character from Persian legend who lost his soul to the devil and took over his father's throne. The devil came to him disguised as one of his subjects, kissing him on the shoulders. Black serpents sprung from the kisses, demanding daily meals of human brains. When anyone tried to cut them off, they returned hungrier than before. Zohak grew very powerful and took over the kingdom of Persia where he became a tyrant for a thousand years. After that a hero called Fraidun managed to banish him to a mountain peak. And that's it there.' Arezu points to the turreted ruins on the hill. 'The locals say that the black serpents, when they couldn't get their daily meal, opened up Zohak's skull and dined on his brains.'

'Cute story.'

Arezu nods. 'There have been forts there since before

Jesus was born. The Shansabani Kings built that sometime before Chingis got to it in 1221.'

'I take it *Chingis* is Genghis Khan and when you say *got to it* what you are trying to say is *destroyed it*.'

'Well, these fortresses were a bit tough for the great khan and his soldiers. The only way into the city was via a single-file track that led through a tunnel in the rock. There were turrets overlooking the track and the guards would send arrows down from the slits within the walls. There were no stairs into the turrets, they were reached by ladders that were pulled up afterwards. It was impregnable.'

'So how'd he do it?'

'I guess an angry Mongol is a determined man. They killed his grandson, shot him with an arrow. Chingis vowed to kill every living thing in this valley including the dogs and rats.'

'And did he?'

'Pretty much. He killed everything and then he destroyed the irrigation canals. It would have taken years for life to start again here.'

'Sounds like a familiar story.'

'It just keeps happening again and again. The city was mined heavily. You don't want to stray too far from the marked path. The mujaheddin fought the Russians and then the Taliban fought the mujaheddin. And now ISAF – the International Forces – are fighting the Taliban. On and on and on.'

'But it's peaceful now?'

'For now. I can't help but feel it's just waiting.'

There is a perfect Russian tank five minutes out from Bamiyan. Young guys in their city clothes and pointy boots are clambering over it and taking photos.

Arezu says, 'It's too far to tow these beasts to Kabul for scrap, so they just rust here.'

The checkpoint at Bamiyan is a formality. They raise the pole and let us through, waving as we pass. We drive through the gatemaker's end of the bazaar where men weld together gate frames, using old sunglasses as eye protection. Everything is grouped together as if competition is good for business. Tin *samovars* and water heaters are piled on the opposite side of the road with wheelbarrows stacked on roofs. Production looks good, but sales are slow. Cobblers sit under trees stitching the soles back on thousand-mile shoes. A fortune teller folds a man's future into a neat triangle and pushes it into his fist. Pharmacies sell out-of-date medicines to illiterate farmers. There is fruit here, too – apples and overripe bananas from Pakistan. Glossy red tomatoes and beans. Men sell poisons and spices side by side. There are bags of lentils and dusty local chewing tobacco.

We take a right at the roundabout and cross the river.

'Where are the Buddhas?' I ask.

'Didn't you hear?' she replies. 'The Taliban blew them to shit.'

'Okay, funny. So where *were* the Buddhas?'

'Over there. You'll see them soon.'

But we don't. Not until we pull into the driveway of the guesthouse and Arezu leads me to the garden.

I see the niche of the small Buddha first – the one they called Shahmama, the mother. It is burnt to gold in the evening light.

'Let's go there,' says Arezu.

'What, now?'

'Yes now.'

I follow her across the field, between the ripening wheat and green vetch. The clover smells like bubblegum and flocks of sparrows rise from the crops and whirr like mechanical toys into the willows.

'My friend Omed saw the Buddhas being blown up.'

'Really, he was here?'

'Him and his friend Zakir. They were watching from behind a rock as the Taliban rigged the statues up with explosives.'

'I heard they used the Hazara to do the dirty work.'

'He mentioned that. When the Buddhas were blown up, his friend Zakir was killed.'

Our way is blocked by a stream and the village kids urge us to cross. One grabs a long-handled shovel and vaults back and forth.

Arezu takes the shovel and crosses to the other bank. 'Come on, it's easy,' she says and passes over the shovel. But my hands slip and I end up shin-deep in the cold stream. I squelch on behind her to the cliff face.

Below the Buddha niche, the caves are blackened with soot. People have lived here since the Muslims pushed the Buddhists out. I close my eyes and imagine this valley filled with the faithful. The pages of Omed's story speak of a wooden mask with jewelled eyes behind which fires were lit. I visualise the chanting monks and the poor peasants looking up in wonder.

'Hey. Ticket!' A guard is walking towards us. 'Ticket.'

'*As-salamu alaykum*, Anwar-*jan*.'

'Arezu-*jan? Chetawr hastid.*'

'*Khub asti.* I am well. Do you remember your English?'

'Little beet,' says the old man, wiping his eyes with a scarf tied around his head.

'This is Hec, he's from Australia.'

'Australayi, good. *Khob.*'

I nod. Take Anwar's hand. He lets go and holds his hand to his heart. I have seen people do this when saying hello as if to show, you are dear to me, I hold you here. I touch my heart in return. Could this be the Anwar in Omed's story; the man who baked him bread and took him to see the Dragon?

'Hec is looking for his friend.'

'Fren?'

'His name is Omed,' I say.

'Many Omed,' says Anwar. 'Many, many, many.'

'This Omed, he had no tongue.' I point to my tongue.

Arezu talks to him in Dari. I hear the word Taliban dropped here and there like a bomb. She shakes her head. 'There was an Omed. He left here for Pakistan before the Americans came. Anwar heard that he had come back, but there was some trouble with a man and he disappeared. His sister, Leyli, lives in the Valley of the Dragon – Darya Ajdahar. Perhaps she knows where Omed is.'

Anwar smiles, his teeth like broken bricks. 'Omed good.' He touches his heart. 'Good.'

'Can we see the Buddhas, Anwar? Salsal and Shahmama.'

'*Balē. Balē. Budd.*' Anwar looks around and quickly hands Arezu the key and a small torch.

The staircase is tunnelled into the rock. The stairs are steep as they twist up to the Buddha's head.

'You know Anwar used to live in one of the caves,' says Arezu.

'I think he is the man Omed wrote about, Arezu.' I don't know why I feel the need to verify Omed's facts or why it gives me such a buzz when I do.

'The Taliban used Anwar to load the big Buddha up with dynamite. Then they made him push the plunger that tore him down. He said it was like killing his father.'

I think about my own father. In the departure lounge at Tullamarine, for the first time in my life, I caught the fear in his eyes. He, the man who believes in stone and steel, in its permanence, was terrified for me, the fragility of my bone and flesh. And inside this porous cliff I can hear him muttering his curses over the senselessness of the violence against these statues.

We come out on a landing. 'Follow me,' whispers Arezu and she disappears into a room.

Inside, the roof is domed, carved out of the cliff and plastered with gypsum and straw. I can see the traces of Buddhas around the dome, repeated over and over. Arezu shines the torch over the roof. Their faces are missing. 'The early Muslims believed that by striking the face from the idol, they could remove its soul.' She moves the torch into a niche. Here I can see the blue outline of the Buddha, his golden halo. 'The Taliban were just the last in a long line of intolerant assholes,' says Arezu. 'But they had dynamite as well as a divine right. Come on, I'll show you Salsal.'

We walk along the base of the cliff. It is pocked with

hundreds of caves and niches. Some are closed with doors. 'What's in those?' I ask.

'Probably more paintings. They keep the best ones hidden so people don't break them from the walls and sell them. The archaeologists took most of the good stuff for the Kabul Museum. But during the war, what the mujaheddin and the Taliban didn't sell, the Ministry for Virtue and Vice broke into pieces.' She squints up the valley. 'We're losing the light. There are landmines on the track, we want to be up and back before dark.'

I stand at the feet of the big Buddha; all that remains is a giant sole. Above me, the niche rises fifty-five metres.

Arezu puts her hand on my shoulder. 'Mullah Omar said he was just "breaking stones" when he gave the order. Thirteen hundred years they stood and then they were gone in two weeks. They tried with tanks and mortars, but the Buddhas held on. Finally they got in the experts from Pakistan who had them wired up with explosives. Most of the Muslim world pleaded with them, but the bastards went about their business. They said that no one had cared about the Afghan people before, why was everyone making such a big deal about some rocks.'

'Can we go up?' I ask.

'Of course. But we should be quick.'

The track leads up the hill to the right-hand side of the Buddha niche. There are white rocks marking the safe path.

'Don't step off the track,' says Arezu.

I mime walking gingerly off into the minefield.

'It's no joke, Hec. Really.'

We keep on up the steep path. Bamiyan is at two thousand five hundred metres above sea level and my lungs burn as I climb. We enter a doorway and walk up and around the back of where the Buddha's head once was. Below, the wheat fields are egg-yolk yellow, the Koh-e Baba range smeared with snow.

'What's that?' I ask, pointing to a hill just beyond Bamiyan.

'Shahr-e Gholghola – the City of Screams. Another of Chingis' wastelands.'

'It's amazing that this was a Buddhist kingdom for hundreds of years. You'd think some of that peace and non-violence would have rubbed off.'

'We need to go,' says Arezu. 'We still have a minefield to get through.'

That night I read the opening of Omed's story to Arezu, holding the typed pages up to the kerosene lantern. She sits quietly, listening and sipping the contraband Coronas we have chilled in the well. The robber moon is sifting through the ruins at Shahr-e Gholghola. I feel tiredness like grit in my eyes. It is late when I finish and we turn into our separate beds. The snick of her lock is a final punctuation.

WE SIT ON THE CARPET in Leyli's house. But it is not her house, not really. She is the second wife of an old man, a greybeard. He is in Mazar-e Sharif on family business or Leyli would never have seen us here, could never have welcomed us as she has done with *chay* and hard bread. She whispers to Arezu that she hopes he will die soon. Then she will take the burqa from its nail on the door and go to town to beg.

Her son climbs into her lap. She strokes his hair and sings to him. The house is dark inside. It will be cold in winter. In the dusty courtyard, the old man's first wife eyes us suspiciously, her veil clenched in her teeth.

I ask Leyli through Arezu, 'Where are your father's books?'

She replies, 'My mother burnt them for warmth. I can no longer read. My children will never learn, my husband forbids it.'

'How did it come to this?' I say. 'You were supposed to marry Zakir.'

'I am not translating that,' says Arezu.

'Why not?'

'That is your story. It's not the truth. Zakir died, remember, you read what Omed wrote. You cannot change history, Hec.'

'Ask her where her mother is.'

I pat my knee for Leyli's son to come and sit, but he just looks at me with wary eyes.

'She says her mother died the year after Omed left. Of a broken heart, she says. Wasim went to war aged twelve. A month before the Taliban were driven from the valley. She hopes he is living in Iran. The youngest, Liaquat, is being raised in a madrassa in Peshawar.'

'And what about Omed?'

Leyli looks at me when I mention his name. She asks through Arezu, 'Do you have a brother?'

'I am an only child,' I answer.

'My brother was not the bravest, or the strongest. He was not thought to be the cleverest or the fairest. But after my father died, he was our backbone. We loved him, all of us. He was gentle and kind. He would help anyone. When he left, it was as though someone had poisoned the well.'

Arezu has taken her time with the translation, picking through her words to get the right ones. I feel the need to pull out my journal and write down that last phrase, but I know how that would seem. Maybe it is the journalist in me, or is it the writer that makes me like this? That gives me this overwhelming need to gather and hoard words, to hang them round my neck like an amulet.

'Where is Omed?' I ask.

'The last I saw him was four years gone. My husband would not allow me to speak with him, but I overheard him say he was going to Band-e Amir.'

The first wife appears at the door. She barks something at Leyli.

'We should go,' says Arezu.

'Why?'

'It will go badly for Leyli if we stay.'

'But she must know more.'

'She doesn't, Hec. She has given us everything. Now it is time to leave.'

Arezu kisses Leyli on each cheek. They are scarred and her eyes have dark rings beneath them. Omed once wrote of her beauty. I offer her my hand to shake, but she shrinks behind her veil. I place a fifty dollar bill in her son's lap. Leyli passes it back to Arezu.

'Her husband will question her about this money.'

'How will he know?'

'She says he knows everything.'

We leave the hut and fall back into the glaring sunshine. The Valley of the Dragon is a barren place. Even the goats and children seem lifeless. As we pass, they barely lift their heads.

'Let's go to the Dragon,' I say.

The Dragon's tears fizz on my tongue. As they move to my throat I feel their sadness. The deep melancholy begins its slow descent.

I press my ear to the long cut made by Ali's sword. The dragon moans, cries, deep within its calcified head. Death is not a full stop; here the dead are mourning themselves.

I look over the pools of dragon tears to the Koh-e Baba

– the Grandfather of Mountains. The sky is a fierce blue. 'It isn't fair,' I say.

Arezu pulls her sunglasses from her eyes. 'No, it's not, Hec.'

'We should be able to do something for her. She's Omed's sister.'

'We can't, Hec. It's just the way it is.'

'Why does it have to be this way?'

'It doesn't always, but for now it is. Change can't happen overnight. This country has been under the cloud of war for thirty years.'

'That doesn't excuse what is happening to Leyli down there in that village.'

'It's not an excuse. It's just an explanation. And it's not my fault either, Hec.' Arezu touches my hand. 'Let's go down.'

She leads me down the rubbly slope to Hazrat Ali's shrine. There is an old shepherd inside, boiling water for *chay*. He asks us to join him and we sit on the dirt, cross-legged, looking out its arched doorway. Twigs crackle on the fire. The shrine fills with smoke. He only has one cup and he serves us first.

'Ask him why he comes here,' I say.

Arezu puts the question to him and he sits quietly for a moment before answering.

'He says they come here every year when they move the flock. From when he was a young child. He remembers his grandfather making *chay* in this shrine. Once they were caught for three days by early snow.' Arezu paused while the old man spoke again.

'He says, Hazrat Ali brought peace to this valley. It has come again.' She hands me the cup. 'Here, have some tea and stop moping.'

The tea is scalding hot. It feels good. 'So do we go to Band-e Amir?' I ask.

'No.'

'Why no? Leyli said Omed went to Band-e Amir.'

'That was four years ago. He could be anywhere now.'

'We need to look.'

'*I* need to do some work, Hec. I'm not on holiday.'

'Neither am I.'

'I know, sorry.' She takes the cup from me and hands it to the shepherd. '*Tashakor, Baba-jan.*' The shepherd pours himself a cup and waits. He knows something is going on, a deal is being struck.

'Okay, I'll arrange a car for tomorrow and then that's it. You're on your own.'

Kissing her would outrage the shepherd. I smile instead.

We go to the bazaar for water and fruit for the trip. Arezu haggles with the hawkers, winning extra apples and dried apricots.

'Come here, I want to show you something,' she says, loading me with bags of fruit. We take a turn in the bazaar towards the river. Here is a lesser bazaar – a place for shoes and stringy meat and cheap plastic tubs.

'In here,' she says and we duck into a tiny shop. Along one wall there are pills stacked in bottles and behind a low table sits a Sikh with a neat turban. His finger marks a spot in a worn book, its torn pages filled with scratchy writing.

'Sanskrit,' he says. 'The original.' He offers us some cushions. 'Come and sit. My name is Baba Singh and I am an astrologer.' We take our seats and he sends a boy for cans of warm Mirinda and when we offer to pay he insists, 'You are my guests.'

'So, you're a fortune teller?' I ask.

'I am most certainly not a fortune teller, I am an astrologer. A fortune teller pretends to know the future by lines on a hand or the pattern of tea. Astrology is a science, an ancient science.'

'How much do you charge?'

'It is up to you.'

'Really?'

Arezu elbows my ribs.

'Yes. But I can get up to five thousand afghani for one reading.'

'I don't have five thousand afs.'

The Sikh smiles, showing bare gums. 'Then pay what you feel.'

I pay him a thousand and it seems like a lot of money for something that I am going to get sooner or later anyway. I give Baba Singh my birthdate.

'And your time of birth, please?' he asks.

Arezu snickers, but I look at the astrologer and say, '10.21 a.m.'

It seems impossible that I would remember this, but Mum would talk about my birth like it was some miracle she had witnessed.

My life changed forever at 10.21 a.m. on 14 July 1988. Midwinter with the swans honking down on the river and me rushed from the boathouse to the Mercy. You came with that swan-honk inside you, bright red like someone had rubbed you with towels. The story always began that way. From there it branched to one of the thousand stories she saved for those silent times when there was just her and me.

Baba Singh scrawls the details into a filthy notebook with the nub of a pencil.

'Okay,' he says, shutting the book and looking at me with his watery eyes.

'What about my fortune?'

'It will be ready tomorrow.'

'But we leave for Band-e Amir tomorrow,' says Arezu.

'Then come along by this way and I will have it ready.'

Arezu brings out her camera. 'You need a photo with Baba Singh,' she says.

Baba Singh rummages about under his books and draws out a pair of false teeth. He pops them in and we get the photo.

'What happened to your teeth, Baba Singh?' I ask.

'The Russians threw me in prison in Moscow. I was drunk. Russian vodka is cheap and very good. They kept me there for five weeks, thinking I was a spy. This was in 1976. They knocked out my teeth.' He shrugs.

Arezu walks me to Shahr-e Gholghola for the sunset.

We cross the bazaar, through the timber yards where families skin green poles with old sickles. Through the wheat and vetch, the odd tall hemp plant tossing its shaggy head in the breeze. We cross the bridge at an old fort and pick up the road to the City of Screams. There is little more than donkey traffic on the road, and the occasional cyclist or motorbike. The sun is at our backs as we start to climb the hill. It is steep and the mine clearance team's white rocks wind past turrets and caves.

'Look at this,' says Arezu, touching her toe to a tin can full of empty anti-aircraft shells as thick as thumbs. 'The mine clearers turn up all this stuff. Sometimes they find an old spearhead or coin. They don't leave those behind.' There are small piles of pottery here too, green and brown glazes, the handle of a terracotta water pot, blown from their hiding places by mortars and mines. And there is a shoe, its sole torn from the upper, nails exposed like kitten's teeth.

We climb higher and at the top there is a police checkpoint and a very sad donkey. We sit for a while on the policeman's *toshak* where it is obvious that he passes his day sleeping. He wants to see our ticket, but Arezu sweet-talks him from doing his duty. She takes me to the northern edge of the ruined city and we dangle our legs over an old wall overlooking Bamiyan. The hills are like a camel-hair blanket on an unmade bed.

'And now it is time for another story, Hec.'

'I like stories.' I try to appear cute, like an irresistible toddler in an oversized dressing gown.

'You sitting comfortably?'

'Yup.'

'Once upon a time, this citadel was ruled by a king called Jalaluddin who had a beautiful daughter. Unfortunately, the king also had a taste for younger women and his daughter didn't approve. So Daddy built her a palace all her own.' She points over her shoulder. 'To the south near Kakrak. She had it decked out with nice carpets, shiny things, slaves. They still call it the Qala-e Dokhtar – the daughter's palace.

'Around that time Chingis, the "Universal", Khan was through destroying Shahr-e Zohak and so he made his way

here and laid siege to the city. But the city held strong.'
Arezu launches a stone into the valley.

'The daughter, fancying her chances with the Mongol king,
shot an arrow with a note into his tent. It told him of a
spring that supplied the fortress with water.'

'Nice girl.'

'She was a charmer. Chingis dammed the spring with felt
and the city fell to his sword. And that is why it's called the
City of Screams.'

'What about the daughter?'

'She dressed up big time for the Khan, her finest Chinese
silk, perfume behind each ear, gold and lapis jewellery. She
expected something big. And she got it.' Arezu pauses.
'Chingis had her stoned to death for betraying her father.'

'He was a hard guy to please.'

'He had some anger issues he was working through.
I don't think he was cuddled enough as a child.'

The sun is busting some big moves on the horizon. The
moon is behind us, all full and pouty-lipped. I want to kiss
Arezu. This is the time.

Her face is towards the setting sun and a warm glow runs
from her cheekbone to her jaw – a perfect range. I lean in
towards her and she turns to me. She looks surprised, like
this is something that I have been planning without her
permission. Then her eyebrows lower and crease, her dark
brown eyes accuse me. *Here in the open?* they say.

The blood of the king's daughter spills over the valley.
The sun is flailing the rock we sit on. There is silence, but
I can hear screaming. It is far away, but certain. It is leach-
ing from the rocks.

The donkey brays as the guard leads him down the path

for water. And we are shaken from this small moment that has come between us. And I can see she also feels ashamed. I want to say, *Nothing happened. No one saw.*

'We should head back before the sun gets too low,' says Arezu. 'Crossing the river in the dark is a bitch.'

So we head down from the City of Screams back to Bamiyan. We cross the river on the two-plank bridge behind a woman in a burqa and her son with an armful of *naan*. Then we go to our separate beds while the desert moon ripens over Shahr-e Gholghola.

THE TOYOTA COROLLA IS THE new donkey. It is small and tough, almost indestructible. It is not a beautiful car, but a thoroughbred wouldn't take these roads. Its tyres are bald. The windscreen is cracked. Its seats are covered with carpets.

I collect my fortune before we leave. It is written on a single, lined sheet of paper. Arezu wants to read it, but I want to save it for Band-e Amir. Because some things need ceremony. It's not like the cookie I opened all those years ago with Dad. The slip of paper pushed inside a dough bubble by some nimble-fingered factory worker. *Every great journey begins with one step*, it read. But even that came true.

Sameer, our driver, likes his music. He likes it loud. His stereo is not up to the job. The woofers and tweeters have rebelled. They are now growlers and squawkers, punk imitations of what they once were. But the beat goes on. And on. And on. It only stops when he ejects the tape to bang the dust out of it.

The roads of Bamiyan aren't kind to cars. There are old shells abandoned in villages, trucks with broken backs that have turned into playgrounds for kids with 'snot' on their upper lips. *Qarghana*, a small round shrub, is carried down from the summer pasture above the Shahidan Pass to dry on roofs for winter fuel.

'See the caves,' Arezu points to a cluster of holes in the cliff. Washing hangs on lines and trails of smoke rise from cooking fires. The doors are made from old oil tins, bashed flat and joined together.

'They're beautiful. It is amazing to see people still living in caves in the twenty-first century.'

'You are seeing it through your tourist's eyes. Shut them now. Go on.'

I close them, even though I feel ridiculous.

'I want you to think about the winter when the snow creeps down from the mountains to lie until the spring.'

'I love the snow.' My eyes are closed on a different dream. 'We'd go to Mount Buffalo when I was a kid. Icicles hanging like swords from the chalet eaves. Cross-country skiing and my old man with a hot chocolate moustache.'

'There's no time for skiing, Hec. It takes too much energy just to stay warm, to stay alive. A couple of months in, it gets so cold you bring the animals inside. They shit and piss on the floor, but you are glad of the heat. You burn *qarghana* and the cow pats you dried in the summer. But the heat is never enough. The rock swallows it.'

Arezu pauses to make sure I appreciate how cold it is.

'You have five children,' she says.

'I don't think so.'

'How old are you?'

'Twenty-two.'

'Then you have four. One of them, your youngest daughter,

has tuberculosis. The smoke from the fire makes her hack her lungs out, night after night. You hate yourself for wanting the noise to stop. She won't make the winter even if you had the money for medicine.'

'It's a cheery little scene.'

'These places are beautiful to you, Hec, because you don't see them as an Afghan sees them – as a home for the poorest.

'It was a bad season for the crops. The rain came late and then at harvest. Much of the wheat was rotten. The potatoes are small. Your children moan at night, their bellies tight with hunger.'

'Okay, Arezu, that's enough, I get the picture.'

'Do you?'

'Yes. I feel guilty for living in a house, for having decent food every day. For saying I didn't like peas when I was a kid even though my mum told me there were kids starving in Africa.'

'That's the first time you've mentioned your mum.'

'I didn't know you were keeping score,' I say. Then quickly add, 'So what can I do about it? The mess this place is in.'

'Just do what you are doing, Hec. Do what you are best at. Write. Tell the world how it is here. Tell them how it really is – that there are Afghans who are tired of war and they are cold and they are hungry and they are sick. But also there is joy and life here. That it is not as simple as the world thinks it is.'

We continue driving, the road forcing our elbows together. A lock of Arezu's hair has escaped from her veil and I feel the urge to tuck it back in.

'Here's a story for your book, Hec,' she says, turning to

me. 'Once there was a cow eating some hay. A frog came along, and the cow, feeling in a playful mood, dropped some hay on its back. The frog was flattened to the ground. It looked up and said to the cow, "Why did you do that?" and the cow replied, "I was only playing a game." The frog shook his head at the cow and said to him, "To you it may only be a game, but this is my life."

'The frog is the Afghan people and the cow is everyone above, all those in power – corrupt politicians, foreign armies, and even some of the NGOs.'

'And what's the answer? More aid money? I've seen where it goes, all those greenbacks and euros and roubles. There are a lot of big white 4WDs here with big white NGO workers and their drivers and their security and their interpreters. It's a business isn't it?'

'It's not a perfect system, but it is all we have at the moment.'

'And what do you do, Arezu? How do you help?'

'I do what I can to improve education. So that ignorance cannot get a hold on the people again. Knowledge is a weapon.'

'And where does the cash for this knowledge come from?'

'From people back home who have the money, but not the time.'

'It must be nice to be you.'

'What do you mean?'

'To be perfect. To be right.'

'Look, Hec, I don't know where this is coming from.'

'You're talking to me like I am an invader. That I'm just taking stuff like everyone else. I paid for this story you know. I lost a friend.'

'We all lost someone to this war.'

'Then that means I get membership to your little club.'

'Hec, stop being such an ass.'

'Arezu, stop being so American.'

'I resent that. You know, sometimes I hate this country. It has stolen some of the most important people from me: my aunt and uncle killed in the Battle of Kabul; my grandfather shot by the Russians; two cousins murdered by the Taliban. But I can't deny that I am part of it and it is part of me.'

'But you can leave whenever you want.'

'But I choose not to.'

'Well good for you. How very noble.'

'What do you think would happen if all the Afghans who were educated left this country? Believe me, when a teacher gets forty bucks a month, it is hard to argue when the good ones want to leave. If those who could just got up and left, what would happen, Hec?'

'They'd send money home?'

'Possibly. But you'd also lose the ability to educate. And without that, without knowledge, the people listen to those mullahs who use their sermons to prepare them for jihad. Suddenly you have eleven-year-old boys with plastic explosives strapped to them. Believe me, I've seen it.'

'Why do you even bother? The problems are so huge.'

'Remember the *kaftar*, Hec.'

'Stuff the *kaftar*. The *kaftar* is nothing. It was just a bird with a brain the size of a walnut, who tasted freedom then flew right back to its cage.'

'What are you saying, Hec?'

'It's a metaphor, Arezu! Seeing as you like them so much. These people you are helping, how are you so sure they won't turn round and shoot you when the Taliban roll back into town?'

'Because they're good people, Hec, caught in bad situation.'

'For thirty bloody long years and a lot of it of their own making.'

'Can it, Hec, you're talking out your ass.'

'At least I'm talking.'

'You have some anger issues.'

'Yup, I'm like a modern day Genghis-bloody-Khan.'

'And stop with the cussing.'

'Cussing now, how very *Little House on the Prairie* of you.'

'Oh, man, you are going too far—'

Sameer pulls the Corolla to a stop in a cloud of dust. He turns off the ignition and speaks quickly to Arezu in Dari.

'What did he say?' I ask.

'He wants us to get out.'

'Why?'

'He says we are being rude.'

'Rude?'

'Rude.'

I open the door and we both clamber onto the road-side. It is barren here. While we were arguing, the car was winding its way up the calf's intestine of the Shahidan Pass. I barely noticed. We sit ignoring each other while Sameer smokes a cigarette. He finishes and goes to the boot, takes out a huge yellow melon and cuts two wedges for Arezu and me. It is delicious and cool. Arezu's chin is glistening with juice. I wipe it with my scarf.

'Sorry,' I say. 'Sorry about the *Little House on the Prairie* and the stuff about your friends wanting to kill you.'

'I'm sorry too. Sorry for being so... I dunno, uptight.'

'You're not uptight. You just care.'

'I do.'

'Friends?' I offer her my sticky hand.

She takes it. Her fingers are like lotus petals. But stickier. 'Friends,' she says.

'I appreciate you showing me around.'

'I like showing you around. And I'm sorry about the lessons all the time. I just want you to know...well, everything. If you're going to write about it, I want you to get it right.'

'I will.'

'I know you will. I trust you.'

'Do you?'

'Of course.'

And I don't understand why I do it, but I blurt it all out then. All about Mum and about her leaving and then I am crying like a child on the side of the road in Afghanistan, of all places. And I feel like I am dissolving into this place, that I am turning to dirt and pretty soon the people will mould me like clay and I will become a pot or a pipe or a Buddha.

I tell her that Mum was too big for her life; that she hurt too much. And I tell her about the West Gate and how once it was a special place, but now it is tainted. How, like Shahr-e Gholghola, it trapped the screams of those who fell.

The tears come and come and they bring that unique ache with them. My face feels wind-bruised. My cheeks and eye sockets burn. This is not a romantic sorrow. There is no Hollywood lighting. This is dark and troubling. It is claw and gut and blood and pain.

'She jumped,' I say. And it is the first time I have ever said those terrible words out loud. It has been the biggest secret that I have ever kept. She jumped and when she fell towards that water, the vacuum she created sucked the words from me. It is the thing that kept Dad and me apart and, in a way, brought Omed and me together.

'She jumped,' I whisper again because now it has been said it will always be said. Now it is the truth.

Arezu's hands slip into my lap and grab my fingers. She holds them to her so I know what life means, so I can feel her warmth and her heartbeat. She doesn't say anything, just waits while the tears keep rolling from me.

They stop eventually and give way to great tugging sobs which in turn leave me breathless. In the distance, a great string of goats files over the wide plain. Nomads moving between pastures. Just looking at them makes me feel tired. How can they stand such endless movement?

I rub my eyes dry on my scarf. Sameer is looking at me out of the corner of his eye as though I am the biggest pussy he has ever seen. I feel in my pack for the book of Pashtun women's poetry that Dad gave me at the airport. I open it at one of the *landays*, the two-line poems of love and war:

> *Oh my love, if in my arms you tremble so.*
> *What will you do when a thousand lightning bolts*
> *flash from the clash of swords?*

I am not built for this land. I feel small and a long way from home. Arezu still has my hands clasped to her as if I may be grabbed by the wind at any moment. As if I am a kite or an autumn leaf. Does she believe in this version of courage, I wonder? That it is wrong for a man to cry or to feel fear or sadness? What sort of a man does she expect? My tears have soaked into her shirt. Does this bond us or does it push us apart?

A flash of brilliant blue appears between the folds of hills.

'Band-e Zulfiqar. The Dam of Hazrat Ali's Sword,' says Arezu.

Out of the car, the lake looks like a slice of sky caught in the teeth of the mountains. I want to be there. The water reminds me of home, of days at the beach.

I write in my journal:

> *Shells and sunscreen. Mum turns cartwheels on the hard-packed beach. A blue-ringed octopus Dad captures in a jar. Beach huts and sleeves of ice cream. Pockets of sand migrate to the suburbs.*

Can it possibly be that these memories are losing some bite? That one day I will be able to think back on my childhood and only feel happiness? Maybe the tears on the side of the road were like the aloe Mum would smear on my burnt calves.

I jump back in the car and beep the horn.

'What's your hurry?' shouts Arezu. 'Sameer is taking a leak.'

It's true. He is squatting down in Afghan peeing style, trying to hide himself behind a rock. 'Come on, Sameer!' I yell. He shouts something back in Dari and Arezu laughs, but I don't ask for the translation.

The road is slowly being rebuilt and as we get closer to the lake, it peters out into a maze of small tracks improvised by cars trying to get around the works. Here the transformation from Toyota to donkey is complete, with the little car bucking and braying its way down to the lakes. It is like driving through talcum powder – a dust so fine it creeps into the car even with the windows shut. I am sweating and my face is streaked with mud.

We come to a fork. 'Band-e Pudina, Band-e Panir, this way,' says Sameer. 'This way Band-e Haibat, Qadamjoy Shah-e Aulia.'

'What?'

Arezu translates. 'Qadamjoy Shah-e Aulia means the Place Where Ali Stood. Shah-e Aulia is one of Hazrat Ali's names, it means King of Saints. There is a shrine to him by the lake.'

'That's where we want to go. To the shrine.'

We head down the hill and cross the bridge below the dam wall. There are families picnicking here, spreading their carpets and blankets and roasting *kabob* over wood fires. Kids jump in the shallow streams and pools leading from the waterfall. The dam wall is over fifteen metres high and streaked yellow with sulphur.

We walk from the car park, leaping small streams until we reach the shrine. By the shore, plastic pedalos in the shape of swans wait for customers. There is a speedboat called *Donald Duck* parked by the track. We sit on the wall in front of the shrine, above the trinket sellers and bathers exposing more flesh than I have seen the whole time I have been in Afghanistan. And I unfold my fortune from Baba Singh.

The paper is completely blank. I turn it over and flick it with my finger as if, by some miracle, words will appear.

'I paid a thousand afs for a blank bit of paper!' I say to Arezu. 'No wonder the Russians knocked out that old charlatan's teeth.'

'*Charlatan*?' mocks Arezu 'How very *Anne of Green Gables*, how very *Sherlock Holmes*.'

I ball up the paper and throw it towards the water. A dog ambles up and sniffs it.

'That's littering,' says Arezu. 'This is a national park, you know.'

I have come here for answers. For an end to this story; Omed's story. If I can just see him one last time I can ask him everything. We can finish this story together. Slip that keystone into the arch. Complete the bridge we began all those years ago.

'Hec, I know this is hard for you. You set yourself an impossible task, finding one person in a country that is in chaos. A country where everyone is missing someone.

'I know you thought there would be some kind of great reunion with Omed. Maybe there still will be. But even if you don't find him, don't you think you have enough to write his story? You have walked where he walked. You talked with Leyli. Maybe it's enough.'

She looks out at the lapis lazuli of Band-e Haibat. 'Do you know the story of how Hazrat Ali created these dams?' she asks.

'Arezu, I don't need another story right now.'

'I think that is exactly what you need, Hec. Now listen.' Arezu takes my hands in hers and looks into my eyes. I wonder if we should be holding hands, here at the shrine of a saint. An old woman comes to the door of the shrine to watch.

'There was once a king called Barbar who ruled this land with an iron fist. For many years he had tried to get his slaves to build a dam so his city could have water. But try as they might, the slaves could not complete the dam. At the same time a young man owed a great sum of money to the king that he could not repay. Barbar had the man's wife and children imprisoned until he could come up with the money. So the young man went in search of Hazrat Ali.

'Together, the young man and Hazrat Ali came up with a plan where he would tie up Ali and offer him to Barbar as a slave.

'Well the king agreed to buy the slave for his weight in gold. But there were three conditions.'

'There are always three conditions,' I say.

'The first was that the slave had to build the dam. The second was that he had to kill the Dragon of Bamiyan and finally, Hazrat Ali should be shackled and brought before him.'

'Sounds simple enough.'

'For Hazrat Ali maybe, but the king put one more condition in place. All of these things needed to be done in one day.'

'I still reckon Ali will do it.'

'Everyone laughed and laughed at the king's joke.'

'Well, it sounds like he was a funny guy.'

Arezu keeps ignoring my heckling. 'Hazrat Ali wasn't laughing though. He booted off half of that mountain top,' she points to a mountain, 'and made the dam of Band-e Haibat. Then he sliced off some more mountain with his sword to make Band-e Zulfiqar. His groom built Band-e Qambar. And inspired by Ali, the slaves finally finished Band-e Gholaman. A nomad woman offered a cheese to Ali for his great work and he placed the gift in the water to form Band-e Panir. And beside it, where mint still grows, Band-e Pudina.

'But downstream the lands had become dry, so Ali drew his fingers across Band-e Haibat's wall and five streams began to flow. Then he marched off and killed the Dragon and returned to stand in front of Barbar, who was so amazed that he converted to Islam.'

'Quite a guy.'

Arezu shakes her head at my glibness. 'See that woman there.' She smiles at the old lady by the door of the shrine. 'Her ancestor was the nomad who gave the cheese to Ali. Her family looks after the shrine.'

'Ask her if she knows Omed.'

Arezu speaks with the woman. She shakes her head and points up at the lake. They talk for a time and Arezu places both her hands on the woman's shoulders. Then she comes back over to me.

'There was a man called Omed from Bamiyan. He hasn't been here for some time.'

I feel my shoulders drop.

'She said he might have gone to live with the *pir* – the holy man – who lives in a cave up by Band-e Zulfiqar.'

'We have to go.'

'It's quite a walk.'

'We have to go.'

'Hec, we can't be on the road after dark.'

'We'll stay here tonight.'

'Where? I can't stay in the *chaikhana*. It's not safe for me.'

'I need to talk to this *pir*.'

'I guess there's no talking you around.'

We buy some water and a slab of *naan* and, leaving Sameer with the car, begin the walk around the lake. At this altitude, the sun tears the skin from your neck and arms.

I cover up with my scarf, but it is suffocating. We walk for a long time – the length of Haibat and then up past the shallow ponds of Pudina and to the reedy shores of Band-e Panir, the Dam of Cheese. From there, the track winds up the cliffs towards Zulfiqar. It is rubbly and dangerous. I wonder what would happen if we broke a leg, or worse, out here.

After a while, the blue sword of Zulfiqar appears before us and soon we are skirting its shores. The cave is set high on the cliff overlooking the lake. We get to it by a zigzagging path.

There is a wooden door on the cave and I knock. I hear a shuffling inside. I knock again. The door opens slowly to reveal an old man. This is where the saying 'as old as the hills' comes from. His skin is the same colour as the hills that surround him, its folds and contours are borrowed from the mountains.

'*As-salamu alaykum*,' I say.

He replies, '*Alaykum asalam*.' And on you, peace.

He beckons us inside. There is a dog living with him and, by the smell of things, it doesn't go outside much. It growls as we sit down and the old man smacks it on the muzzle. He sits smiling at us. We smile back.

'Ask him about Omed,' I whisper.

'Shhh,' she says. 'It would be impolite.'

'So we just sit here looking at each other?'

The *pir* gets up and, placing some twigs on his mud stove, puts on a blackened kettle. When it is boiled, he uses his woven cap to pull it from the heat. I look around at what he has: a kettle, two chipped mugs, a tin plate, a woollen blanket and a battered copy of the Qur'an.

He pours tea, offering us the two cups, and seems to relax once we bird-sip a little. Without prompting, he begins to talk. Arezu listens intently, and when I ask her what he is saying she just holds out her hand to silence me. He talks and talks, as if he has been storing this conversation for a long time. When he stops, it is silent for a moment in the cave. The dog yawns, its long pink tongue curled like a wood shaving.

'What did he say?' I ask Arezu.

'He says, he was born in Herat and was the son of a carpet weaver. He lived all his life there and was happy. When the time came, he was married and had three children. When the Russians first arrived they thought things would be good. But soon the masters turned on their servants and the troubles began. He was asked to join the mujaheddin, but he refused. He had a wife and children. He didn't want to die. But the Russians had spies everywhere. One day your friend was your friend, the next he was turning you in for a reward. They questioned him inside his house. His children were scared. When the soldiers pulled the veil from his wife, he found bravery. He shouted at the Russians, "How can you come to this land and treat it so badly? What have we done to you?" They beat him. They told him to confess to being a mujaheddin or they would kill his family. He thought they were bluffing.'

The old man strokes the dog. He looks straight at me and in his eyes I see the blood and the fire. I see how quickly a piece of lead can enter a body and change the course of everything forever. At every turn a story. And it comes to me quite suddenly that maybe all these stories are perhaps the one story. That possibly these small tributaries I have waded across feed into the one great river that is, that will become, Omed's and my story. I pull out my journal and take notes just in case.

'Then he joined the mujaheddin,' Arezu continued. 'And the years became a blur. Sleeping in caves, eating hard *naan* and dried meat. No laughter of women or children. Just the business of killing. And one day they came across a mosque in a village that had been bombed by the Russians. There was a holy man in there, a *pir*, but he had lost a lot of blood. The villagers were weeping and trying to stop the flow with rags. The *pir* gave him a copy of the Qur'an and told him he must stop killing. By then he had killed a hundred men, or more, and not thought once about them. But that night, he snuck away from camp and started walking east. It took him months but when he arrived at Band-e Amir, he stopped walking.'

'Does he know Omed from Bamiyan? He came here once with his father many years ago, maybe he met him then. Tell him that we think he may have come back here recently.'

Arezu talked to the old man. He nodded and began to speak. He talked for a long time, pausing to hawk and spit out the door, and once to scribble on the cave floor with a stick. When he had finished Arezu turned to me.

'He knows the boy. He came when he was young with his father. They camped nearby in a cave. He fell into the water and the *pir* had to save him. That was a long time ago.'

'Was that all he said?'

'Wait, I am getting to the rest.' Arezu sips her tea. 'He came back here, before last winter. He was older, much older. The Taliban had stolen his tongue. It was hard for them to talk because he had no words. He could only write his thoughts in the dirt with a stick. His dirt-words said that it was unsafe for him in Bamiyan, even with the Taliban gone. That there was a man there who wanted to kill him.'

'The Snake. So he ended up back in Bamiyan too. I knew it would be bad for Omed to come home. He did it to protect my father and me.'

Arezu continues, 'He lives on the far side of the lake. The *pir* hardly sees him. Sometimes there is some smoke. He doesn't know how he survives the winter. He has no animal to keep him warm.'

'I have to go there,' I say.

From the square of light we can see the other side of the lake. It looks hazy and very far away.

'We can't be out after dark, Hec.'

'Arezu, I am so close. I can't give up on him again.'

'It's too dangerous.'

'Go back with Sameer. I'll be okay.'

'You don't speak the language. You don't know the customs. How can you think you'll be okay? Word will have gone around that a foreigner went out walking and hasn't returned. Sure, this is the safest province in Afghanistan, but these are a poor people. And you are just dollars on legs.'

'I have to do it.'

'And what about me?'

'You'll be okay. Go to Sameer and drive back to Bamiyan. There is still time before nightfall.'

'That is not what I mean. What if something happens to you? What do I do?'

I place my hand on her shoulder. 'No one will hold you responsible for me.'

She shrugs me off and stands up. The ceiling of the hut is so low that she has to crook her neck. It makes her fury seem worse: a hooked weapon, a bend of barbed wire. 'You are so stupid sometimes!' she shouts.

I watch her from the door as she stumbles back along the path, leaving clouds of dust behind her. The *pir* mumbles something to me that I cannot understand. It could be advice about goats or girls or about the danger of walking alone.

I walk alone. It is not like walking through a forest or a city where the path ahead is obscured. Here everything can be seen for ten kilometres, from the turreted mountains to the broken-biscuit shoreline. I feel exposed. I wonder what the range of a Kalashnikov is? And who could be hiding behind the rocks?

I whistle a tune that comes up from my nervy depths. Why exactly whistling should make things better is beyond me. Perhaps it is just company of sorts, a cheerful but slightly stupid friend.

Dad and I would watch the Monty Python movie *Life of Brian* every weekend. The final scene was the best: where Brian is being crucified with a bunch of others and his mum turns up and says (we'd put on her shemale voice), 'Go ahead, be crucified. See if I care.'

And then we'd whistle loud until our cheeks hurt: *Always Look on the Bright Side of Life.* Loud enough that it would seep through the door of Mum's room where she would be curled on the bed. And it would cover her like a balm, like aloe on sunburn.

From the far shore I can see the cave of the *pir* like a mouth opened to the lake. Ahead is the small jumble of mud walls that the old man had pointed out.

Each step becomes a heartbeat and I feel the distance between Omed and me closing. It has been seven long years and so much has changed, yet so much has stayed the same. I remember when I met Omed in the candle factory, when he had first showed me what bravery meant. How he had stood up for what he believed. In the end that had been his undoing.

As I get closer, the walls form three collapsed buildings. A fourth, still standing, has a rough roof of saplings and mud. The place will soon disappear back into the land it was coaxed from. There is a thin wisp of smoke coming from an opening in the roof. I breathe deeply.

The door is made of sticks bound with loops of wire. This is no more than an abandoned summer camp for herdsmen. On one corner of the roof, a meagre crop of *qarghana* is drying. I knock. It is an absurd little noise in this big space, no more than bird-chitter or the rub of a cricket's legs. The door opens on its wire hinge.

A man with a moustache appears. He hides his body behind the door, but I can see its outline through the branch bars. He looks at me as if daring me to speak. Inside, the *qarghana* fire crackles. There is no other sound.

I reach out slowly with my hand. Omed's hand comes to meet it. Our fingers touch and wrap over each other. We stand there for a while looking at each other over the bridge we have formed. A bridge that has crossed so much distance and difference, and survived for so many years. Then he opens the door and pulls me to him, hugging me so tight I think he may break my ribs.

The room has so little: a couple of hessian sacks on a bed made of tree branches, a woollen coat on a peg thrust into the wall. Omed pulls the pot from his tiny fire and makes us a glass of *chay*.

I don't know where to start. I don't know if he realises that I can speak. He is still locked in his silence and will be forever.

I pull out my journal to show him a photo of my father I have stuck between the pages. He grabs it from me and flips through the pages, smiling, as if recalling something sweet.

He scribbles in the air with his fingers and I pass him a pen. He begins to write, slowly and fluidly, relishing the touch of the pen on the page. Each loop is an arabesque, each plunge, a dive from a highwire. I read over his shoulder like a peeping Tom.

I have waited for this day, my friend. I never stopped thinking of you or the kindness you and your father showed me.

He hands me the journal and I say, 'I can speak now, Omed.' But he shakes his head and pushes the pen into my hand. So I write my response:

I have waited for this day too. Our friendship meant so much to me at a time when I most needed it. We started a bridge between us when we met. Today we can lay the last stone.

It is a very slow way to speak and the words are there forever. It is a high-stakes conversation.

Omed rises from his spot on the floor. He picks something from a stone shelf. He holds it in his fist above my hand. As I open my palm, he drops it in.

It glints in the firelight. I grip it between my thumb and forefinger so it can draw the warmth from the fire. It is the fish-jewel that the fisho gave me all that time ago. The same jewel that I gave to Omed when he left. He picks up the pen and writes again:

I knew one day you would collect it.

I unwrap something of my own. Something I brought from home that will complete his story. It is a metal arm with the letter 'e' stamped at one end from Mum's typewriter – the one he wrote his story on when we lived beneath the same roof. It is to replace the one that was missing from his father's typewriter when he was a boy. I write:

This is for your father. To lay his story to rest, to complete it.

He grabs the pen quickly.

It is you that must tell his story. I have entrusted it to you.

With the pen back in my hand, I do not know what to write. I consider each word before I put it down.

It is an honour to tell his story. And to tell yours. I don't know if I have the ability to do it well.

The pen is back in his hand.

You will do it well because your heart is in it.

The pen is still, but the ink it has left dances under the fire-light. Outside, the sun is setting. I talk then and my voice is a bucket in a deep well.

  'What happened to the Snake?'

He paid to have me shot when I returned to Bamiyan. I came here to wait. He was killed in a knife fight in Badakhshan. I heard it was over a shipment of opium. He lived like a snake and eventually he swallowed his own poison. The Talib had been forced from the valley. I hope they will never return. It was a matter of waiting.

'And now you can go home, Omed.'

My home is here now. My family is scattered.

'I met Leyli.'
  Omed's eyes brighten. He writes:

Was she well?

I don't know what to say. She wasn't sick, that much is true, but that is only part of the story. Do I need to tell him what he already knows, that Leyli, the daughter of an educated man, is the second wife of a greybeard? That she has for-gotten how to read and is raising illiterate children on stale bread and *chay*? That the power of the written word means nothing in her village? 'She is well,' I lie. 'You should go to her.'

Omed circles the words: *My home is here now,* as if it is an incantation that will protect him from the snow and bullets.

When dark comes there is nothing to do but sleep. In the dark I cannot read the thoughts that Omed places so carefully on the page. He has no light, except that of the fire, and he feeds it sparingly.

I hear Omed's breath slow and deepen. The outline of his body is a dark island on the floor next to me. I fling out my arm and find the end of his shirt with my fingers. I grip it tight and fall asleep myself.

The sun comes across the lake like it is running from something. I have been sitting on the shore for an hour waiting for it. A light breeze hits the water and I feel as if I can breathe for the first time in over a week. I have done what I set out to do – I have found Omed. All that is left is to write it all down. That is the easy part.

I flip open the journal. There is nothing more scary and exhilarating than this fresh page. The possibilities are endless. I write the date and *Band-e Zulfiqar*. I draw Ali's sword under it, long so it touches both margins. I grip the pen between my teeth and make myself comfortable on the rock.

Over the lake, the *pir*'s cave is oozing smoke. I remember the story of him diving down to save Omed when he was a boy. Did Omed ever learn to swim? He feared the water for so long, but now he lives beside it. I will ask him when he wakes.

I need to start the story. But where? I shut the journal

and glance over my shoulder back at Omed's hut. He is in there sleeping. I should wake him and ask him. How does the story start? And where does it end?

Sooner or later I need to draw a line beneath the last word and say: *now this is the beginning of a new story*. The trick is knowing when to separate. When to make that cut.

Omed appears at the door. He walks down with his *chay* pot to the edge of the water. After he has filled it, he takes my journal and looks at what I have written. He smiles at me and shakes his head. On the same page, he writes:

> In winter, the lake freezes. I cut a hole in the ice and fish. The *mohi* are cunning, but they taste good cooked over hot coals.
> Pilgrims have heard of me and bring me gifts of flour and rice. It is curious they think my silence is holy.
> I am lucky. This place is more beautiful than anywhere I have known. I am at peace. I am free.

I know what this peace means, how hard Omed has fought for it and what a huge victory it is after a life of restlessness and sorrow. It is not a perfect ending, but it is the best that could be done.

We breakfast on *naan* that Omed makes himself in a *tandoor*. The sparks cling to his moustache as they once did to Anwar's beard. The bread is good – soft and warm, with a fine crust and the odd fleck of ash. We share a cup of *chay*, breathing the steam off as we sit with our backs against the rock wall.

I know I must say goodbye. I shuffle the things around in my pack, looking for a parting gift. My hand falls on the journal that Dad gave me. I have only filled in twenty or so pages. How small my experience seems when written on the page. I think of the haiku I learned in school, how the Japanese masters could fold an entire world into three simple lines.

I tear out my pages and hand the book to Omed along with my pen. The ink will outlast the paper. I will have to send more from Australia.

Omed points out the path I must take. I mustn't backtrack. It is important to keep going forward.

I turn after a few minutes of walking to see Omed's silhouette against the burqa-blue flash of the lake. One hand is high, waving, the other grasps the journal and pen. He is the keeper of my story as I am of his.

I make the Shrine of Ali by lunch. I am so hungry I could eat a liver *kabob*. There is one *chaikhana* in the dusty street above the shrine. The sign reads: *CLEAN RESTAURANT*. It has *Rooms and Delicious Food*. I am full of hope.

Under a flapping tarp I am served *qabli pulao* and a saucer of gristly lamb. I order a *naan* and pour myself yet another *chay*. I have no idea how I am going to get back to Bamiyan. As I am looking down the street, a mirage appears through the midday haze.

'You didn't really think I'd leave you.' It is Arezu with Sameer in tow.

I try to downplay my smile. I try not to hug her in front of these people. I try to pretend that I would feel the same way if it was just Sameer who had stayed. *It is only relief*, I say to myself.

I write a new ending in the car on the way home on the backs of the pages I tore from my journal. Omed returns to Bamiyan and he marries a girl he has always known. Wasim becomes a writer and together with Omed they start a small printing company. They finally complete their father's work, documenting the legends and poems of the valley. Leyli marries Zakir; it turns out it was just a flesh wound. And if Zakir doesn't die, then Omed doesn't mess with the Taliban and he doesn't have to leave. He never meets the Snake. And the Taliban leave the valley forever. And everybody, lives happily ever after. The end.

But it's not a story. It has no tension. Nothing happens. And if life were that simple, what would we learn?

'What are you stopping for, Sameer?' asks Arezu.

'Checkpoint.'

'There wasn't a checkpoint on the way in,' I say.

'Keep driving, Sameer,' says Arezu. There is an edge in her voice.

'There are rocks on the road.'

'Drive over them, Sameer!' shouts Arezu.

It is a big ask for the little Toyota. And then I see the guns. And uniforms.

'It's okay, Arezu,' I say. 'It's the police.'

'I have a bad feeling about this,' she says.

'Relax, they just want to check our passports.'

We stop and a policeman comes to each side. They have Kalashnikovs. They shout something in Dari. 'I don't understand,' I say.

'Passpot. Passpot.' He jabs me with the muzzle of his gun.

I bring out my passport. He looks at it and hands it to a friend. I notice there are four other guys not wearing uniforms. This is bad.

The other guy in uniform is rattling Dari at Sameer. His hands are trembling on the wheel. If Sameer is afraid then I should be shitting myself.

My guy shines a torch in the back at Arezu. She pulls her veil over her face. 'Passpot!' he screams at her.

He grabs her passport and hands it to his friend. 'Amrikayi,' he says – American. He shoots some Dari at me.

'I don't understand.'

'He is asking if I am your wife,' Arezu hisses.

'No. No!'

'Ne?' says the man.

'*Balē. Balē,*' says Arezu and then rattles off some more Dari.

He spits on the ground and his machine gun glares at her.

'What is going on?' I ask.

'He wants to know if I am a spy. Why do I speak Dari? Why do you say I am not your wife when I say I am? Why are Americans in this country?'

'Are they Taliban?'

'Talibaaaan. *Balē,*' says the cop, leering at me.

'I don't think they are. They're just bandits.'

'*Just* bandits?'

'Well it gives us a better chance of living. They'll only shoot us if we don't give them money. If they were Taliban they'd take our money and then shoot us for being infidels.'

'How do we tell what they are?'

'Offer them some money. If they let us go then maybe they're not Talibs.'

'Good plan.' I peel off fifteen hundred afghani and hand it to my man.

He shows it to his friends and laughs.

Arezu slaps my head. 'Is that what you think our lives are worth – thirty bucks? These boys aren't playing, Hec.'

I give them the whole lot, minus the stash of dollars I have in my jacket. They get us out and make us lie face-down on the dirt. Sameer is crying. I am numb. This can't be happening to me. I am an Australian citizen. Surely, my embassy will save me.

They go through the car and get everything, including my jacket with its stash of greenbacks. Then they get us off the ground and start us walking. Every now and then I feel a gun between my shoulder blades. It is cold. My body is charged. I can feel fear in my root canals. A car starts and is driven away. We keep walking.

My mind fills the gaps. *They are taking us away to execute us. Shut up! A knife is cheaper than a bullet. No, no! If they shoot us and miss can I play dead? Are there rules to this? Shut up, Hec! If I do play dead, will they notice? Will they check our pulses?* And on and on like this.

It gets dark, but there are no stars. The night wedges in my lungs and I feel like retching. I feel like purging this valley, this country, from my body. It is a poison I have swallowed and now it is going to kill me.

At some point I can't feel the rifle at my back. I keep going for a minute because my legs don't know how to stop. Then I turn and stare into the dark. Into more and more dark. The only sound is the river, muttering Dari curses over rock.

'Well I guess they weren't Taliban,' I say to Arezu and Sameer.

And we laugh. Not that it is funny. Not that any of it is funny. We laugh because we are alive. And at that moment nothing else matters.

'Shall we go back for the car?' I ask.

'Have you lost your mind?' says Arezu. 'We got away once. Let's leave it at that.'

'So what now?'

'We walk until it gets light and then we hitch a ride.'

The ride appears in the guise of a rubble truck and we climb on top. The cloud lifts as we move down the valley. We are reborn.

AFTER DINNER, WE WALK TO Shahmama – the mother Buddha. Sparrows flood from the wheatfields, their beaks and bellies full of seed.

'When my dad was young, they used to eat sparrows,' says Arezu. 'His mother would bring them home on a string from the bazaar. They would roast them and eat them whole, crunching the bones.'

'Yum.'

We cross the stream on a fallen tree and stand beneath the Buddha niche. Arezu reaches out and takes my hand.

If I were a Persian poet I would tell her that her lips are like sweet figs, her breath like musk. But in truth she is a drug, a ball of opium, slipped into milk.

We run back through the fields, laughing like children. Dogs nip at our heels and yellow-backed finches fly ahead of us.

We undress in our room. Her skin tastes of dust. Her dark hair is a waterfall. Moonlight crosses her body. She whispers in my ear. Something in Dari that I cannot understand.

How did we get to this point? I wonder. *Is it just the close-ness to death that makes me feel so alive?*

When we are lying still beside each other I say, 'You know the bridge my mum jumped from?'

Arezu props herself on her elbow. 'Where did that come from?'

'That bridge had killed before.'

'But she jumped, Hec.'

'I looked it up after the fisho told me.'

'Hec, what is a fisho? What are you talking about?'

'It was in 1970 when they were building the bridge. Two bits didn't join up properly so they bent one side with concrete blocks. It didn't work out as they hoped. The bridge buckled and fell. It killed thirty-five men.' I suck in a quick breath of air. 'I remember reading how the survivors couldn't believe their eyes. What they thought of as solid steel didn't behave as it should; it turned blue and fluid. Some of the guys rode it forty-five metres to the water. I've stood beneath that bridge and it's a long way to drop.

'Have you ever felt like that, Arezu?'

'Like what?'

'That sometimes the things you thought were concrete and steel suddenly change?'

'I get that a lot.'

'What is your secret, Arezu?'

'Pardon?'

'The day we met. You said everybody here has a secret. What is yours?'

'I don't have one, Hec. I told you, I am an open book.'

I laugh, but it is then that I know Arezu is, and will always be, a mystery.

'Do you think this bridge we've built to each other is strong enough?' I ask.

'You writers always have to be so cryptic.'

'Stop avoiding the question.'

'I don't know, Hec. Really, I don't.' She rolls onto her back so that her silhouette is etched by moonlight. 'There's a place in north-east India that is the wettest on earth,' she says. 'Villagers plant strangler figs on riverbanks. They care for them for years, training the tendrils across strips of bark until they reach the far side. Generation after generation keep it going, helping the tendrils back and forward, placing earth and stone as a walkway. Eventually they have a bridge that cannot be washed away by floods. It is a living part of the land.'

'Is that what we've done? Have we started this bridge?'

'Maybe. I think it might just take time and patience.'

'Come to Australia,' I say impatiently.

'You know I can't leave, Hec,' she says.

I list the reasons why she can and why she should and every one of them sounds hollow.

'Hec, how can life in Melbourne or in Wichita compete with Afghanistan?' says Arezu. Her head is now on my chest and I can feel the words inside me. 'For all the bad stuff that has gone on here, it is a place at the start of something new, that might just be very good. I want to be a part of that.'

e

We don't sleep that night and in the morning we have our simple breakfast of *naan* and *chay sabz*. We kiss goodbye in our room, but not in the bazaar when we *say* goodbye. These two moments serve different purposes. In the bazaar we present our public face that cannot touch or kiss. Behind walls, she and I can be us. These are the rules. I wonder how long Arezu can play by them and what will happen if she does not.

The *Tunis* is packed and I am shoved in the back between a fresh-faced student wanting to practise English and a hard-bitten ex-mujaheddin. I push my earbuds deep and switch on my iPod. I scan the crowd outside for Arezu, but she is gone.

As we cross the Shibar Pass, the song in my head is REM's *Leaving New York* – another of Mum's favourites. I know Arezu is from Wichita and I am leaving her in Bamiyan, but that song could be about leaving anywhere or anyone. It's that sort of song. There is such sadness and longing in every line. But sometimes, it's not easier to leave than to be left behind.

Dad and I are under the West Gate again. But this time is different. The past is no longer a burden. I have placed the final stone; I have mortared it with words. The arch is complete.

The bird is not frightened as I bring it from its cage. I tie the fish-jewel carefully around its leg with a strand of red cotton. Its heartbeat quickens. It can taste the sky. The feathers on its wings quiver with the excitement of it. I touch its head with my lips and close my eyes, remembering when Arezu did this on the dusty Pul-e Khishti above the Kabul River.

Then I toss the dove up. It rolls on its back, falling for a moment before turning and opening its wings. And it beats them, and with each beat it stirs the breeze. And it rises. Up by the pylons. Up to the snaky underbelly of the bridge. It is a flash of brilliant white in everything that is dull and industrial about this place.

When the sky is the colour of newsprint it will slice it apart with its wings. When there is lightning it will take it in its beak. It will not return to captivity. It will move forward forever.

'What's the story with the pigeon?' asks the old fisho.

'It's a dove. It's a story about wishes and hope,' I say. 'Arezu and Omed.'

'Aye, yer a funny lad,' he says, shaking his head and rebaiting his hook.

'Come on,' says Dad. 'We need to get to the airport.'

We traipse up through the she-oaks to the car.

'Fancy grabbing something to eat on the way?' Dad asks.

'Sure.'

'Your shout?'

'My shout,' I say.

Hector Morrow
Melbourne

AUTHOR'S NOTE

If this novel contains in some small part the dust and light of Afghanistan, it is because I was lucky enough to travel there in July–August of 2009. Like Omed, I discovered that dragon tears fizz on the tongue, how heavenly bread, fresh from a wood-fired *tandoor*, can taste and just how achingly blue the waters of Band-e Amir truly are. Like Hec, I sat dumbstruck in a *chaikhana* on my first day in Kart-e Parwan, watched the sunset from the City of Screams and took the grit and fumes of Kabul into my lungs. There was so much of my journey that could not make it to these pages, so many incredible people and experiences. But I hope I have managed to convey part of the spirit of Afghanistan, so that when you pass an Afghan on the street or read about them in your newspaper, you will know them as a people with huge hearts, modest dreams and great courage.

Tashakor (thank you) to the Australia Council for the Arts without whose generous support I would not have been able to make this trip or write this novel.

For those who wish to read more about my journey, please visit the archive of my Afghan blog (Blogistan 2009) at www.neilgrant.com.au

ACKNOWLEDGEMENTS

This book has been a journey in itself. Along the way many people have helped in its creation and I would like to acknowledge and thank them.

AUSTRALIA

My family and my friends – who told me I was crazy but supported me anyway.

Eva Mills, Erica Wagner, Jodie Webster (Allen & Unwin) – who didn't give up on me.

Sonja Torode and Nicci Grant – for their keen eyes and kind words.

Jane Keogh (refugee advocate).

Jenny Bourne (Rural Australians for Refugees, Port Augusta).

Jacki Whitwell (Refugee Council of Australia) – for introducing me to the world of the refugee and to the plight of the Hazara people.

Sardar Shinwari – who spent three and a half pivotal years in Baxter Detention Centre.

The Asylum Seeker Resource Centre – where I have taught and learnt.

The Dunmoochin Foundation – who gave me a creative space in which to dream and write.

Bill Cassidy (Nortan Olympia Waxes) – my candle guru.

AFGHANISTAN

James Springer and Dawn Erickson – for teaching me how to drive in Kabul and steering me on the right path in every other way.

Marnie Gustavson (PARSA Afghanistan) – for her kindness in driving me to Bamiyan and showing me the good that can be done by motivated people.

Tahir and Zohra and their beautiful children – who live in the shadow of the Buddha caves in Bamiyan and cared for me while I was there. Especially Tahir, who interpreted as I was dressed-down by the Chief-of-Police in Bamiyan.

Yasin Farid (PARSA Afghanistan) – a brave Afghan working for the betterment of his country.

Atollah – who drove us for ten tortuous hours to Bamiyan then rescued my mobile phone from a muddy stream.

Hamidullah and his plucky little Toyota – who drove me to Band-e Amir and the Valley of the Dragon and discovered the hidden Buddha faces with me in Deh-i-Ahangaran.

Samir – who chaperoned me in a *Tunis* from Bamiyan to Kabul.

If you read this book and feel that you would like to help refugees or Afghans in their homeland here are two organisations that I have had personal dealings with, and I have seen the tremendous difference they make to people's lives.

PARSA AFGHANISTAN

Who do on-the-ground projects with widows, orphans and other disadvantaged groups within Afghanistan.
www.afghanistan-parsa.org

ASYLUM SEEKER RESOURCE CENTRE

Australia's leading asylum seeker organisation. A multi-award winning, independent and non-federal government-funded human rights organisation who work at the coalface assisting some of the most disadvantaged people in the community.
www.asrc.org.au

NEIL GRANT was born in Scotland in the Year of the Fire Horse. He learnt to speak Australian at the age of thirteen when he migrated to Melbourne to ride kangaroos. He finished high school at the International School of Kuala Lumpur then spent years blundering through Indonesia, Israel, Yugoslavia, India, Nepal, Thailand, Greece, Italy, the UK and Tasmania. To research *The Ink Bridge,* he travelled (quietly) through Afghanistan.

Sometimes he escapes to write and dream in a mudbrick cottage he built himself on the Far South Coast of NSW.

Neil has three children and lives in Cottles Bridge, Victoria.